LETHBRIDGE-STEWART

THE LAUGHING GNOME
FEAR OF THE WEB

ALYSON LEEDS

CANDY JAR BOOKS · CARDIFF
2018

Fear of the Web © Alyson Leeds 2018
The Forgotten Son © Andy Frankham-Allen 2015/2018

Characters and Concepts from 'The Web of Fear'
© Hannah Haisman & Henry Lincoln
Lethbridge-Stewart: The Series
© Andy Frankham-Allen & Shaun Russell 2014, 2018
Fiona Campbell created by Gary Russell

Doctor Who is © British Broadcasting Corporation, 1963, 2018

Range Editor Andy Frankham-Allen
Editor: Shaun Russell
Editorial: Keren Williams
Licensed by Hannah Haisman
Cover by Martin Baines & Will Brooks

Printed and bound in the UK by
CPI Anthony Rowe, Chippenham, Wiltshire

ISBN: 978-1-912535-11-8

Published by
Candy Jar Books
Mackintosh House
136 Newport Road, Cardiff, CF24 1DJ
www.candyjarbooks.co.uk

This book is dedicated to:
Kenneth Percy Winn Leeds (1930-2013)
'Not an officer, but nonetheless a gentleman.'

PREVIOUSLY...

THE CHECK-UP WAS BOOKED, AND TEA WAS ON THE WAY. Fiona Campbell felt ready to weather any of Alistair's arguments as she returned to his room.

'All done. I've arranged for the doctor to come round at–'

Fiona stopped. Clamped a hand to her mouth.

Brigadier Bishop and Dame Anne were sprawled on the floor. And her ex-husband, Sir Alistair Lethbridge-Stewart, was slumped in his chair, his head fallen to one side.

Fiona rushed over to him. 'Alistair! Alistair!' She cupped his head in her hands, gently patted his face. 'Alistair!'

There was nobody home.

Pulling herself together, Fiona pressed two fingers to Alistair's neck in search of a pulse. There. A little slow, but distinct through paper-thin skin. His breath was light and steady on the back of her hand, as if he were only sleeping.

Reassured for the moment, she moved quickly to check on Brigadier Bishop and Dame Anne. Her assessment of the two proved they were in a similar condition; all three were unconscious, yet, on the face of it, unharmed.

As if only sleeping.

Fiona's mind flashed back to the graveyard earlier

that day, to when she had returned from her walk around the church to find her ex-husband slumped in his wheelchair, the grotesque gnome cradled in his lap – so quiet, so still. With thoughts of the funeral they had just attended still fresh in her head, Fiona had naturally feared the worst. She recalled how she had tried so desperately to wake Alistair, how a deep chill had settled around her heart when he was unresponsive. Her mind had turned to her daughter and her grandchildren... To the loss they would endure if Alistair died so suddenly.

But then she had felt faint with relief when his eyes had opened and, after a moment's confusion, had rested on her, bright and clear as ever. He had come back. Something had happened, though; she had recognised the signs immediately in Alistair's expression. He had been *away*, somewhere else, and while he had been gone something significant had taken place. And now it had happened again, only this time two of his oldest friends had somehow been caught up in it – whether intentionally or by accident was anybody's guess.

Fiona considered her next move with care. Doris, Alistair's wife of almost fifteen years, would need to be notified. And then the rest of his family; Albert and his family. Kate and hers... So many.

It was fair to say that in recent years Fiona had become a little more enlightened as to the true nature of Alistair's work, as they worked out their own complicated history. She had become well-versed in not jumping to any conclusions about any given situation. In casting her gaze around the room, she noted that there was no sign of a struggle or forced entry; no indication of immediate danger, no foreign item in evidence, save that ghastly gnome Alistair had picked up earlier in the churchyard. It was now on the floor by Brigadier Bishop's feet. He must have dropped it.

Such practicalities established, there was little else

Fiona could do, save make her charges as comfortable as possible. Falling back on her Girl Guide training, she set about putting both Dame Anne and her husband into the recovery position, taking care to support their heads correctly as she did so. Next, she took the blankets from Alistair's bed, tucking one securely around his waist and legs, and used the others to cover Brigadier Bishop and his wife.

Smoothing the blanket over Dame Anne's shoulders, Fiona studied her sleeping face. A few strands of grey hair had been dislodged from Dame Anne's usually so neat bob, and Fiona gently tucked them back in place behind her ear.

Pushing herself up from the floor, her knees clicking with arthritis, Fiona crossed back to Alistair's bedside and pressed the emergency call button. With the sound of hurried footsteps approaching down the corridor, the former Mrs Lethbridge-Stewart sat down to worry, and to wait.

CHAPTER ONE
One Tin Soldier

EMIL JULIUS SILVERSTEIN'S EVENING HAD NOT GONE AT all according to plan.

It was a crisp Tuesday night in late winter; the air outside the Silverstein family home in South Kensington was clear and chill. His son, Malachi, was out with his fiancée, attending the preview of some new up-and-coming gallery in the West End. Silverstein had been looking forward to spending a quiet night in his study, re-categorising his collection of Bronze Age arrowheads; just him, a blazing fire, a well-matured camembert, and a vintage bottle of port freshly decanted in honour of the occasion.

After forty years in the art world – dealer, collector and connoisseur – Silverstein had finally decided last summer to step back and allow Malachi to take on the day-to-day running of the business. Even so, it was still relatively rare for Silverstein to find himself with the opportunity to simply relax and indulge his passion for antiquity.

Instead, at around half past six, Silverstein's plans had been derailed beyond hope of salvation. He had hardly swapped his dinner suit for his smoking jacket and carpet slippers, when the front doorbell had started ringing frantically. Grumbling at the distraction, Silverstein had nevertheless gone to answer the door. Whoever the caller was, it was possible that he would have been able to get rid of them fairly swiftly and press on with his evening.

On opening the door, however, he was surprised to be confronted with the sight of Professor Edward Travers, breathless and flustered in his porch.

'Is it here?' Travers had immediately demanded, by way of greeting.

'Is what?' Silverstein had asked, bewildered. The professor was fair bristling with agitation.

'The Yeti, man! Quickly now, we need to check!'

Not waiting for an invitation, the scientist had barrelled his way inside. Caught off guard, Silverstein could only follow like a piece of driftwood in the wake of Travers' overbearing personality, too stunned to utter any protest.

Travers had made his way straight to Silverstein's private museum – his Hall of Curiosities, as he liked to call it – and had come to a halt in front of the robotic Yeti. As ever the beast was in place on its pedestal, exactly where it had been standing for the last thirty years, ever since Silverstein had bought it from Travers.

At the sight of the Yeti the professor breathed a great sigh of relief, as if he genuinely believed that the creature would be missing, but the air of distraction had still not left him. Having caught up with Travers, Silverstein attempted to get an explanation as to what all the fuss was about, and what Travers meant by turning up in such a fashion. True, he had grown used to the professor's abrupt nature over the years, but this was something altogether different. He had not seen Travers for months, and the man's sudden appearance would not be without reason.

Travers, however, instead of explaining calmly, immediately flew off in a tirade, declaring that the Yeti was dangerous and that he must at all costs have it back, citing some electronic mumbo-jumbo about 'waves' and 'reception'. That, of course, only had the effect of turning Silverstein's bewilderment to bafflement, and then towards irritation. Each time the collector tried to reason with Travers, the professor started again; insisting, pleading, demanding, even outright begging that Silverstein surrender the Yeti to him.

Eventually Travers calmed down, but he refused to move from the museum, instead falling into a pattern of pacing, muttering inaudibly to himself, only stopping every now and again to lapse into a pensive silence.

Two hours later, now seated at his desk, Silverstein wondered what he should do. He had abandoned Travers to the Yeti a while back, retreating to his study to attempt at least some of his cataloguing – but the thought of his unwanted house-guest prevented him finding any pleasure in the activity, and certainly no enjoyment in his port.

He laid down his pen with a heavy sigh, removing his glasses and rubbing wearily at his eyes. He supposed he could call the police, but some remaining respect for the friend Travers had once been made him baulk at the idea. Malachi had looked in on his way out, off to pick up Rachel before heading to the gallery. At the unexpected sight of Travers, Malachi had cast his father an enquiring look, but Silverstein had simply shaken his head, waving him on his way. For all Travers' bluster, the professor was a gentle soul, and at the time Silverstein had been sure he would blow himself out in the end.

He now wished he hadn't been so dismissive. Malachi would not be back for hours, and so he could not expect any help from that quarter. Travers' family would be of no use either; his son, Alun, was busy lecturing in Oxford, and his daughter, Anne, herself a scientist, was somewhere half a world away. He simply had to trust that something would turn up.

Edward Travers had not been the same since his interests had changed to electronics during the last War, in Silverstein's opinion. He and Travers had known each other for years, both being enthusiasts of anthropology and cryptozoology. Once upon a time the professor had been a frequent visitor to Silverstein's home, where the art dealer had set up his museum of curiosities when he first came to London – oh, so many years ago now. It was Silverstein who had stepped in to help Travers after his disastrous expedition to Tibet, offering to buy the robot Yeti as a means of keeping the professor from bankruptcy. Travers had been grateful at the time, using the money to take the dive into electronics, where he had subsequently made his fortune.

And then things had changed. Slowly at first, almost imperceptibly, but something had begun to dog Travers' mind. His visits had become less frequent; shorter, far less genial. The death of Travers' wife during – but not a result of – the War had not helped matters, either. Margaret Travers had always managed to keep a reign on her husband's greater excesses of character, but after she was gone the professor's demeanour had shifted to something more proprietorial; patronising, even. Always Travers had come back to the Yeti with an intensity that bordered on the obsessive; as if it were still his, as if he were only lending it to Silverstein out of some superior sense of charity – as if Silverstein had not bought and paid for it outright, and it was not he who had done Travers the favour!

Things between the two men had long since cooled significantly when, just this last year, Travers had suddenly buried himself away in his work, practically becoming a hermit. Now months later he had re-emerged, and once more he was fixated on the Yeti, only this time demanding its outright return.

A deep frown creased Silverstein's brow. Always,

always, it came back to that dratted Yeti! Not that Edward Travers had the right to demand anything of him anymore, or *ever* had... And yet here he was again, larger than life, and twice as insufferable as before.

The ringing of the doorbell broke into Silverstein's thoughts, startling him out of his reverie. Rising from his chair and hurrying into the hallway, he cast a glance back down the corridor. Travers was still with the Yeti, back turned and broad shoulders stooped. Silverstein let out a frustrated sigh as he made his way to the front door, wondering what new turn his evening would take. There was at least none of that frantic jangling like before, so whoever this visitor was seemed content to wait patiently for an answer – though why they would be calling at this hour was a mystery in itself. Maybe Malachi had decided to return early, having forgotten his key?

Cautiously, Silverstein undid the latch and opened the heavy front door a crack.

Standing on the other side was a young woman with short, dark hair, cut in a fashionable bob. The features of her heart-shaped face were somewhat fey-like, her dark eyes alive and intelligent. She was wearing a pair of sturdy knee-high leather boots and a deep blue capelet, the collar of which was pulled up against the winter chill.

'Mr Silverstein?' she enquired politely.

'Yes,' Silverstein replied, a little stunned. He did not recognise the young lady, yet at the same time there was something oddly familiar about her. Try as he might, though, he could not place her. 'Er, who are you?'

A slightly uncertain expression crossed the woman's face. It seemed *she* at least had expected him to recognise her. 'Anne Travers. Is my father here?'

Anne Travers. Of course it was. Anne, whom Silverstein had last seen as a girl, now grown-up, so much like her mother. Silverstein breathed a mental sigh of relief, offering up silent thanks to whichever of the Patriarchs had sent her here in search of her father. Yes, Anne would be able to deal with the professor, he was sure.

'Yes, he's here.' A look of relief crossed Anne's face, and Silverstein stood to one side, letting her in and closing the door behind her. 'Come and see him, and take him away. He's a fool. An old fool!'

Not that Silverstein himself was really in a position to call anyone 'old'. Neither he nor Travers were getting any younger, but in this case he felt more than justified about the 'fool'.

Anne nodded her understanding, apparently taking his calling her father a fool in her stride, and headed straight for the museum, instinctively knowing that was where she would find him. It seemed she still remembered the way from her childhood visits to the Silverstein house, and the thought made Silverstein feel a brief spark of fondness for those days. He and Travers used to take their children around the museum, showing off the prize exhibits, Travers bringing the exotic specimens to life with tall tales of the daring expeditions that had finally captured the beasts – and the children would listen, wide-eyed and fascinated. Despite all that had happened in the intervening years, it was one of Silverstein's most treasured memories.

'Father?' Anne called out gently as she stepped into the room, Silverstein following close on her heels. The professor did not seem to hear her, apparently lost in his own thoughts.

Not in the least perturbed, Anne crossed over and stood directly in front of him so that he could not fail to miss her. 'Father.'

Travers responded this time, surfacing from whatever brown study he had fallen into. His face was puzzled, a deep frown creasing his brow.

'Anne?' he asked gruffly. 'What are you doing here?'

'Looking for you,' she said.

'Oh?' Travers didn't seem to be any more enlightened.

'You were supposed to be meeting me,' Anne prompted.

The professor's frown deepened. 'Was I?'

'At the airport.' She spoke deliberately, as if she were talking to an errant child. It seemed to have the desired effect. Travers turned from her, tucking his chin into his scarf, like a scolded schoolboy.

'Hmm.'

'Father, what is the matter?' An edge of impatience crept into Anne's voice. 'You sent me a cable saying you're in grave trouble, and I've flown half the way round the world–'

'Trouble!' Travers' distracted air was gone in a flash, as if someone had thrown a switch in his head. The professor turned to his daughter, suddenly animated, focused. 'Yes, a great deal of trouble. It's *that thing!*'

He gesticulated wildly at the Yeti. It was now Anne's turn to look confused.

'The Yeti?' she asked, clearly inviting her father to explain, but Travers didn't seem to notice the invitation.

'You're a stupid old fool, Julius Silverstein,' the professor grumbled, letting out an irritated huff.

Silverstein resisted the urge to roll his eyes. It seemed Travers had now resorted to insulting him. Always Julius whenever he was annoyed, never Silverstein's actual first name.

'Oh, me the fool?' he said. 'You would like me to be the fool and give you back my Yeti, hah?'

'You must, man,' Travers insisted. 'Don't you understand? It's dangerous!'

Silverstein gave a dismissive scoff, turning to Anne in exasperation. 'For thirty years it stands here in my museum, and now he tells me it is dangerous!'

'I wish I'd never brought it back from Tibet,' Travers growled by way of response.

Anne spared Silverstein a sympathetic look. Clearly she was beginning to find her father's behaviour just as ridiculous as he was. 'Father,' she said, attempting again to get the professor to explain himself. 'What has happened?'

'Well, he won't listen to me. This silly old goat won't listen to me!' Travers snapped petulantly. 'I've told him, warned him. Damn it, he knows it's a robot!'

Anne sighed. Silverstein would have found her patience commendable, had he not already had more than his fill of Edward Travers for the evening. 'But, Father,' she said calmly, reasonably. 'The Yeti isn't dangerous. Well, it can't work unless it has a control unit.'

Silverstein nodded his agreement. He knew all about the control spheres; the tremendously sophisticated pieces of machinery that worked the Yeti. Silverstein had never believed Travers' claim that they were powered by some alien influence that had long since left Earth – still didn't believe it – but one thing was for certain; none of the units would ever work again, and that without a sphere the Yeti was only so much metal and fur. Anne, sensible Anne, knew exactly what she was talking about.

Yet at that moment a strange look entered the professor's eyes, as if he was seeing something far beyond the walls of the room they were standing in.

'But I've done it, Anne,' he said hoarsely. 'I *have* reactivated a control unit.'

The news was certainly unexpected. Overcoming her astonishment, Anne's face lit up with excitement; ever the scientist, like her father. 'Oh, Father, this is wonderful news!'

'Is it?' The distant look left Travers' eyes, bringing his attention back into the here and now. Unlike his daughter, he seemed anything but happy with his break-through. 'Yes, yes, I suppose it would be, except for one thing.'

'What?'

'The sphere – it's gone! It's disappeared!' Travers rounded on Silverstein again, his face a picture of desperation. 'Look, you must let me have the Yeti back, Silverstein! Oh, make him understand, Anne!'

Silverstein could only stand there, speechless. All of a sudden Travers' desperation to recover his prize made so much more sense. The Yeti was a fabulous piece of machinery in and of itself, but a working robot... It would be utterly priceless. So, in the end all it came down to was money. After a lifetime of converting works of art into cold, hard cash, this was something Silverstein understood implicitly. Travers wanted the Yeti back so he could exhibit the complete device to the scientific community; more fame and fortune for Edward Travers, and in so doing he would happily rob Emil Silverstein blind. It was an outright betrayal.

'Oh, I understand,' Silverstein said coldly. 'I buy the Yeti off you thirty years ago, and now it is valuable, yes? You try to scare me, take your Yeti back. Why? Money. You want to rob me!'

'Oh, all right, I'll buy the thing back, if that's what you want!' Travers exclaimed, exasperated – but it was too late for that, now that Silverstein had guessed his purpose.

'No, no, no, no!' Silverstein shook his head, wagging his finger for emphasis. 'Is priceless; the only one in the world. It's mine!'

'Fool!' Travers growled, doubtless furious at being thwarted.

Silverstein felt his blood rise in response. For a few moments they traded insults, until finally Anne intervened.

'Father!' She was clearly shocked.

Silverstein turned, flinging out a hand in disgust, both at the situation and Travers. 'Take him away! Out of my house!' He stalked over to the mantelpiece, not trusting himself to be near the other man for a moment longer.

'Father, look,' Anne intervened again, drawing her father to one side – away from both himself and the Yeti, Silverstein noticed. 'Perhaps you've made a mistake? You've put the sphere away somewhere in your laboratory and forgotten it. You've done it before, you know.'

She was doing her best to placate her father, keeping her voice low, calming, rational. As before, the tactic seemed to work. Travers deflated a little, tucking his chin into his scarf again.

'No, no, I've looked everywhere,' he muttered.

'Let's go home and look again, shall we? You know what you're like.'

The professor still looked unconvinced. 'Yes, well. But suppose–'

Sensing that she was making headway, Anne moved in to press home her advantage. She smiled, patting her hand gently against his shoulder. 'Let's go and have a quiet dinner and you can tell me all about it,' she said cheerfully. 'Then we'll go home, and we'll look for the sphere.'

'Hmm. Well. All right,' Travers agreed grudgingly. But then, quite suddenly, he turned back to Silverstein and raised his voice. 'But I warned you, Julius, I warned you!'

That was the last straw for Emil Silverstein, his temper flaring uncontrollably. 'Get out!' he snapped at them both. 'Take him away! Nobody destroys Emil Silverstein's collection! Nobody!'

Anne reacted instantly, recognising that the time for tact had passed. 'Come on, Father!' she said briskly, grabbing Travers by the arm and ushering him from the room, not giving the professor the least chance to rally himself into resisting.

He followed Travers and his daughter, practically chasing them down the hall and out onto the front porch. 'No, the Yeti's mine! You can't scare me with your wild stories!' Nobody treated him like this in his own home, least of all Edward Travers, who he had once called a friend. 'Get out! Out! Out!'

He slammed the door shut behind them, the loud *bang* as the wood connected with the frame echoing through the house. Silverstein turned and walked back along the hallway shaking his head, still furious. He could not recall ever feeling so angry in his life. Heaven alone knew what went on in Travers' mind these days – Edward Travers certainly appeared not to know!

Even so, he shouldn't have taken it out on poor Anne. With Travers and his daughter finally gone, Silverstein began to feel a twinge of guilt over his behaviour. It was clear that she had been doing her best to keep her father in check, and that she herself was worried for his wellbeing. And with good reason, it would seem.

From considering Anne Travers, Silverstein's thoughts naturally turned to his son. Would he himself one day become such a burden to Malachi? Old age could certainly play cruel tricks on a man, though a burden shared among family was much easier to cope with. Malachi would soon be married, and to a very suitable match. Silverstein liked Rachel; she was a sweet girl, if a little flamboyant at times, but then so many girls were these days, weren't they? True, he would have preferred her to be Jewish, but when it came to that Silverstein didn't really have a leg to stand on, having married outside the faith himself. He spared a thought for his dear Edith, no longer with them for many years now. Just like Margaret Travers.

Yes, Rachel would make Malachi an excellent wife – and who knew? Maybe very soon there might be grandchildren to dote on and show the wonders of the Silverstein Collection?

Silverstein sighed and shook his head once more. Well, he may have lost most of his evening, but there were still a few things that required his attention before he retired. A shame about his cataloguing... A small supper was in order, and then to bed, maybe reading a few chapters of his book first. Malachi would not be back for a while yet, probably stopping off at a club with Rachel for a nightcap, and he was well past the age that Silverstein would even consider waiting up for him.

He walked back down the hallway with a measured pace, blowing out the candles as he went. Malachi was always on at him to replace the candles with electricity, convinced that it was only a matter of time before he accidentally burned the place down. Silverstein could only smile at that. Back in the old country he had grown up with gaslight and candlelight, and both behaved well enough if you respected them. Besides, many of the artefacts had been fashioned in an age when they could only be viewed either by daylight or candlelight; electric light was harsh, and would only be unkind to his collection in return. No, Silverstein liked the thought that he was seeing the objects as their creators had intended them to be seen, as had the eyes of countless generations before him. Somehow it brought the exhibits to life.

A sudden splintering crash made Silverstein jump, his hand jolting the candelabrum he was holding and spilling hot wax onto the tiled floor. The sound of breaking glass was unmistakable, and it had come from the museum.

Silverstein swallowed the lump that had risen in his throat. Had Travers somehow given Anne the slip and returned to steal the Yeti by himself? That in itself was madness. The Yeti was heavy and unwieldy; Travers would barely be able to move it on his own. The professor must have truly gone mad!

'Travers?' he called out. 'Travers, is it you? I'm not frightened by your stupid tricks!'

The tremor in his voice, though, clearly said otherwise. Beforehand, Silverstein had been buoyed up with righteous anger in the face of Travers' bellicosity, but met with just a sinister silence… Suddenly the house felt very big and very empty.

Silverstein forced his legs to move, and took a few cautious steps towards the museum. 'Travers, I know it's you! I'm not a fool!'

Still there was no reply – nor any other sound, for that matter. Perhaps it wasn't Travers after all? Perhaps it had just been some kids messing around, throwing stones at windows for cheap thrills? Yes, that seemed more reasonable; just stupid kids up to stupid tricks.

But as he stepped into the museum, heart hammering in his chest, Silverstein became aware of a high-pitched electronic beeping just at the edge of his hearing. He looked around in bewilderment, trying to locate the source. Where on earth could it be coming from? It seemed to be moving, getting louder…

It was right behind him.

Slowly, Silverstein turned, and found himself looking up to meet a pair of glowing red eyes.

A scream of abject fear tore itself from his throat as the Yeti brought down its monstrous paw with a roar.

CHAPTER TWO
Hang on to Yourself

SHE IS FALLING, SPIRALLING DOWNWARDS, DRAGGED
*irresistibly into the black gullet of the gnome. A great, howling
roar rings in her ears as she is swept up, away. She tumbles
through darkness and light, drowning in noise. In the distance
she is sure can see – or feel! – her husband and Sir Alistair,
both of them falling with her. Now accelerating rapidly through
time and space, screaming past her and through her – so fast,
too fast to bear. She wants to close her eyes against the
onslaught, but she has no eyes to close. She wants to cry out,
but she has no voice. Too much, too much. Her mind and body
are turned inside-out and back-to-front, racing onwards ever
faster…*

And then everything stops.

The world returns around her.

Someone is holding her hand.

'Darling?'

Dame Anne Bishop sat perfectly still, her thoughts
reeling as they slowly caught up with the rest of her. Now
that the rush was over, information began to filter
through to her senses, little by little grounding her in her
surroundings. She was sitting upright on what felt like a
settee, her legs tucked neatly underneath and crossed at
the ankles. She hadn't been sitting beforehand; she had

definitely been standing.

What on earth had just happened?

Someone was sitting next to her, holding her hands in theirs. She turned to ask them what had happened, only for her voice to die in her throat when she realised that the person sitting next to her was a stranger.

He was holding her hands in what she supposed was meant to be a comforting manner; he was roughly in his early thirties, fairly handsome, with slicked-back dark hair, deep brown eyes and an aquiline nose. His gaze was utterly focused on her, his face a picture of concern.

'Rachel?' he asked.

Anne blinked in confusion. Rachel? Who was Rachel?

She felt cold all of a sudden, and her body gave a violent shiver. Something was wrong, though. She felt strange, out of kilter, as if she were somehow detached from the moment she was living in. A side-effect of whatever she had experienced, perhaps? Hard to tell, seeing as she still didn't know what that might have been. Her eyes were heavy with make-up – too much make-up, by the feel of things – and her cheeks were wet, as if she had been crying. But why would she have been crying?

In the meantime, the young man's concern had turned to outright worry, doubtless as she hadn't replied to him; though why he thought her name was Rachel, Anne could not fathom. Around her she was becoming aware of other people in the room; a low murmuring of male voices, the soft shuffling of shoes on parquet, bodies milling around at the edge of her vision. Yet she had not been in such company a moment ago, and it should be somebody else holding her hand.

Bill. Where was Bill?

The name was as good as a rallying cry.

Almost instantly Anne's head cleared and the memories began to come back to her. She and Bill had been paying a visit to Alistair at the nursing home; it had been Joan Pemberton's funeral that morning, and they had decided to drop by especially, fearing that Alistair may need a little 'bringing out of himself' afterwards. He had lost a lot of friends over the years – as had they all.

Alistair had been telling them about his 'falling asleep' after the funeral, and how he believed it to be connected to the gnome he had found lying discarded in the churchyard.

Anne felt another shiver crawl down her spine. The gnome was a grotesque little thing, but at the time it hadn't seemed anything special or particularly uncanny. She remembered the strange circular engravings on its base, and felt a strange familiarity looking at them. What had Alistair said? Something to do with the past…?

'Darling? Rachel, can you hear me?'

Terribly nice though the young man was, and clearly concerned for her welfare, Anne was beginning to get more than a little cross with him. Even on brief acquaintance he had no business calling her 'darling', especially as she was old enough to be his grandmother! She was just about to tell him to let go and show a little respect, when she happened to glance down at their clasped hands. Her words dried up in her throat again, eyes widening in shock.

The hand the young man was holding was not Anne's hand. It couldn't be. Her hands were old, a mess of veins beneath too-thin wrinkled skin. This hand was young, smooth and soft-skinned, with perfectly manicured nails far longer than Anne would ever have deemed practical. More significantly, this hand was wearing an engagement ring; a large, showy cluster of diamonds which glittered coldly at the slightest movement. And yet Anne could feel the sensation of the young man's hand; feel the gentle pressure of his fingers, the comforting warmth of his skin against hers and the weight of the ring on the finger as if it were her own.

19

With a growing sense of alarm, Anne dared to look further downwards. She was wearing a navy blue mini-dress, just long enough for decency, it seemed. Long, shapely legs were covered by the thinnest of hosiery – fifteen denier, she thought absently, if she were any judge at all. Bare arms, short skirt and flimsy tights; no wonder she was feeling chilly! A pair of stylish but utterly impractical stilettos on her feet finished the ensemble.

There was no doubt about it; she was not in her own body.

Heart pounding in what was not her chest, Anne did her best to keep her expression neutral as she turned her attention back to the young man. When she had first seen him, she hadn't recognised him at all; yet now that she looked at him properly, he seemed strangely familiar. There was something about the set of his features that plucked at her memory, and a name floated at the back of her mind from oh so many years ago now. What was it? She *did* know this man, or had at some point in her life, and had known him pretty well, she was certain…

In her mind she could picture an old black and white photograph; in it the young man was standing beside a smaller, balding man with thick-rimmed glasses, sporting the same aquiline nose and sharp eyes. Julius – no, that had been her father's name for him – *Emil* Silverstein. Which meant that this young man had to be–

'M-Malachi?' she asked in disbelief.

She had not seen Malachi since… Well, not since far too many years ago, and they had not parted on the best of terms. But if this truly was Malachi Silverstein, then logic dictated that he should be older – *much* older! He and Anne were of an age after all, and by all rights he should now be in his seventies. No, it just didn't make sense. None of it did.

Malachi's brow creased with fresh concern, and he rubbed his thumb gently across the back of her hand.

'Don't worry, darling, I'm here,' he said firmly, reassuringly. 'You've had quite a bit of a shock; we all have. It'll be all right, I promise.'

'Mr Silverstein?'

Both Malachi and Anne looked up, the latter very grateful for the interruption, as she was too stunned to form any sort of response. The man who addressed Malachi was middle-aged, skinny and slightly taller than average height. His short, dirty-blond hair sported a severe parting over his left eye, his chin covered in a thin layer of stubble. He was wearing a dark grey overcoat that might once have been considered fashionable in the 1950s, and there was a spiral-bound notepad and pencil clasped in his left hand. Anne's mind readily supplied the word 'policeman'.

'We're just about finished here, sir,' the man said. His manner was brusque and his voice rough around the edges, his face bearing the haggard expression of a man who had recently been dragged out of bed and thoroughly resented it. 'If you wouldn't mind, I'd like to leave one of my men stationed here overnight, just to be on the safe side.'

'Thank you, Inspector,' Malachi replied crisply, confirming Anne had been right in her suspicions. Malachi, however, sounded anything but grateful. 'Miss Ashcroft has had a terrible shock, and I must get her home.'

Anne took advantage of Malachi's momentary distraction to get a better look at their surroundings. She recognised the room as being the front parlour in what had once been the Silverstein family home in Kensington, though Malachi had sold the place decades ago, following his father's death. She remembered it vividly; the Regency-style furniture, the antique Persian carpet, the pattern of the wallpaper…

There were policemen coming and going from the

room; uniformed officers and plainclothes alike. Again, Anne felt something at the back of her mind trying to get her attention; some element that she could not quite put a name to.

'Which I appreciate, sir,' the inspector continued, with what seemed like commendable patience. 'And you'll be free to do so shortly. Just for the record, have you since noticed anything else that's missing?'

'What? No. No, nothing that I've seen,' Malachi answered distractedly. 'Just that damned Yeti!'

The word brought Anne's attention back to Malachi and the inspector. *Yeti?* An intense feeling of dread began to creep over her as she continued to listen in to the conversation.

'And you're certain you don't know of anyone who would want to steal it?' the inspector prompted.

'No! Well… I suppose the professor–'

'Professor…?'

'Travers. Professor Edward Travers,' Malachi explained, somewhat exasperated. 'He was the one who brought the Yeti back from Tibet; he was here before I went out, arguing with my father. But that doesn't mean–'

Anne didn't hear the rest of the sentence, as Malachi's voice became drowned out by the sound of her own heartbeat pounding in her ears.

The Silverstein house, a break in, a stolen Yeti…

No. It *couldn't* be!

Before she fully knew what she was doing, Anne leaped to her feet, ignoring Malachi's cry of alarm, and headed to where she knew the museum used to be. Cursing under her breath, she kicked off the useless high heels and ran down the hallway in stockinged feet, slipping and sliding as she came to halt outside the open door to the museum. A young constable stood guard just inside the door, but was so startled by her sudden appearance that he only had the chance to begin a token protest.

'Miss,' he stuttered. 'Please, you can't! We haven't covered–'

Anne ignored him, pushing past and stumbling into the room, stopping short with a gasp.

The scene that presented itself to her was one that she knew all too well. Many years ago she had studied the photographs from the police investigation into the murder of Emil Silverstein in an attempt to work out for herself what had happened, and it was as if she had stepped into one of the frames.

Around her were the taxidermied animals, suits of armour, tapestries and glass cases of ancient artefacts she remembered from her childhood, caught in relief by the stark flash of the crime scene photographer's camera. The French windows on the far side of the room had been shattered, the empty frames hanging drunkenly off their hinges. In the centre of the room, surrounded by three further policemen who were directing surprised and irritated glares towards her, stood the plinth where Silverstein had displayed his prize exhibit. The plinth was empty.

And there lay the mutilated body of Emil Silverstein, face and front lacerated almost beyond recognition; fresh blood having soaked a dark red pool into the Persian carpet where he had fallen.

Anne was dimly aware that someone was shouting at her, taking hold of her shoulders and trying to pull her away from the scene, but she stood fast. The singing in her ears grew louder, drowning out all other sound, and her breath came fast and shallow. Her vision narrowed in on the grisly tableau, as if she were viewing it through the wrong end of a telescope, and the ground seemed to shift beneath her feet.

The last thing she was aware of, as the world began to fade to comforting blackness, was a man shouting a name.

'Rachel! Rachel!'

But who was Rachel?

About forty miles away from the drawing rooms and tree lined-streets of Kensington, and a few hours later, Private Daniel Arkwright of 1 Para – 'Noah' to his friends – was on duty in the guardroom of Browning Barracks, Aldershot. It was a chilly night, no mistake about that, and he was glad to be inside in the warm; for the present, at least. At the moment it was his turn to be inside with Sergeant Calder and Corporal Jackson; Privates Shaw and White were out on the gates, whilst Tovey and O'Brien were walking the inside of the perimeter. Arkwright had another half an hour before he switched over with White, and he was not looking forward to going outside again.

Browning Barracks had only been completed last year, and 1 Para had moved in not long after. Since the beginning of the decade the military garrison at Aldershot had been in a constant state of rebuilding, the old brick Victorian buildings of both the North and South Camps being demolished and replaced with brand new modern buildings; concrete, glass, plastics and all mod-cons. On the whole, Arkwright was not entirely convinced by his new home. There had been no doubt that the old buildings had been hopelessly outdated, no longer fit for needs of a modern Army; and yet the private could not help but feel that there could have been a slightly better design than a series of featureless rectangular blocks. Call him old-fashioned, but it all felt a bit soulless to him. Maybe, given a chance to settle down, it would improve in time?

Arkwright himself was still something of a new feature in 1 Para. Two months ago he had earned his wings, and had finally been able to ditch the hated green oval patch from behind his cap badge that denoted a man yet to complete his parachute training. The euphoria had quickly worn off, however, once he'd transferred to Aldershot and he had settled back into the mundanity of everyday military life. Guard duty wasn't the worst of it. Still, there were worse places to be, and the news was that the battalion was gearing up for deployment – though, as yet, exactly where they might be going was anyone's guess.

Where Private Arkwright was headed, he thought gloomily, at least in his immediate future, was towards a very empty wallet.

'Unbelievable,' he complained, throwing his cards down on the table in disgust. 'Un-bleedin'-believable!'

Sitting across from him, Jackson looked on in resignation as Calder raked his modest pile of winnings across the formica, a triumphant smile splitting his craggy, weather-beaten face.

In the background the small transistor radio on the shelf above the desk was tuned into *Night Ride* on Radio 2, Jon Curle introducing *Wichita Lineman* as the next song. Rumour had it that the Powers That Be had been persuaded to purchase a television for the guardroom, though how long it would be before that materialised was a running joke in the Mess.

'Cheer up, old son,' Calder said brightly, as Glen Campbell softly crooned he could *'hear you singin' in the wire'*. 'Not like you was going to spend it on anything worthwhile.'

'How'd you know, Sergeant?' Arkwright grumbled.

Calder raised what were left of his eyebrows. ''Cause I've seen that bird you're stepping out with, and trust me, you ought to ask for your money back.'

Arkwright's only response was to mutter something inaudible under his breath.

Calder wagged a warning finger. 'Oi, enough of that.

Honestly, Noah, I'm doing you a favour.'

Though exactly what sort of favour this might be was never clarified, as at that moment the RT crackled into life and Private White's voice sounded over the airwaves. 'Heads up,' came the warning. 'It's Little Spence.'

The three men inside immediately sprang into action. In one deft move Calder swept his winnings off the table and into his pocket, picked up the cards, and began laying out a game of Patience. Jackson retrieved the battered paperback book from over by the kettle, while Arkwright, likewise, started flicking through the magazine he had unwisely discarded earlier in favour of the poker game. About half a minute later the door opened and in stepped Captain Ben 'Little Spence' Knight, OC D Company. The duty officer for the evening.

'At ease,' he said, automatically waving the men back down again as they simultaneously rose from their seats. 'All quiet, Sergeant?'

'Yes, sir,' Calder replied, settling back down again. 'Quiet as the grave. Quieter, even.'

Knight eyed the cards Calder had laid out on the table, not for one moment fooled by the tableau of virtuous inactively he had been presented with on his arrival. 'Teaching Arkwright and Jackson the error of their ways, Calder?'

'Oh yes, sir,' Calder replied, grinning. 'Always make sure to set an example, sir.'

'And how much did they err this evening?'

Calder's grin widened. 'There'll be plenty to forgive come church parade on Sunday, sir.'

'I'm sure the Padre will be delighted,' Knight remarked dryly. Calder was an old rogue – what was sometimes generously referred to in the battalion as 'a character' – but fairly harmless with it, and the captain was experienced enough to know exactly when to turn a blind eye. Pleasantries exchanged, he walked over to the desk to take a glance through the visitor and log books.

'Any news on our deployment, sir?' Jackson hazarded, looking up from the book he was pretending to read. The captain honestly wondered why the corporal bothered; no one would ever believe he would choose to read a book like *Wuthering Heights* of his own free will.

'Not yet, Jackson,' Knight said briskly, flicking through the last couple of pages. As Calder had said, no incidents or visitors had been logged since the late afternoon. 'The CO expects to receive the orders next week.'

'Farleigh in B Company thinks it'll be Libya,' Arkwright chipped-in. 'Reckons that things are hotting up over there a bit more than the Brass're letting on.'

'Probably means we'll end up in Northern Ireland, then,' Jackson scoffed.

Knight couldn't help but grimace at the thought. Lance Corporal Farleigh had a reputation for being spectacularly wrong about nearly everything, from racing tips to the weather forecast, though he never let that stop him from trying. After a decade or so of relative quiet, things were beginning to turn ugly again, and despite the assurances of Terence O'Neill and his Ulster Unionist Party government, everyone in the Forces knew that it was only a question of *when*, not *if*, they would be sent to intervene. Still, despite Jackson's snide remark, Knight knew for certain that whoever Whitehall sent it would never be them; that wasn't what the Paras were for. Wrong regiment, wrong place.

'Well,' he said. 'Whether we'll be sunning ourselves or freezing our socks off, I'll probably only find out just before you chaps do.'

What Ben Knight knew, however, that his men did not yet know, was that wherever 1 Para would be sent, he and D Coy would not be joining them. They would be staying behind to form the core of a new Special Forces Support Group, under the direct command of Colonel 'Old Spence' Pemberton. Apparently, the RAF and Royal Marines were in on it too, the whole thing being co-ordinated by General Hamilton at Strategic Command, Fugglestone. It had been on the cards since last September, but as ever with such things, it took a while to organise.

As yet Knight did not know all the details, but Old Spence had confided in him enough to learn that their brief was to counteract 'new and unusual threats to national security', which to the captain's mind had a somewhat ominous ring to it.

In the background *Night Ride* came to an end, giving way to the news, and Knight realised it had to be coming up to the early morning closedown. It wouldn't hurt to stay and catch the latest bulletin.

'Turn that up, would you?'

Jackson obliged, leaning back in his chair to twist the knob, and Robin Boyle's measured voice filled the small room.

'*...though the Secretary admitted it would raise questions in the House. The millionaire art dealer and collector, Emil Silverstein, was found dead in his home in South Kensington late last night. Police have issued a statement saying that Mr Silverstein was killed during a break-in. The thieves are reported to have stolen a life-size model yeti; a priceless artefact brought back by an expedition from Tibet in 1935. So far there have been no arrests. The London School of Economics remains closed as students...*'

The rest of the broadcast fell on deaf ears as the soldiers exchanged baffled glances.

'Did he say, "model yeti", sir?' Jackson asked.

'That's what it sounded like,' Knight said.

Arkwright looked puzzled. 'What's a yeti?' he asked.

'What? Oh, it's a mythical creature that supposedly

lives in Tibet,' Knight explained. 'Supposed to be half-man, half-ape. Lives high up in the mountains in lonely, isolated spots.'

Arkwright's eyes widened to almost comical proportions. 'And this bloke *had* one?'

'A model of one, it would seem.' Knight frowned. 'Dashed odd thing to steal, though.'

'Probably wants it to go with his clockwork Loch Ness Monster, don't he?' Jackson quipped.

'That'll do, Corporal,' Knight said firmly, but the smile playing at the corners of his mouth belied his tone, and the corporal grinned in response.

Calder chuckled as he finished playing out his spread, sweeping the cards and shuffling them. Looking up at Knight, he indicated the deck. 'Deal you in, sir?' he asked.

Knight let slip a snort of amusement, but lifted an eyebrow in warning all the same. 'Don't push your luck, Sergeant,' he said, turning to make for the door. 'The Padre may be in the business of forgiving, but the CO's not.'

Calder grinned in response, but it was clear enough that he'd got the message.

'Fair enough, sir,' he acknowledged, and started laying out another game of Patience. 'Goodnight, sir.'

'Goodnight, Calder.'

Once the door had shut, Arkwright slowly released the breath he hadn't realised he had been holding.

'Chancing that a bit, weren't you, Sergeant?' he asked incredulously.

'What, him?' Calder shook his head. 'Nah, Captain Knight's a decent sort. For an officer, that is.'

'Yeah, not like that flathead Major Dempsey,' Jackson grumbled. 'Proper little-jumped up–'

'Anyway,' Calder cut in, before Jackson could warm to the subject. 'What was all that, Noah? "What's a yeti, then?" Ain't you seen the film?'

'What film?'

'Peter Cushing, *The Abominable Snowman*.'

'Oh, that. Nah, I couldn't.'

'Couldn't?'

'I were only seven, Sergeant.'

'Stone the crows.' Calder rolled his eyes. 'I'm playin' a bleedin' nursemaid!'

The comment slid off Arkwright, more than used to digs at his age. 'So, a yeti's an abominable snowman? Why didn't he just say that?'

'Officers for you.' Calder grunted. 'Always go for the fancy words.'

'You wonder who'd would want to steal it, though,' Jackson said, chucking his book onto the desk, unread. 'And who'd *make* a model yeti in the first place?'

Calder shrugged. 'Lord knows. Probably some guru up a mountain knocking 'em out as souvenirs for the tourists.'

'Shouldn't have thought they'd get many tourists in Tibet.'

'That'd be why it's priceless.' Calder checked his watch, then shoved his empty mug in front of Jackson. 'Brew up. Your turn.'

Muttering only a token protest, Jackson collected the mugs and made his way over to the kettle. As he passed the radio, he noticed that the news had given way to the weather, and he turned the volume down.

Beneath the sounds of running water and general chatter the announcer carried on unheeded.

'*...will continue into Thursday afternoon, with scattered showers. Motorists in Central London are warned against isolated patches of dense fog in Kensington, which are unlikely to clear before mid-morning...*'

CHAPTER THREE
The Fog

DAME ANNE STARED UP AT THE STARK WHITE CEILING above her, and blinked. When that failed to give her any clue as to where she was, she turned her head to one side, in the hope that the rest of her surroundings would prove more helpful.

She was lying in a hospital bed, which admittedly came as no great surprise. On waking, Anne had thought she'd recognised the particular combination of not-too-comfortable mattress and highly starched linen, which only came with institutional bedding; the old-fashioned brushed nylon nightie she was wearing was something of a giveaway, too. She was not in a ward, however, but a private room – and a quite recently decorated one at that, judging by the faint smell of fresh paint lingering beneath the sharp tang of disinfectant. To her left was a small wooden bedside cabinet, on which was placed a carafe of water, a somewhat 'retro' (Anne hated that word!) Sony Digimatic digital clock, displaying the time of 10:23, and a hideously large bouquet of red-orange roses in a vase. To her right there was a solitary modern-style armchair upholstered in cream leather-effect vinyl, and a window gave her a view of what looked like a sort of urban green or common, over the far side of which stood a Victorian gothic church with a square tower. Her immediate surroundings seemed quiet, the muffled sound of human voices and movement coming distantly from elsewhere in the building, while outside she could just about discern the steady rumble of traffic, albeit deadened by the thick glass of the window.

Brief reconnaissance conducted, Anne returned her gaze to the ceiling and attempted to shuffle her thoughts into something resembling order – though as her head felt as if it were stuffed with cotton wool, this did not prove to be quite so simple a task as usual. Despite the setting, she was not yet particularly alarmed; there were no IV lines, nor any sort of medical monitoring equipment, and besides a little grogginess and a mild headache she was actually feeling remarkably well. Sense dictated that, whatever had happened to her, she would not be in any immediate danger.

So, not being in any dire physical condition, she moved on to consider what had caused her to be here. Facts, evidence, logical progression of events; these were the things that always grounded Doctor Anne Travers (as she still called herself professionally) whenever she found herself adrift. She trawled back through her most recent memories, or what she *assumed* were her most recent memories. From visiting Alistair, to fainting in the private collection of Emil Silverstein…

Had her life turned out any differently, she would probably have come to the conclusion that she was either dreaming or had gone mad. Anne, however, knew better. Dreams were seriously overrated when it came to detail, and 'madness' was often a term employed by the small-minded for things they could not be bothered to try and understand. With all the strange and mysterious things she had witnessed over the decades, both wonderful and terrible, she had learned never to jump to any sort of conclusions regarding relative sanity.

First things first, she told herself. Before she figured out when and where she was, she needed to establish whether she was back to normal, or still in the body of a younger woman.

Folding back the blankets and sheets, she sat up and perched on the edge of the bed. A quick glance down at long, shapely legs, smooth hands and a slender waist told her all that she needed to know – although this time there was no sign of the diamond engagement ring. A thin, slightly paler band of skin on the fourth finger of her left hand did however prove that she had not imagined this detail.

Curiosity now starting to get the better of her, Anne looked around to see if there was anything she could use as a mirror. There was nothing in the room itself, but then these private units usually had a small en suite which would undoubtedly have something. A small door set into the far corner of the room looked promising, and she got up and went over to investigate. Sure enough, on opening the door she was met with the sight of a white enamel bath, a toilet, and a rail on which were hung a selection of pink, fluffy towels, and a small washbasin with a mirror hanging over it. Bingo!

Pausing only to steel herself for a few seconds, she marched straight over to the mirror to see what she could see. The young face that stared back at her was definitely not hers – not even a young 'her' – nor was it that of anyone she knew.

She studied the features in front of her critically; blue-green eyes, petite nose, shoulder-length blonde hair, the long eyelashes still showing traces of mascara. Opening her mouth revealed a full set of strong, healthy teeth, which had undoubtedly been bleached to get them that white. The girl was certainly beautiful, in a very conventional 'bright young thing' sort of way, and a small, treacherous part of Anne's mind whispered the word 'jackpot' – which she immediately quashed, irritated and embarrassed. Whatever had happened to her, *that* was certainly not the attitude to take!

Her cheeks burning, Anne exited the bathroom. Well, that much was clear. Next would be figuring out exactly where, and quite possibly when she had ended-up. She suspected the 'why' would not be quite so easy to discover, but one step at a time.

Returning to the foot of the bed, she picked up the clipboard hanging there to study 'her' patient notes. The top sheet bore the printed header for the Royal Brompton Hospital, and the name written on the form read:

Miss ASHCROFT, Rachel Veronica

Anne picked up the clipboard and began to scan through the rest of the paperwork. 'Miss Ashcroft' had been admitted at 23:19 hrs on 4th February 1969, unconscious and suffering from shock. The patient had remained unresponsive until 23:53 hrs, when a period of delirium was noted, and for which a Doctor Raymond Farleigh had administered a sedative. Anne wrinkled her nose in disapproval, already deciding that she didn't care for Doctor Farleigh.

Further checks had been carried out on 5th February at approximately half-hour intervals by nurses E Richards and C Gupta, both of whom noted that the patient seemed to be resting peacefully with no deterioration in her condition.

Interestingly, the name listed under 'next of kin' was that of Mr M Silverstein (fiancé), which Anne found a little peculiar. If this was indeed 1969 – and, so far, all the evidence pointed towards this being the case – then it was highly unusual for an unmarried woman to have a non-blood relative as her next of kin. She recalled being vaguely aware that Malachi had been engaged around this time, though only having heard the news second hand from Alun while she was working in the States, she had never been told a name. When she'd met Malachi at his father's funeral after the London Event, however, he had been single again.

And she had certainly never heard the name Rachel Ashcroft.

According to the notes, the last nurse's check had been carried out at 09:57 hrs. Anne glanced at the clock on the bedside table and saw the display now read 10:31, which most likely meant that she would soon have company.

Replacing the clipboard, Anne sat down on the edge of the bed to mull everything over.

As she saw it, there were two main possibilities as to what was happening to her; firstly, that this was some kind of virtual reality experience or waking dream, or secondly that her consciousness had indeed been sent back in time and transplanted into another body. Anne had already pretty much ruled-out the first option; simulated realities, natural or artificial, were rarely this consistent, and even the most sophisticated technology was not infallible. There were always clues, if you knew where to look for them, as Anne knew well from past experience. Patterns repeating where they shouldn't, instrumentation that didn't behave as correctly, geographical absurdities, text that was nonsense, inconsistencies in the passage of time... All the clues, or lack thereof, indicated that this was not a simulation.

Which left the second option, which was not as far-fetched as it might otherwise have sounded. Anne's own experiments with astral projection and thought transference had long ago proved that the human consciousness was not quite so inseparable from the human body as conventional thought dictated. That her own mind was now elsewhere was a fairly easy concept for her to accept, although it did not necessarily make the prospect any less disturbing.

She hated to be blasé about it; she was an old hand at time travel, thanks in no small part to the Doctor, but to travel back through time and wake up in somebody else's body… That was a new experience.

The sound of brisk footsteps approaching broke into Anne's train of thought, and she looked up just as the door opened to admit a young Indian nurse. Seeing that Anne was up and sitting on the side of the bed, the nurse smiled.

'Oh good, you're awake,' she said brightly, stepping into the room and shutting the door behind her. 'My name is Nurse Gupta. I've been looking after you since early this morning. How are you feeling, Miss Ashcroft?'

Anne gave a purposefully weak smile in response to the query, taking a guess at what sort of character 'Miss Ashcroft' might be. Whoever Rachel Ashcroft was, it would be best to play along for now.

'A little tired,' she replied. The words emerged from her mouth, but they were in an unfamiliar voice. And yet still her usual well-travelled accent. It was a horribly peculiar sensation. 'Please, where am I? Why am I here? What happened?'

Nurse Gupta's brow rumpled with concern. 'Do you not remember?' she asked.

Anne shook her head, and did her best to look worried. 'No, I… I'm afraid I don't,' she lied. It was probably the quickest way of discovering more about her current situation without arousing suspicions – or people thinking she was unhinged.

'You poor thing.' The nurse adopted an expression of sympathy. 'You're at the Royal Brompton Hospital. You were brought in to us last night, had something of a nasty shock. Don't worry; it was nothing too serious, and you're very much on the mend now, but you were unresponsive for some time. Your young man was quite beside himself.'

Again, Anne forced herself to raise another watery smile. She appreciated the nurse's answer, which was carefully couched to not bombard the patient with too much information – and to test what she did remember it would seem, referencing Malachi as her 'young man' and not by name.

'Is Malachi here?' she asked, deciding to take her cue from the nurse.

Nurse Gupta shook her head. 'No, not any more. Doctor Farleigh sent him home last night when it became clear you wouldn't be awake any time soon. He'll be relieved to hear you're up and about.' She nodded to the flowers that were taking up most of the bedside cabinet. 'Those arrived for you first thing.'

'Can you tell me why I fainted?'

The nurse shook her head. 'I'm afraid I don't really know the details. Probably best if you wait for Doctor Farleigh to look you over first; he'll be able to tell you more than I can. And it's possible you might remember of your own accord before then. Now, you sit still there as there's a couple of little tests I need to do, then we'll see if we can get you some breakfast.'

As if it had been listening in, Anne's stomach twinged and gave a very audible growl. Now that food had been mentioned, she found that she was absolutely starving, and she felt her cheeks go hot again.

Nurse Gupta grinned. 'Breakfast a priority, then!' she said, laughing as she took a thermometer from her top pocket and gave it a shake. 'All right, Miss Ashcroft, just sit still and let's pop this under your tongue.'

Anne did as she was told, submitting as the nurse took her temperature, measured her pulse and checked her pupils, then asked a few cursory questions as to whether she was feeling nauseous or dizzy, which Anne was not. As she sat there, she tried to recall what little she had known about Malachi's engagement, which was admittedly next to nothing. Even after Emil's funeral, Malachi had never liked to talk about it, only ever muttering that it had ended badly and simply been 'a dreadful mistake'. At the time that had piqued Anne's curiosity, but seeing the closed look on Malachi's face she had decided not to press him, reasoning that he would talk to her when he was ready to; but, as had often been the case in her life, events had conspired against them both before that could happen.

'Everything all right?' she asked, as Nurse Gupta finished updating the notes on the clipboard.

'All fine, you'll be pleased to hear,' she replied, smiling. 'Temperature a little high, but that's not unusual. Now, I'll go and tell Doctor Farleigh you're awake, and fetch you something to eat. I shouldn't be long.'

So saying, she replaced the clipboard and headed back out into the corridor. She shut the door behind her and, once again, Anne was left alone with her thoughts.

Rising from the bed, she crossed over to the window. She took in the wintery scene below; the bare branches of the trees swaying lazily back and forth in the wind, patches of fine frost still coating the grass where there were shadows, a few skeletal autumn leaves that had escaped the attention of the park keeper dotted here and there. Anne shivered and pulled the collar of the nightie closer around her neck. This was definitely 1969; no illusion could possibly be this good. Every detail was perfect; from the sky-blue Hillman Minx with an old-style registration plate parked on the road below, to the solitary 'Keep Britain Tidy' leaflet fluttering mournfully along the pavement.

It had been a cold but clear day when Anne left the future, but the sky here seemed darker, overcast by fast-moving clouds which hinted at later rain. The question now was what had been the purpose of bringing her back to the past – though, judging by the circumstances, the trap, as she was beginning to think of the gnome, seemed to have been laid for Alistair.

He had found the statue (or it had found him), and

he had been abducted by the gnome – though he hadn't got so far as explaining what had actually happened.

Although Anne was by no means privy to everything Alistair had done after he had left the Fifth Operational Corps, she knew enough of Brigadier Lethbridge-Stewart's career and the formidable reputation that went with it. She knew that he had made many enemies; powerful enemies, some of which had considerable abilities to mess with reality, and not only due to his close association with the Doctor. For most of his life Alistair had been practically walking around with a target on his back, and it seemed retirement hadn't robbed him of his inability to stay out of trouble.

While Alistair had not managed to describe what had happened to him with the gnome before, Fiona had told her and Bill what she had seen. He had 'fallen asleep' in his wheelchair, but in such an attitude and so deeply that Fiona had genuinely feared for the worst. It had taken a good couple of minutes for her to rouse him. From what both Alistair and Fiona had described, it sounded as if, like her, Alistair's consciousness had been taken elsewhere while his body had remained in the present, vacant. If only he'd had the opportunity to explain…

Then again, Anne thought, might that have been exactly *why* the gnome had laughed again at that moment? Perhaps it had been 'listening in', and had re-activated to prevent Alistair from letting on? But no, that didn't really fit either. If the gnome had been a trap, then why return Alistair's consciousness to his body at all? Something else was going on here, some other purpose to the gnome – but Heaven help her if she could guess at this moment what it might be!

Turning away from the window, Anne walked back over to the bed and sat down on the edge. If her supposition was correct, this time it was she, Alistair, and Bill who had been transported by the gnome. For this reason alone, she was very grateful that Fiona had chosen that moment to step outside and see about tea. Though Alistair's current wife, Doris, was far more experienced with this sort of thing, Fiona was by no means the helpless sort. She would know who to go to for help, and see to it that their bodies were taken care of while they were… elsewhere.

Well, Anne thought, letting go of a sigh. Here she was; back in 1969, stranded in another woman's body, with very little clue as to how she got there, or how she was to get home. It also begged the question, if three of them had been taken at the same time and by the same method, what would have happened to the boys on their arrival?

And did she have a hope of finding them?

To say that fog was not unusual on the streets of London was something of an understatement. Truth be told, as any aficionado of Sherlock Holmes films would doubtlessly have agreed, it was probably the city's signature weather. Every winter the warm air and smoke from thousands upon thousands of the capital's domestic and industrial chimneys collected in the low-lying Thames Valley, sending great clouds of yellow, sulphurous smog rolling up the river and into the city.

Sergeant Daniel Walker of the Metropolitan Police remembered the Great Smog of '52 vividly. Things had become better of late, the effects of the Clean Air Act of 1956 which had forced industry and residents to convert to smokeless fuels finally starting to show some effect. The last really bad incident had been seven years ago, but '52 had easily been the worst of the lot. That December the smog had crept into the capital like a thief in the night, causing chaos and carnage for three days running, robbing close to four thousand people of their lives before a stiff westerly wind had swept it out into the North Sea. The fog itself had been so thick as to have a physical presence; greasy, cloying, as if you were walking through a forest of damp towels, and you would get home to find yourself covered in a layer of thin, grey grime. It had seeped into buildings – hotels, theatres, department stores and homes – all invasive and smothering. The livestock at the Smithfield Show had suffocated in their underground pens. People had stumbled around in the eerie darkness, metal and muslin breathing masks clamped over their noses and mouths, barely able to see where their feet touched the ground. And, of course, the criminal elements had taken advantage of the chaos; burglars, looters, and bag snatchers all striking with impunity, appearing and disappearing like phantoms, utterly untraceable in the fog.

Walker had only been on the force a year in '52, and he knew his experiences of that December would stay with him for the rest of his life. He remembered being called to one house by a worried neighbour, where he had found the entire family had been asphyxiated; the father and children upstairs in bed, the mother and pet dog stretched out on living room carpet. The youngest, a little boy, had been only eighteen months old. It had taken two hours for anyone to be able to reach Walker to relieve him and take away the bodies, as the only way that the ambulances could possibly navigate the streets had been for a member of their crews to walk in front, guiding them with flares in the almost pitch darkness.

Londoners knew about fog. It was a traditional foe, and as such they knew how best to get by whenever the winter weather turned against them. Sergeant Walker had therefore been somewhat surprised when he had been called to Cadogan Street, just off the Brompton Road, on account of disruption caused by a patch of mist.

Not knowing quite what sort of 'disruption' he would be facing, the message having not been that specific,

Walker had taken young Constable Varney with him as beat partner. They had arrived at the south end of Cadogan Street to find a gaggle of twenty to thirty residents and passers-by gathered together, over-spilling the pavement and clearly agitated. Bisecting the street was a pall of thick white fog, which on investigation was found to be about a hundred yards wide and a quarter of a mile long, having seeped into the neighbouring Denyer Street and Rose Street.

Apart from its unusually localised situation, there didn't seem to be anything peculiar about the mist at all; but soon it became clear that this was not the opinion of the residents of Cadogan Street. And not just the residents, either. Cadogan Street was a minor thoroughfare; something of a rat-run for those who wished to avoid traffic on the Brompton Road. Vans and cars had been turning off Draycott Avenue to come up the street, on what was obviously their usual route but, when approaching the fog, the drivers had all stopped short, slamming on the brakes with a look of utter confusion on their faces. Then, having shaken off their surprise, they had all turned their vehicles around and driven off furiously in the opposite direction, some choosing to honk their horns at the huddle of bystanders in irritation as they went. Every single driver, without fail. No one wanted to go into the mist.

'Uncanny,' a portly middle-aged man in a brown woollen overcoat and red scarf stated firmly. 'Bloomin' uncanny is what it is.'

There was a murmur of agreement from the rest of the group, and Sergeant Walker shot PC Varney a sideways glance. On arrival Walker had clocked the man, who rejoiced in the name of Ronald Slim, as the local busybody; and after two minutes in his company, the sergeant was very much of the opinion that he had guessed correctly.

'Mr Slim,' Constable Varney said, with what Walker thought to be commendable patience. 'Uncanny you may think it, but a patch of fog doesn't really present an active menace to the public. Nor is there anything we can particularly do about it.'

'So why isn't it moving?' Slim demanded. He clearly wasn't impressed by Varney's youth, and rounded on Walker. 'Feel that wind? What sort of fog hangs around in a wind? Should have been long gone by now.'

'You have a go at it, Ronald,' some unknown wag shouted from the back of the crowd. 'Put some of that hot air of yours to good use!'

A ripple of laughter went through the bystanders, and Walker could see Varney was trying to keep a straight face as Mr Slim's features turned almost as red as his scarf. Yet, despite the remark, and much as Walker hated to admit it, Mr Slim did have a point. A stiff breeze had been blowing in from the west on and off all morning, which meant by all rights the mist should have cleared hours ago. Even now Walker could see that the air was not disturbing it in the slightest, unlike the discarded section of broadsheet newspaper he could see fluttering gently along the opposite pavement. Unless it wasn't just mist...

'Suppose it could be a gas leak of some sort?' Varney suggested, apparently having the same thought as Walker. 'Could be coming up from a pipe beneath the road.'

But Walker shook his head. 'No. If it were gas we'd smell it, even from here, and it'd still move with the wind.'

No smell of sulphur either, so it definitely couldn't be smog. And, truth be told, the longer they stood there, the more Walker began to feel that there was something eerie about the mist. He couldn't really explain it, but he had an uncomfortable feeling, deep down in his guts, that made him want to get as far away from the street as possible.

It felt… evil.

Walker immediately berated himself for that thought. Evil fog? Nonsense! He was there to maintain public order and get to the bottom of what was happening; letting his imagination get the better of him was not the way to go about it.

'What about the people inside?'

The sergeant frowned, and turned to the speaker; a young woman wearing a tartan skirt and a navy blue duffle coat. 'Inside where?' he asked.

'The people inside the houses in there.' The woman had a somewhat nervous expression on her face. 'I'm next door to one, and I haven't heard or seen anyone all day. Usually you hear someone, especially with the baby.'

Walker felt a sense of dread starting to creep up on him. *Especially with the baby.* Why hadn't the blasted woman led with that?

'Nothing at all?' he demanded.

The woman shook her head, frightened by the suddenly thunderous look on the sergeant's face. 'No, nothing!'

Walker searched the faces of the onlookers. 'Has no one gone in to check?'

The question was met by a guilty silence. Suddenly no one in the crowd wanted to meet his eyes, even the bellicose Mr Slim became uncharacteristically demure. Walker recognised the signs; he had seen it many times throughout his career. They were frightened, all of them. Whatever this mist was it had got to them, and they had backed away and banded together for safety, desperate for someone outside of their little community to come in and solve their problems for them. And you couldn't be angry at them, much as Walker wished he could be. Solving other people's problems, after all, was what he, Varney, and all the rest of their kind were paid for.

Walker turned back to consider the fog. Still it was sitting there, still as impenetrable as before, still as much a looming presence. It definitely wasn't smog; he *knew* what smog looked like, felt like, smelled like, and this wasn't it. But there was something wrong with it. Very wrong.

'All right,' he said softly. 'I'll go in and take a look.'

A collective sigh of relief went up from the crowd, but Constable Varney looked far from reassured.

'Sarge?' he queried, his intonation implying that his sergeant was about to make a grave mistake.

'There's only one way to settle this nonsense,' Walker said stiffly. He cast an irritated glare at Slim, who had been puffing himself back up to start pontificating again, and effectively silenced him. 'Most likely it *is* nonsense; but it's our duty to check on those people all the same.'

'But what if it's not safe, Sarge?' Varney insisted. 'Shouldn't we call for back-up? Get someone down here with some special gear? If it is toxic–'

'–we'd most likely not be standing here,' Walker finished. In fairness Varney did have a point, but Walker kept seeing in his mind the image of a small form lying far too-still in a child's bed. No, Walker wouldn't wait any longer.

Turning both himself and Varney away from the crowd's scrutiny, he lowered his voice. 'Look, lad, even if it is fumes, it's a small patch; I won't be in there long enough to be overcome. We'll keep in touch via the radios. If I do find someone, I'll call out and you can get some back-up.'

For two years it had now been the national standard for every police officer to be issued with the new Pye PF1 two-piece Pocketfone, replacing the earlier, much bulkier mobile box sets and complementing in-car units. Like everyone else on the force, Walker had been all too relieved at the introduction of personal radios. Even with separate hand-held receiver and transmitter, it was much more convenient to be able to immediately call for assistance, instead of having to find a Police Box or, if really desperate, whistle for help and hope someone was close enough to hear.

Walker turned back to the crowd, who were watching them expectantly. He nodded to Varney, taking out his issue torch and switching on the beam.

'All right, I won't be long. Keep an ear out, and get someone along to deal with that traffic.'

So saying, Sergeant Walker stepped briskly into the mist. After only a few paces, he and his torch beam were lost to the gloom.

Darkness closed in from every angle, as if he had just stepped from day to night. *Black cat in a coal hole*, Walker thought bitterly. The beam from his torch was barely making any impression.

The mist pressed in, but didn't seem to offer any sort of resistance. Walker knew well the damp ghost-like caress of smog against the skin, but it was as if there was nothing around him except thin air.

The sergeant continued to advance cautiously, his footfalls on the tarmac sounding muffled to his ears. Save those, and the sound of his breathing, there was nothing else to hear; no wind, no traffic, no birds, and most definitely no human voices.

'Hello!' Walker called. 'Is anyone there?'

His voice seemed to go no further than the end of his nose, utterly deadened. It was as if he was walking through a cloud of grey cotton wool.

Starting to feel more than a little unnerved, Walker fumbled for the transmitter button on his radio.

'28BS to 381, do you read me?' he said, using his and Varney's identification numbers. Walker waited for a reply, but there was nothing. He tried again. '28BS to 381, do you read me?'

Silence met him again; not even a hiss of background noise. Walker thumped both the receiver and transmitter, just in case something had worked loose. Though they shouldn't have. They'd been working fine not long ago, and the batteries couldn't have run down already.

Just then Walker spotted a shape on the ground outside one of the houses. From where he was standing, it looked uncomfortably like someone slumped on the doorstep. A fresh sense of alarm overtaking him, Walker jogged over to take a closer look.

It was a woman in her forties, hair in curlers, dressed in rubber gloves and pinny, as if she had just stepped outside from doing the washing up – only she was covered from head to toe in swathes of fine white filaments. Walker frowned. What was that, spider's web? No, it was too thick and too much for that, and he'd hate to meet the spider that made such a web!

'Varney.' Walker tried the radio again, dropping the formality. 'I've found one. Doesn't look in a good way. Varney? Can you hear me, over? Blast it, Varney!'

Still there was nothing, and Walker swore under his breath. Stepping closer to the woman, he moved to brush aside some of the web so that he could check for a pulse and see if she were still breathing. If so, he could carry her out and return to search for the others…

But the moment his hand touched the web, Walker found himself completely paralysed; rooted to the spot and unable to move a muscle.

Beneath his hand the filaments began to glow and pulsate, and Daniel Walker could only watch in horror as the web swept up his arm.

CHAPTER FOUR
A Dangerous Realisation

THE DOOR CLICKED SHUT AND DAME ANNE GRIPPED THE arms of the chair, her knuckles turning white, utterly incandescent with rage.

How dare he? How dare *he?*

She had just been paid the promised visit by Doctor Raymond Farleigh, who it transpired was the hospital's consultant gynecologist. He had breezed in without knocking, flanked by the Sister in charge of the private rooms, and borne down on Anne with a grin that put her in mind of nothing less than a white-coated shark.

'Ah, Miss Ashcroft. Good to see you awake.'

As Anne had suspected, she had taken an instant dislike to the man; all high-handed and patronising, cut-glass accent, calling her 'my dear' and addressing her as if she were a child. It had taken all of Anne's self-restraint to bite her tongue when Farleigh had smugly explained to her that young ladies were often prone to fits of hysteria when under strain, and that a little peace and quiet would see her perfectly well in no time.

Admittedly, she had not helped her case by still claiming to be a little 'muddled', though pretending to have remembered more about the previous evening's event, but that this man was a respected gynaecologist was both laughable and horrific. And when he had taken hold of her hand, patting it gently while he reassured her she would be perfectly fine while he was looking after her, it was positively nauseating. It had been only a brief touch, barely a few seconds, but it was both unexpected and unwanted, and the way he had looked at her... It was one thing to remember how bad it had been when she was younger, but to revisit it was entirely another.

How on earth did we stand it? Anne asked herself, her mind reeling. But, of course, the answer had been that they hadn't. She had, on the whole, been lucky in her friends and family, fighting tooth and nail to establish herself in her own right, and surrounding herself with people who respected her for her mind and as an individual. Even Bill, when they had become engaged, had never once considered that she would have given up her work once married; yet another of the many reasons she had loved him, and why their marriage had lasted thirty-nine years so far. Or would... once the Anne Travers out there finally met him next month.

Outright chauvinism had dogged her early career, and quite a part of her later career too; every opportunity that she had been refused, which had gone to a less experienced male colleague, every unthinking use of 'Miss' instead of 'Doctor', every unwanted touch, every leering glance, every cat-call or wolf-whistle... And then, if you did find the courage to complain, you were simply dismissed, or told you were making a fuss over nothing, or might have done something to encourage such advances.

Thank God for First Wave Feminism, Anne could only think. True, the twenty-first century still had a long way to go where equality was concerned, but at least a woman no longer had to face the prospect of a senior medical practitioner basically telling her that she had suffered an attack of 'the vapours'.

At least, not unless said medical practitioner was *looking* to have their name and professional reputation dragged through the mud.

Wanting to vent her rage, Anne was sorely tempted to hurl the vase of flowers across the room and imagine she was aiming it at Doctor Farleigh's head. It would make a very satisfying noise and mess – glass, water and roses flying all over the place – but on the downside it would draw attention to her, and would probably be viewed as a relapse of 'hysteria', which was the last thing she wanted.

Curse her unfailingly logical brain. So, she settled for angry pacing instead, folding her arms across her chest and treading a path between the window and the door, muttering a few choice expletives under her breath.

One positive thing that had come from Doctor Farleigh's visit – *Just the one!* Anne thought bitterly – was that she did not seem to be suffering any ill-effects from her ordeal; or 'fainting spell', as Doctor Farleigh had put it. He had declared her medically fit and asserted that she would be free to return home the following day, as the extra rest wouldn't do her any harm.

Anne reflected that she would never have got the extra day in her present, with a pared to the bone NHS desperate to see beds vacated as quickly as possible.

The hospital had informed Malachi that she was up and about. He would be calling by during visiting hours that afternoon, which was a prospect that Anne dreaded; not in the least because meeting someone so close to her at such a crucial point in her past carried with it an inherent danger.

Still, maybe she could persuade Malachi to get the hospital to discharge her that evening? Physically she was perfectly fit; there was no need for her to stay there. What she needed to do was get out and begin investigating, try and remedy her situation – and she couldn't 'remedy' anything from a hospital bed.

That Alistair had returned from his trip beforehand seemingly of his own accord was something of a comfort, but Anne was not so willing to leave things to chance. With any luck she might find a clue as to whether the others were there with her, and together they could determine a way to return their consciousnesses to the future.

She could, she supposed, discharge herself, but that would cause far too many complications. Besides, where would she go? She couldn't return home – to *her* home, the Travers' family home – not in the body of a complete stranger. Meeting her own consciousness (even in a different body) might prove disastrous as far as causality was concerned. Alistair had once told her of an incident back when he was teaching at Brendon School, when a past and future version of himself had met and triggered something called the Blinovitch Limitation Effect. As far as Anne's research had been able to decipher, this was interpreted as a 'short-circuit in time', though in her opinion the thinking behind the theory was a little mathematically woolly. Nevertheless, the meeting had cost Alistair's younger self severe mental trauma, and Anne was not willing to risk that happening to her. No, the quickest way to work out an escape plan was to get herself properly discharged, and the easiest way to do that would be through Malachi.

Thoughts of the Travers' family home put Anne in mind of her father and, as ever, she felt the familiar sense of loss and regret. The pain far less keen, but still there. She had lost two versions of him, but that first time... Her *actual* father. Even after all these years she remembered how much it had hurt; how she had watched, helpless, as the brilliant, loving man her father had once been began slipping away. How it had been almost more than she could bear, seeing him look at her and knowing he saw a stranger. She was eternally grateful that she'd had Bill with her to support her, not to mention Ruth, Alun, Sally, and Samson – even Alistair, in his own unique way.

They had all rallied round and become the family she had so desperately needed at that point, when she had felt so lost and alone. She had come to terms with everything eventually, but it had taken time. Far too much time. Even when the time had come – so brutal, and so needless an end! – saying goodbye to him on the astral plane had not really helped.

And now here she was, revisiting it; the first link in the chain of events that led to Edward Travers' untimely death. His possession by the Great Intelligence, his capture and experimentation on by the Vault, which started the deterioration of his mind, which had then led General Gore to put him in the gateway machine deep beneath the Cheviot Hills, which had served as his tomb – at least until 1980 when his body was freed by the Great Intelligence and taken back to Tibet…

Anne stopped in her tracks. Quite suddenly a thought had hit her; so suddenly as to almost have physical force. It was certainly enough to take her breath away.

Accepting that this was really 1969, before London was evacuated, then her father was still alive, his mind undamaged. In a couple of weeks his mind would be possessed by the Great Intelligence. But what if…? Could it be possible…?

Within her head, the thought was taking root. Anne knew well the risks of messing with the accepted outcomes of past events; had seen enough attempts by misguided scientists, despots and aliens that had ended in near-disaster. But change *was* possible; small changes, not enough to disrupt major events.

The London Event had to happen; Anne was brave enough to acknowledge that. It was what had brought her and Alistair together, and opened their eyes to the realities of their world and beyond. That meeting could not be jeopardised. Her younger self had to be co-opted into the scientific team of the Special Forces Support

Group, under Colonel Pemberton, she had to go to the Fortress at Goodge Street and continue to fight the Intelligence and the Yeti as the Web tightened around them. So many people would die; Pemberton, Captain Knight, Staff Sergeant Arnold, Craftsman Weams, Corporal Lane, Corporal Blake... But her father did not need to be possessed by the Intelligence. They would all have ended up at Piccadilly Circus despite that, and the Intelligence would be defeated.

Her father's possession was not a vital link in the chain, so if, somehow, she could get a warning to him and stop him from becoming the Intelligence's puppet...

Forty years of regret surged to the surface, and she knew that yes, yes she *could* do it! It was dangerous, foolhardy, even. But if she was careful, made sure she covered her tracks, kept herself at a remove...

She could stop her father from losing his mind. He would stay whole, not slip away into a ruin. She could save the soul of Edward Travers.

Doubt crept in. Did she have the right? Anne had seen enough examples of human ingenuity gone wrong to know that just because you *could* do something, didn't mean that you *should*. If she did this, would she be any better than the numerous villains she and Alistair had fought over the years?

Anne glanced out of the window, clenching her jaw in determination. Yes, she was. Because she was not some power-crazed Schädengeist seeking a new world order, not some profit-driven monster like Vorster, and she was certainly not some self-proclaimed gatekeeper of knowledge like General Gore. She was Dame Anne Bishop, daughter of Professor Edward Travers, and she was simply going to give her father the chance to live out his final days with the dignity he deserved.

And, unlike Schädengeist, Vorster, Gore and all the others, *she* was going to succeed.

'Anything, sir?'

Lieutenant Maximillian Dawlish of the Royal Engineers lowered his field glasses. He glowered at the Mist, as if it had personally insulted him. 'Nothing. Not even a flicker!'

Standing beside him, Staff Sergeant Albert Arnold let out a hiss of breath between his teeth. About forty yards in front of them, the three sappers armed with flamethrowers directed uncertain glances in their officer's direction. They had just subjected the Mist to a good thirty-second burst of flame, but it appeared to have had no effect whatsoever. Not a single ripple of movement, let alone any sort of reduction. The Mist was just as static and dense as before.

Dawlish muttered under his breath in Polish. His family's first language had been English for almost a century now, but he resorted to Polish when in need of a particularly filthy word. Ordinarily he was not one to let his feelings get the better of him, especially on operations, but this particular job had had him at too much of a disadvantage from the start.

The lieutenant and his platoon had arrived at Cadogan Street two hours ago, dispatched in response to a formal request for assistance by the Metropolitan Police; a request which was as unexpected as it was perplexing. It only served to baffle Dawlish further when it transpired that someone high up had detailed him to this assignment by name.

'They want someone who's dealt with "weird",' his major had informed him coldly, on receiving his orders earlier that afternoon. 'And you've dealt with "weird".'

As much as he would like to, Dawlish couldn't take issue with that. What had happened up at MoD Kettleness last autumn certainly fell into the category of 'weird', although he wouldn't have said he had really 'dealt' with it. Sheer dumb luck had guided him through that mess. But this was an entirely different kind of weird, and Dawlish was feeling well out of his depth. This was definitely more the speed of the Porton Down lot.

'Rum business, Staff,' he grumbled.

'Bloody uncanny business, sir,' Arnold said with a growl.

Dawlish raised a humourless smile. He liked Arnold; a steady, reliable sort, who wore his experience and rank like a second skin. Fair with the men, but not one to drive. Just the sort of fellow you wanted at your back when things got rough. As Dawlish had discovered for himself at Kettleness.

He removed his beret, rolling it up and securing it beneath one of his epaulettes with a sigh. 'All right, men,' he said wearily. 'Fall back. NAAFI break. We'll try something else.'

Maybe a smoke and a brew would provide inspiration? But as the sappers were helping each other off with the flamethrowers, Corporal Smith came trotting up from the direction of Draycott Avenue. Judging by the uncertain expression on his face, he was not the bearer of good news.

'Sorry, sir,' he said, throwing a quick salute. 'We've got company, and they're asking for you.'

Smith turned and pointed to the end of the road, where a military Land Rover was just pulling up at the other side of the secondary roadblock, the first having been set up at the junction to the Brompton Road. Dawlish swiftly re-pocketed his lighter and cigarette and put his beret back on. With any luck it might be a messenger coming to tell him that a boffin in a lab somewhere – someone who *actually* knew what they were doing – had come up with a solution to the problem. He could hope, anyway.

The Land Rover doors opened, disgorging two

figures in Army fatigues, and Dawlish instantly clocked the maroon berets and wings. Officers as well, the pips on their shoulders denoting a colonel and a captain. The lieutenant frowned, his hopes for answers instantly evaporating. What the blazes were Para officers doing here?

'With me, Staff,' he said quietly.

Dawlish unhooked the binoculars from his neck and passed them to Smith, then headed over to meet the officers, Arnold falling in behind him. As he approached, he saluted the colonel.

'Good afternoon, sir.'

'Good afternoon.' The colonel returned the salute smartly. 'Lieutenant Dawlish, I presume?'

'Yes, sir. How can I help you?'

The colonel extracted a folded piece of paper from his top pocket, which he handed to Dawlish. 'I'm Pemberton, CO 1 Para, and this is Captain Knight. From now on this operation is being handled by the Special Forces Support Group. You and your men will be under my command.'

For a moment Dawlish was too stunned to reply. *Special Forces Support Group?* But none of his men were commando trained... Remembering the papers in his hand, he unfolded them and took a read. Orders for Colonel Spencer Pemberton, 1 Para, to take direct command of the investigation into the Mist, with authorisation to requisition whatever troops and resources he judged were necessary for the task.

It was the most extraordinary *carte blanche* that Dawlish had ever seen, but there was no denying the official paper – nor the authorising signatures at the bottom of the page, the sight of which made his eyes widen. He stole a glance at the other officers; the colonel was waiting with polite impatience, while the captain's face was stoic and unreadable.

If this was a wind-up, Dawlish thought, then it was

on a monumental scale. And it definitely wasn't April the First.

Refolding the papers, he handed them back to Pemberton and braced up. 'Understood, sir,' he said woodenly. 'Lieutenant Dawlish, 36 Field Squadron, 21 Engineer Regiment. This is Staff Sergeant Arnold, my SNCO.'

Pemberton acknowledged Arnold with a nod as the staff came to attention. 'At ease, gentlemen. Now that's sorted, would you please give me your report on the situation so far, lieutenant?'

Dawlish nodded and stepped to one side, gesturing towards the Mist. 'This way, sirs. We've evacuated the residents from the immediate area,' he continued, as they came up to where the men were taking their break, Pemberton waving an 'as you were' before they could get to their feet. 'And we've cordoned off to a distance of a hundred fifty yards around the area of Mist which the police are manning, along with an information and first aid post in the local school hall.'

'Have you been able to find out what it is yet?' Knight asked impatiently.

Judging by Pemberton's lack of reaction to Knight jumping the gun, Dawlish guessed the two must have a fairly easy working relationship. The lieutenant cleared his throat awkwardly.

'Well, sir, at this stage it'll be easier to tell you what it *isn't*. It's not coal, or North Sea gas, it's not vapour, and it's not carbon monoxide. We feared it may be some sort of nerve agent, but chemical readings suggest that it isn't toxic – not in any way that they know or can measure. In fact, the air quality in there is slightly better than it is out here. And it isn't moving at all with the wind. It just sits there, as if held by air pressure alone. We've tried a vacuum pump, and that hasn't worked, and as you can see we just attempted to burn it off, but no joy there either. The next stage would be to try for some sort of chemical reaction; only there doesn't seem to be anything there to react. It's completely inert.'

'What about the civilian casualties?' Pemberton asked. 'Has anyone attempted to get them out?'

'No, sir,' Dawlish said shortly. 'Not since that police sergeant disappeared this morning. I thought we'd better attempt to get rid of the Mist first before risking it.'

He knew it would sound bad before he said it and, judging by the looks he received from Pemberton and Knight, Dawlish had not been wrong.

'Risking it?' Knight's voice was laced with contempt. 'I thought you said it wasn't toxic?'

'Not by any means *I* can measure,' Dawlish said pointedly, standing his ground.

'Well, you've got NBC suits, I can see you have. Surely those would do?'

Dawlish suppressed a sigh of frustration. Of course he had thought of that, but there was no point in saying that to Captain Knight. 'There's no guarantee they would, sir,' he explained levelly. 'As I said, the Mist isn't affected by the wind, or anything that we do to it – due to the fact that it doesn't seem to have any physical presence.'

There was a brief silence in which both Knight and Pemberton's attitudes switched from resentful to baffled. Dawlish took advantage of it and pressed on.

'We haven't been able to collect a sample of the stuff. Every time we've tried all we've come away with is a sample of thin air.'

'So how did you get your toxicity readings?' Pemberton demanded.

'Kitted up a man, stuck the instrumentation in the Mist bank and hoped for the best,' Dawlish replied honestly.

'So you're saying that the Mist isn't really there?' Knight asked, after a further beat of silence.

'Oh no, it's there all right, sir,' Dawlish assured him. 'But as we can't do anything to touch it, there's no guarantee that a suit or respirator would keep the stuff out.'

Colonel Pemberton glanced over at the Mist, his face adopting a scowl. *Now you know how I feel,* Dawlish thought mutinously.

'We have discovered one thing though, sir,' he said out loud.

Pemberton's gaze swung back to Dawlish. 'Go on, lieutenant.'

'The police constable reported that his radio went "odd" just after his sergeant entered the Mist. We conducted an experiment, setting up RTs either side of the area to transmit at different intervals and frequencies along the Mist's length. We got absolutely nothing.'

Pemberton's eyebrows rose to meet his beret. 'Nothing?'

Dawlish shook his head. 'Not even static. This stuff, whatever it is, completely absorbs all radio waves.'

'How is that possible?'

'Search me, sir,' Dawlish answered. 'Our signalman couldn't explain it. Especially as we've found out that it's broadcasting on the infrasonic level.'

He paused, noting the blank expressions on the colonel's and captain's faces. Then he remembered he was talking to Paras, and adjusted his explanation accordingly.

'Infrasound is below the range of human hearing,' he said. 'While we can't audibly hear it, there are frequencies just above and below that we can still detect.'

'Like a dog whistle?' Pemberton offered.

Dawlish's estimation of the colonel went up a notch. 'Yes, sir. Only, whereas a dog whistle is at the upper end of the scale, infrasound is at the lower end; anything that registers below twenty hertz. The Mist is broadcasting intermittently at a level of eleven hertz. The closer you get to it, the more you feel it.'

'To what purpose?' Knight asked, his frown deepening.

Dawlish folded his hands behind his back. 'Depends on what it's broadcasting. In nature infrasound is used for various reasons; elephants to communicate between herds, tigers to intimidate their prey.'

'So it's the infrasound that's affecting the victims?' Pemberton reasoned, jumping on board the engineering officer's train of thought.

'Most likely, sir. It would certainly explain the snarl-ups with the traffic.'

Pemberton nodded his understanding, turning to study the Mist once more. He took a few experimental steps closer, then stopped short, an expression of discomfort passing over his face. Knight went over to join him.

'Can you feel it too?' Pemberton asked, lowering his voice.

'Yes, sir,' Knight replied. The stoical captain was now looking somewhat unsettled. 'Like… something's walking over your grave, or creeping up on you.'

'A sonic weapon,' Pemberton mused, and from where Dawlish was standing he couldn't tell whether the colonel was horrified or impressed. 'I've heard rumours… Though I thought the aim was for precision. Doesn't seem a very efficient method of attack.'

'Could be experimental,' Knight suggested, lowering his voice further. 'Terror tactics, widespread panic?'

'Hmm, you could be right.'

Dawlish, starting to feel awkward at the turn the conversation was taking, cleared his throat. 'Um, sirs?'

The other two officers turned around in surprise, seeming to have momentarily forgotten that Dawlish was there.

'Yes, quite,' Pemberton said briskly, as he and Knight walked back over to rejoin him and Arnold. Dawlish reckoned it served as an apology. 'Any idea as to how this infrasound is being projected, Lieutenant?'

Dawlish could only shake his head. 'No, sir. Based on our observations, it shouldn't be possible.'

'Neither should a stationary cloud of mist on a breezy day,' Pemberton quipped. 'But there it is.'

Dawlish's brow creased in thought. 'I suppose there could be some sort of central emitter, the signal of which is somehow being picked up and amplified by the Mist. But if it's a work of technology, sir, it's completely alien to me.'

At that remark Pemberton and Knight exchanged a significant glance, and not for the first time that day Lieutenant Dawlish began to wonder just what sort of rabbit hole he and his men had fallen down.

CHAPTER FIVE
The Days of Sand and Shovels

WHEN VISITING HOURS FINALLY ROLLED AROUND, DAME Anne was more than ready.

She had set her stage carefully. When Nurse Gupta had come in to take her order for lunch, Anne had asked if it was possible to get hold of some make-up, pleading that she didn't want to look a mess for when her 'young man' came to visit. The nurse had been only too happy to oblige her with the 'bare essentials'. A smidge of foundation, some blusher, a hint of mascara and a neutral eyeshadow... Not full war paint by any means, but enough to count as camouflage.

Bundling herself up in the warm pink dressing gown and slippers she had been given, Anne moved to sit in the armchair which she had moved a little closer to the window. She took with her a blanket from the bed and an issue of *Harper's Bazaar* which Nurse Gupta had brought with the make-up, although she was not really all that interested in the latest spring trends from Milan. She sat down, tucked the blanket over her legs to keep out the winter chill, began flicking through the magazine and waited for Malachi to arrive.

Despite her careful composure, Anne felt somewhat nervous and a little ashamed at resorting to feminine wiles to further her plan. It was not something she ever chose to make a habit of, preferring to negotiate on her own merit and her own terms. The Underground, in the

Fortress at Goodge Street, was one of the few times she had done so; taking advantage of Captain Knight's crush on her so that he would allow an expedition up above ground to secure the parts they needed for the signal jamming device. The captain had gone up to the surface... and he had never returned.

Even after all these years she still felt a twinge of guilt over her behaviour towards Ben Knight that day. Could she somehow make it up to him? No, helping her father was as far as she could go. She would just have to live with her bad judgement call forty-two years ago. She had chosen to use him unkindly, and she was about to use Malachi in a similarly unkind way. The prospect of having to flirt with a man who was not her husband, and for whom she felt no attraction whatsoever, did not make it any better. But she had committed herself to her mission. If she was serious about making it a success, then she had to be prepared to do whatever was necessary – and if that part involved deceiving Malachi, then so be it.

While freshening-up in the bathroom, Anne had tried to see if there were any memories she could pick up from her 'host' that might give her an idea as to the life and character of Rachel Ashcroft; but there was nothing, not even a hint. It was almost as if the woman had not existed before the moment of Anne's arrival at the Silverstein house. Which simply could not be the case, and was frankly quite disturbing.

All she had to go on was an impractical outfit and a flashy diamond ring; there wasn't even a handbag to root through, which would have provided some clues. She suspected that it was with Malachi for safe keeping, along with the ring.

Drawing a blank on Rachel, she had instead resorted to remembering what she could about Malachi. He had been an only child, and with his father quite often away on business trips the opportunity to spend time with Alun and Anne had meant the world to him. They had been quite close as children, she recalled, always in and out of each other's houses at weekends and during the summer holidays… And then, as often happens as the concerns of the adult world take over, they had grown up and drifted apart. Their fathers had remained friends of a sort, news still passing between the families; but Anne could not honestly say that she was familiar with Malachi Silverstein as a man. Oh, she'd heard plenty about his business deals, his world-renowned fine art collection, and his eventual status as a venerable Patron of the Arts – but actually *known* him? In all honesty, she had not.

Well, she was about to find out. And probably in more detail then she would ever wish.

Anne turned the page, ignoring the article about Twiggy's latest shoot for Dior in New York, and began to consider the next steps in her campaign of temporal redirection (she deliberately rejected the word 'interference'). Getting out of the hospital was simple enough, but where and how she proceeded from thereon became trickier. She'd had her fair share of time travelling since that first time at Fang Rock, and she knew that successful time travel lay in finding the hazy bits; the gaps in between the major events, where things were grey and muddled. That was where history was made or, in this case, where it could be undone. The trick was to make sure it didn't unravel entirely.

She could not cross her own timeline in person; that much she knew would lead to unwanted consequences. She did, however, have the advantage of not being in her own body, so she would be awarded a little more freedom for interaction than were she here purely as her full 2011 self. After all, for all she knew her colleagues *could* have met a woman matching Rachel's description;

like Schrödinger's Cat, the necessary ambiguity was there, and it was up to her to turn that to her advantage.

She had been seated for about a quarter of an hour before she heard a soft knock on the door. Anne put the magazine to one side (she had been through it twice and still not found anything to interest her), sat up straight, and arranged her features into something resembling anticipation. *Showtime.*

'Come in!' she said brightly.

The door opened, and in stepped Malachi Silverstein. He had changed out of his dinner jacket from last night, swapping it for a not much more casual navy-blue pinstripe suit and baby pink silk tie. Despite the fresh clothing, he had the unmistakable look of a man who had been up all night; his handsome face was drawn, dark bags under his eyes, his jaw not as evenly shaven as it might otherwise have been. At the sight of his fiancée sitting up and out of bed, however, his face broke into a smile of pure happiness, and Anne felt her guts twist into an uncomfortable knot. She recognised a man in love when she saw one. It was a look she'd seen on Bill's face often enough over the last forty-two years. Knowing Malachi's feelings for Rachel as an abstract was bad enough, but seeing it... That was going to make this all the more difficult.

'Darling,' he greeted her, striding across the room, and before Anne knew it, he leaned in swiftly and kissed her on the cheek. Startled, she couldn't help but flinch, although she managed to stop herself from pulling away.

Surprised by her reaction, Malachi drew back, the smile sliding from his face with confusion.

'I-I'm sorry, darling,' he said uncertainly. 'What's the matter? Did I hurt you?'

'Oh, nothing,' Anne hastily reassured him. To emphasise this, she leaned forward and caught hold of his hand. 'Just... just a little tired, that's all. I wasn't expecting it.'

Malachi's smile returned. 'Ah. That's not really surprising,' he said wryly. Putting his overcoat to one side, he sat down opposite her on the edge of the bed. He rubbed his thumb over the back of her hand – the same gesture of comfort that he had used the previous night – fixing her with an admiring gaze. 'I'm so glad to see you're up and about. How are you feeling?'

'Better,' Anne said, trying to stop herself from blushing under his gaze. Only Bill had ever looked at her like that. 'Much better.'

'Good. I managed to get a call through to your father early this morning to let him know what happened and where you are.'

So, Rachel did have at least one parent alive. That could prove awkward.

'Is he coming here?' she asked, but Malachi shook his head.

'No. The Hong Kong business is still ongoing, and even if it wasn't, it'd be at least another week before he could charter a flight back. He sends you his love, and told me to take good care of you.'

Which came as something of a relief to Anne. She would not have to contend with the woman's father, and it answered the question as to why Malachi had been down as her next of kin.

'And don't worry about Mr Trevelyan,' Malachi continued, reeling off the news like he was going through the items of a shopping list. 'I told him what had happened, and he said to take all the time you need to get better. Penny will be able to manage his appointments for a week or so.'

'Oh, that's kind of him,' Anne said faintly. She was a little surprised to learn that Rachel had a job; somehow, she had got the impression that Miss Ashcroft wasn't the type to really need or want one. Just went to prove that you could not judge a book by its cover. Which was a shame, because the cover was all Anne had to go on at the moment.

'And who's looking after you?' she asked him, looking to redirect the subject away from her. Plus, Malachi really did look exhausted, and even at one remove she couldn't help but worry about him. He was, after all, still an old friend. He waved away her concern, however.

'Oh, I'm fine,' he said breezily. He didn't fool her for a minute, though; she had been married to Bill too long for that. 'I wanted to stay until you woke, but they wouldn't let me. So, I fetched a few things from home and booked myself into a hotel.' His smile faltered. 'I didn't want to stay... *there*,' he admitted, clearly meaning his home. 'Not with... everything. I couldn't. Besides, I wanted to be on hand in case you needed me. When you fell last night, I thought for a horrible moment that I had lost you too.' His dark eyes softened, making him look younger, a little fearful. 'I really don't know what I'd do without you, Rachel.'

It took all of Anne's willpower to maintain her smile as she continued to listen, utterly mortified. Here was Malachi, still processing his bereavement and laying bare his heart, and she couldn't even let him know he was talking to the wrong woman. She found herself wishing that the ground would open up and swallow her.

Something of her discomfort must have shown on her face, however, as Malachi's brow once again creased with uncertainty. 'Darling, are you sure you're feeling better? If you need to rest, I'll come back–'

'No, no, please don't,' Anne insisted, seeking to cover the gaffe. She took hold of his hand again and squeezed it. 'Please stay. I... I was just thinking about your father. It's just so awful!'

This, at least, was something that was genuine

between her and Malachi. Back then she had mourned the death of Emil Silverstein like a family member; and though both she and Malachi had lost their fathers to the machinations of the Great Intelligence, poor Malachi was doomed to never know the truth.

'Have the police said anything?' she asked softly.

'Not really,' Malachi replied. He sighed heavily. 'They're pretty much convinced that it was a burglary gone wrong. Dad stumbled in on them, they panicked…' He shook his head sadly. 'I'm sorry, dearest, I don't want to distress you.'

'Oh no,' Anne insisted, giving him an encouraging half-smile. It would be something of a rigmarole to have to ask all the right questions when she already knew the answers; but Rachel didn't, and would doubtless be trying to understand everything she possibly could about the death of her would-be father-in-law. And Malachi needed to process events. She could help him with that much, at least, even if she were deceiving him in other ways. 'It's all right, I'm tougher than I look. Honestly.'

Malachi hesitated a moment, but continued. 'They came armed though, that much is certain from the wounds. Knives, the Inspector thinks–'

Claws, Anne's brain supplied.

'–which makes him think that they're looking for a gang of high end art thieves.'

'Do you think he's right?' Anne asked, out of genuine curiosity. She had never really had the chance to talk it all through from Malachi's perspective.

'Without a doubt,' he said simply. 'As I've said before, our business can get very nasty. Some people will go to immeasurable lengths to get hold of something they want, even if it means taking lives. If there was somebody out there who wanted the Yeti bad enough, they weren't going to let Dad get in their way.'

Anne put a hand to her mouth, and not just for effect.

Though the motive and perpetrator were wrong, the scenario was not so far from the truth. 'I'm sorry,' she whispered, and meant it.

Malachi sent her a sad smile, and patted her hand in reassurance. *Don't worry*, the gesture seemed to say. *It won't happen to me.*

'Thing is, they're not entirely sure how the fellows got in. The inspector said that it looked more like a break-*out* than a break-in. They did find a smashed pane of glass in the higher-up windows, but it's tiny – too small for a person to get through, and much too high up for a standard ladder. They think it's unconnected, probably some kids mucking about with stones.

'The door from the museum was broken down from the inside,' Malachi continued, oblivious to Anne's train of thought, as she substituted his supposition for the facts she knew all too well. 'By something massive and heavy, by the looks of it. Funny thing was they didn't find any blood – usually they can rely on someone getting caught by flying glass. They did find animal hair, though; long-dead, but they haven't identified it yet. The theory runs that they used the Yeti as a battering ram to get out!' Malachi snorted derisively. 'Stupid thing if they did. Why go to all that trouble only to risk damaging their prize on the way out?'

'I don't know,' Anne said, hoping to stop Malachi pursuing that thought. Anything to keep him as far away from the truth as possible. 'Possibly because they were in a hurry, like the inspector said?'

'Probably,' Malachi admitted reluctantly. He sighed, rubbing at his tired eyes. 'Anyway, because there's no sign of forced entry, they think it must have been someone Dad was acquainted with, which ties in with the theory of art thieves. They probably visited him beforehand as clients to case the joint. He wouldn't have let strangers in at that time of night.'

'Do they have any suspects?'

'Not yet. They came by the office to get a list of our recent clients and contacts, but it may take days to chase each one down.' Malachi let out a huff of dry laughter. 'For a bit they thought it was old Travers, but I soon told them they were barking up the wrong tree there! The professor may be a windbag, but he's harmless.'

Anne felt her hackles rise, but held her tongue against Malachi's remark. Had he known who he was really talking to, he wouldn't dare be so flippant about her father. Either way, it helped make her feel a little less guilty for leading Malachi on.

'I should think so too,' she said shortly, as if she were only upset with the police. 'How could they ever think that of Professor Travers?'

Malachi looked at her in astonishment. 'I didn't think you'd met him?'

Blast! 'I was introduced to him once at a party,' she said quickly. 'He seemed such a nice old gentleman.'

Malachi's expression went from astonished to sceptical. 'I wouldn't have thought Professor Travers was the type to get invited to parties. Nor go to them, for that matter.'

'Well, he was at this one,' Anne said crossly, mentally kicking herself. It was a small mistake, and easily covered up, but she couldn't afford to be so careless again. There was so much at stake.

Malachi still looked unconvinced, but he seemed to accept the explanation. 'Well, leastways they now know he couldn't have done it. His daughter, Anne, flew in from America yesterday, and she's been with him the whole time since they left my father's house yesterday. And I trust Anne. I always say she got the lion's share when they were dishing out sense in that family.'

How's that for a back-handed compliment? Anne thought irritably, but she smiled nevertheless.

'So, what will you do now?' she asked out loud.

Malachi shrugged. 'Not much I can do as yet,' he said, suddenly weary again. 'Just keep things running. I identified the... the body this morning, but I won't be able to start making arrangements for the funeral until they've done the post-mortem and the coroner releases him. Under the circumstances, I don't think even Auntie Flo will hold the delay against me.'

He smiled at her again, but the pained expression remained in his eyes. 'Get some rest, darling. I'll come by tomorrow when you're discharged and drive you home. Is there anything you particularly want me to get?'

'Actually,' Anne said, placing an arresting hand on his arm as he made to get up. 'I'd much rather go home today.'

'Today?' Malachi queried, looking puzzled.

Anne nodded. 'Can you speak to the nurses?' she pleaded. 'After all, the doctor said there's nothing seriously the matter with me. I want to get home as soon as possible and recuperate there. Will you arrange it? Please?'

She widened her eyes and fluttered her eyelashes a little, and told herself sternly it was all in a good cause.

'Yes, yes of course,' Malachi said. He seemed a little taken aback. She had clearly wrong-footed him. 'I must say, darling, you're a bit keen to get going.'

'I don't like hospitals,' Anne said quickly, giving a pretend shudder. It wasn't technically a lie; for all she knew Rachel Ashcroft could hate hospitals. 'I always have, since I was a child.'

Malachi continued to look puzzled, but he nodded and stood. 'I'll go and speak to someone,' he said. 'And I'll get you a paper and pencil so you can write me a list of what you want me to bring from your flat.'

Anne smiled. 'Thank you, darling. I can't wait to get out of here and get home.'

'Well, it'll take a little longer than usual, I'm afraid,' Malachi said ruefully, pressing down the door handle. 'Getting back is going to be a bit tricky; they've had to close the Brompton Road due to fog.'

The news hit her like a punch to the stomach. *Oh no.* 'Fog?' she queried, hoping that she was mistaken.

'Yes, there's a thick patch of it spreading across the whole southern end. Utter chaos out there! I'll be as quick as I can.'

Once the door had closed behind him, Anne screwed her eyes shut and buried them into the heels of her palms.

The Mist first and then… the Web!

It had already started.

Len Harris hummed happily to himself as he stuffed another coat into his bag. He had been planning a little raid on the Brompton Road boutiques for a while now; all those lovely high-end furs and jewellery, just asking to be taken. The road closure and evacuation had been a Godsend. *Gas leak*, the coppers had said, and a real big one at that. Which meant they'd had to turn off the electricity for three or four blocks. Which meant Len needn't disable any alarms. Just him, his trusty jemmy, a sound knowledge of the back lanes, and all the time in the world. It was Christmas come early.

''Nother one for you, Cyril!' he said, tossing the full sack to his nephew. Crime was a family business as far as the Harrises were concerned, and at present Len had taken on his sister's boy for work experience.

He heard Cyril grunt softly under the weight of the bag as he caught it. He was a skinny lad; fifteen this December just gone, his hair a bit too long and too fond of scowling, but for all that a keen student. Most of the time.

'How many more, Uncle Len?' he heard Cyril whinge, as he dragged the sack out of the back door.

'As many as you c'n carry,' Len said cheerily, moving on to a new rack and starting to clear that. He was reminded of his old dad telling about his time as an ARP warden during the Blitz. *Rich pickings, my lad, for them that took the opportunity, and well worth the risk!* This was probably as close as Len would get. 'So you just keep cay-vee and I'll do the rest.'

There was no response from the back of the shop.

'Oi! You listening?' Len called irritably. But when there was still no response, he put down the coat he was holding and turned, a frown on his face. 'Cyril?'

Still nothing. Growling, Len hefted the half sack onto his shoulder, and marched out of the back to give the boy a ticking-off. 'Cyril, when I talk to you I–'

He stepped out the back door and found himself immediately confronted by a pair of huge, angry eyes, burning fiercely like headlamps. Len made to scream, but the sound wouldn't come out. He couldn't move. He couldn't do anything anymore.

And then everything went dark.

Placidly, the men who had once been Len and Cyril Harris picked up the sacks of furs, and followed the Yeti.

Into the Mist.

CHAPTER SIX
Yester-Me, Yester-You, Yesterday

'SIR?'

Sir Alistair took a moment to steady himself, waiting for the now-familiar head-rush to subside. Only then did he open his eyes.

He was bending over a large table covered in papers and maps, his arms braced against the edge of it, keeping himself upright. The hands in front of him were young and strong, the muscles of his bare forearms firm beneath sun-tanned skin.

It had happened again. Only, this time, he was even younger.

Looking up from the table, he found that he was standing in a large room, the rough walls and low ceiling of which were decked out in whitewash. There were eight British Army officers of various ranks and builds gathered around the table with him, all of them wearing the warm weather kit which Alistair recognised from some of the more exotic postings of his early career. Despite the combined effort of two electric fans placed strategically on desks either side of the room, the air was close and foetid. Somehow it all seemed terribly familiar, but for the moment Alistair struggled to remember exactly why.

The other officers were looking at him expectantly, as if they were waiting for him to say something – which, Alistair supposed, was quite possibly the case. The set-up had all the hallmarks of a military briefing and, at a quick glance, the highest rank he could see was that of a major. Most likely his 'arrival' had interrupted his younger self mid-flow, similar to how he had found himself in the pub in 1981, mid-drink on a bar stool and waiting for old 'Duffer' Hackett.

A young, blond captain was standing to his left, an expression of concern on his face. 'Are you all right, sir?' he asked.

At the sound of his voice something clicked into place at the back of Alistair's memory. *Sanders*. Captain George Sanders, his regimental adjutant on his final tour of duty with the Scots Guards. Good Lord.

Now that he had placed Sanders, Alistair recognised the other men around the table as officers he had known during his time as CO of 2 Scots; Major Ferguson-Gowe, Lieutenants Felby and Roth, Captain Lennox-Browne, Major Connor… He remembered each and every one of them, and a few more besides who were not present in the room. For Alistair to be there with them, at the ages they appeared to be, he must have gone much further back than before. He hadn't been in the collected company of these men since… since…

Libya, 1969. The year his life had changed forever.

Around him the other officers were getting restless, and Alistair cleared his throat awkwardly. To the occupants of the room it must have appeared that he had momentarily gone faint, and he played into this, wiping a hand briefly across his forehead.

'Yes. Thank you, Sanders,' he said dismissively. 'Touch of the heat.'

It was a flimsy excuse, but it served. Almost instantly Lieutenant Roth appeared at his right elbow, offering a glass of water, which Alistair accepted with muttered thanks. He took a few sips. The water itself was a little on the warm side but still fresh, and he was glad of it –

not least because the simple action of drinking also bought him enough time to compose himself both mentally and physically.

He stole a glance at the papers which were spread over the surface of the table; close-typed sheets of thin duplicate paper, a map unrolled beneath them. Setting the glass down, he shifted the papers to one side in a casual gesture, and he instantly recognised the topography as that surrounding El-Adem, Tobruk and Benghazi.

Yes, he was definitely in Libya. It came back to him now; this was the briefing room at the transit garrison just outside of Tobruk, where he and his men had been stationed for a six-month tour of duty. A furtive glance at his wristwatch told him it was 19:53 hrs; after dinner, so he must be partway through giving 'evening prayers'. Which meant that he needed to take control of the room, and quickly, before anyone started to suspect anything was amiss.

'Now,' he said briskly. 'Where was I?'

'You were just about finished actually, sir,' Major Connor replied helpfully.

That's a mercy, Alistair thought. He probably could have finished the briefing from memory, but he was very relieved that he needn't put it to the test. Clearly his 'landing' this time around was going to be somewhat kinder to him than the last.

'I suppose that's just as well, then,' he said aloud, and meant it. 'Very well, gentlemen, that'll be all. Until tomorrow.'

If the dismissal was somewhat blunt, none of the other officers drew attention to it. They simply nodded, exchanged a few goodnight sirs, and promptly filed out. Before long, the only other person remaining was Sanders.

The young adjutant put down the file he was holding, fixing Alistair with a critical gaze.

'Are you certain you're all right, sir?' he asked. 'It's not like you to get affected by the heat.'

He was right, of course. One thing that had never really troubled Alistair whenever he went abroad was hot weather. He had always had the knack of acclimatising quickly – to the point where a close friend had once called into question his credentials as a Scotsman. Sanders was probably concerned that his superior might be sickening for something. There were worse hazards to a man's health out here than the heat, after all.

'I'm fine, Sanders.' Alistair let a half-smile curl at the corners of his mouth. 'Honestly. Just looking forward to hitting the sack, truth be told.'

For a moment it looked as if the captain would insist that he visit the MO to make sure, but Sanders knew better than to push. Alistair recalled that he had always valued Sanders for his tact; a quality much rarer in aspiring Staff officers than many would ordinarily suppose, and for which, on this occasion, he was particularly grateful.

'Very good, sir,' Sanders replied. He picked up a stack of files from the table, tucking them under his arm. 'I'll not keep you. See you tomorrow, Colonel.'

'Goodnight, Captain.'

Once the captain had gone, Alistair let out a hefty sigh and pulled up a chair from the desk behind him. He sat down, rubbing his hands over his face. Near one that, but better than being blown up – or made to imagine that he had.

So here he was again; back experiencing life as his younger self and, once again, all because of that blasted gnome. It seemed his suspicion that someone was deliberately messing with his past might be well-founded. It certainly wouldn't be the first time. By whom, and what said person or agency hoped to achieve by doing so was still a mystery, but from Alistair's experience the sort of people who could arrange a stunt like this rarely had the world's best interests at heart.

In his mind he conjured up an image of the gnome; a crude figure with a pot belly, puffed cheeks, one eye and a jagged grin. An ugly little thing, but there had been nothing about it to suggest anything but terrestrial origin, save for the way it had tugged at his attention, and the odd circular marks he had spotted on its base. Perhaps those marks had significance? Devil take him if he recognised them, though...

Well, for whatever reason he had ended up here, at least he would have his memories to guide him. In this case, 2 Scots was out here as part of the permanent British establishment that remained in Libya; guarding against the Soviets, and a tactical show of force to help prop up the Libyan Crown against the Arab nationalist movement. Not there to engage, but just to remind people that they meant business. God, in the days when they used to not think twice about such a thing! After Aden, Middle East Command had understandably grown a little more cautious in its dealings, but the American and British bases in Libya were viewed as vital to securing the Mediterranean against Russian aggression.

How times change.

At least on this occasion he would not be stumbling around in the dark, unlike the fog that had surrounded his escapade with Bugayev in '81. The memories of his adult life before the Fifth and UNIT were some of the strongest Alistair possessed. He could certainly bluff his way through his immediate circumstances from what he remembered of the operation from all those years ago – which was quite a bit, actually.

Having said that, it would be good to know exactly at which point in their tour he had returned. He had only stayed three months out of the six before Pemberton had recalled him to London to help deal with the Yeti, but which end of those three months he was at made a great difference.

Searching the room, his gaze came to rest on the desk calendar positioned over the far side of the map table. 7th February.

'Ah,' Alistair said quietly. 'Of course it is.'

Rising from his chair, he paced an experimental circuit around the perimeter of the room. Satisfied as to the renewed strength of his legs, he quickly checked that the door was firmly shut, then dropped down and banged out twenty press-ups; quick and easy, barely raising a sweat. Childish of him, perhaps, but he had not had the opportunity to enjoy his regained vigour on his previous jaunt down memory lane. The simple fact of being able to stand up straight to his full height, of not having to rely on someone else to perform the simplest of tasks, of not needing a hideous cocktail of tablets just to get through a day without pain…

Youth was certainly wasted on the young, Alistair thought firmly as he got back up again, although he had not considered himself 'young' at the time. No right-minded thirty-nine-year-old ever did.

Straightening his shirt, Alistair considered what ought to be his next move. In '81 he'd had a meeting with old Duffer to keep, and then a mystery to solve. If his suspicions were correct, then trouble would undoubtedly present itself to him sooner or later. No need to go chasing after it; all he had to do was wait for it to come to him.

This time around, though, there was an extra factor. If the same rules applied to all parties in this scenario, and Anne and Bill had indeed been transported back with him, then they would now be in their own bodies back in Britain – Anne with her father in London, Bill with the Green Jackets. At least one of them would be out of reach of extra-terrestrial danger; he almost envied Bill, reliving the relative-humdrum of manoeuvres. However, Alistair was not unduly worried by this prospect of Anne and Bill being in the past. They were seasoned operatives who knew how to take care of themselves, and they knew the dangers of interfering with established events; fixed points in time and space. Although, Alistair seemed to recall something about how the Doctor had once said that the London Event was a 'fracture point' in time, which never sounded good to him. Whichever it was, Alistair could trust Bill and Anne to be careful.

He gave a small smile, knowing how happy Anne would be to see her father alive and well again. The professor's first untimely death had hit her hard – had hit them all hard – and Alistair hoped that she would draw some comfort from the reunion, however brief it may turn out to be; help her to remember him as he was, that sort of thing. Yes, Anne and Bill would be perfectly fine.

With no immediate danger threatening, Alistair reflected that his best move was to carry on as if nothing was out of the ordinary; retire to his quarters, get a good night's sleep, then see how things stood in the morning. Whatever else happened, he was temporarily responsible for a battalion again, and he wasn't about to shirk his duties.

That decided, he turned to leave, but he had only taken a few paces when he stopped in his tracks. Suddenly there was a nagging sensation in the back of his mind that something was not quite right, was somehow missing from this scenario... And then his eyes lighted on the glengarry and swagger stick that had been placed neatly on the desk by the door. He smiled. *Ah yes, of course.*

He put the hat on, brushing a thumb over the Scots Guards cap badge as he did so, and tucked the stick firmly under his right arm. There, that was better.

Now properly attired, Colonel Alistair Lethbridge-Stewart stepped smartly into the corridor and headed for the entrance to the inner courtyard. He met no one else, which was to be expected, as the only other people in the building at this hour would likely be the duty officer, and whichever unlucky soul was manning the comms room. Though he hadn't stayed here long, Alistair still recalled the layout of the compound perfectly; offices and Ops and Briefing rooms this side in the main block – stores, armoury, and NAAFI hut dotted around the edge. The Officers' quarters were almost directly opposite where he was now, next to theirs and the Sergeant's Messes; a short walk in a straight line across the open courtyard. No one would bother him. That was one of the privileges of being the boss.

As he approached the interior door, he paused. As was customary in Army bases, there were full-length mirrors fixed strategically at the exits so that it was possible for any passing soldier to check their uniform was correct. 'Tarting stations', Alistair always privately called them, and he caught sight of his reflection in the one next to the door into the courtyard.

Now, Alistair had never been one to indulge his sense of vanity, but it had been well over a decade since he had worn a uniform, and even longer than that since he had worn one on active service. In his case vanity won over, and he retraced a couple of steps to take a proper look.

In the mirror he saw a man in his prime. A trim figure in a uniform that not only fitted, but flattered in its cut. Jet-black hair without a hint of grey, a neat military moustache, a strong jawline not yet softened by enforced inactivity, and not a wrinkle in sight. Alistair shamelessly took a moment to admire what he saw, fixing the picture in his mind for when this was all over. As he looked, he felt a slight constriction in his chest.

'Make the most of it, old chap,' he murmured quietly.

The Lethbridge-Stewart in the mirror returned a wicked smile.

Leaving his reflection be, Alistair stepped outside and made his way across the compound, enjoying the sensation as the cool night air hit his skin. The sky above was bright with a multitude of stars, putting him in mind of an explosion in a jeweller's shop.

Now that's something you don't see anymore, Alistair reflected sadly. Towns and cities were constantly alight now, blocking the heavens from view and depriving millions of a beauty they didn't even know was there. Were people to turn the lights off, they would be astonished by how much more they could see.

A distant gale of laughter brought his attention back to earth. The sound of lively conversation reached Alistair's ears, and it appeared to be coming from the direction of the Officers' Mess.

Alistair halted, and stood pondering for a moment. These days he wasn't allowed to drink. At the home the nurses kept him on a strict regimen, all in the noble cause of prolonging what precious little time he had left. There was a glass of brandy at his bedside, but that wasn't for him. *That* was waiting for the Doctor, if he ever chose to claim it. Alistair could not remember the last time he drank in the company of fellow soldiers, and it had been donkeys' years since he had been able to avail himself of a Mess account...

And he never had finished his pint in '81, had he?

Smiling to himself and humming *Lily the Pink*, Alistair changed direction and headed for the Officers' Mess, a definite spring in his step.

Colonel Pemberton studied the map of Central London on the Ops Room wall with a growing sense of misgiving.

They had requisitioned the church hall of St Joseph's

up the north end of Cadogan Street, converting it into a makeshift command post. Officers and men went back and forth, passing on orders and bringing in updates about the continuing situation, which after twenty-four hours was not particularly encouraging.

'How much ground does it cover now?' Pemberton asked of Knight, who was standing at his elbow, clutching a sheet of typewritten paper.

Knight checked the report. 'Gained another two hundred yards in both directions, and picking up speed,' he intoned. 'Dawlish confirms that it has stopped expanding width-ways and is moving along a linear path.'

'That's something, I suppose,' Pemberton muttered darkly. Not much, but he'd take it.

On the map, the area covered by Mist had been shaded in red; through Chelsea, Brompton and Kensington. Around it blocks of buildings had been coloured blue, marking them as inside the ever-expanding evacuation zone. Pemberton frowned, thinking of the major disruption across the city and the hundreds of people already displaced. His orders from General Hamilton had been to keep the operation discreet, but they were fast approaching the point where concerns for public safety would overtake those for secrecy.

'Any word on that chemical weapons expert, sir?' Knight asked.

'No,' Pemberton said stiffly, still studying the map. That was the latest fiasco.

The Ministry sent one of their 'finest' in chemical weapons to take a look at the Mist. He had arrived that morning; a shabby-looking, ruddy-faced fellow by the name of Bloodnock, whom both Knight and Pemberton were astonished to discover held the rank of major. Bloodnock had cheerily asserted that he'd 'Soon sort this for you chaps!', roundly dismissed Dawlish's own findings, suited up in the most outrageous NBC suit any of them had ever seen, and trotted off into the Mist clutching some sort of space-age monitoring gadget. No one had seen or heard from him since.

Knight made a noise of irritation. 'Damn fool.'

While Pemberton agreed with the sentiment, he chose not to make any further comment. There were far more pressing concerns than the missing Major Bloodnock.

'I had a call from General Hamilton,' he said, redirecting the subject. 'As Dawlish's theory might be the key here, he's sending us an expert on radio waves.'

Knight pulled a face. 'Hopefully this one won't wander off.'

Pemberton raised a half-smile. 'Apparently this one comes on personal recommendation,' he said, crossing over to the rickety pasting table that served as his desk. 'Civvie, mind. Doctor A Travers; Cambridge boffin, just returned from a big project across the Pond.'

Despite himself, Knight looked impressed. 'He sounds a bit more promising, sir.'

'With any luck he will be,' Pemberton said archly, crossing back to the map. 'God knows we need a breakthrough.'

It was at this point Corporal Lane came trotting across from the comms desk, brandishing a note. Judging by the look on his face, it was not good news.

'Urgent, sir,' he said, passing the paper to the colonel. 'Two new patches of Mist reported. One on the Edgware Road, another at Notting Hill Gate, both spreading rapidly.'

It took great restraint for Pemberton not to snatch the note from Lane's hand. He read through the hastily-written lines, which gave little detail beyond what Lane had told him. Notting Hill, spreading north and south. Edgware Road, spreading east and west.

'New orders,' he said briskly. 'Extend the cordon to

those areas and begin evacuation. Get Dawlish to Notting Hill ASAP. He might catch sight of anything resembling a detonation device before the Mist patch gets too dense.'

'Sir!' Lane acknowledged, and doubled it back to his station.

Meanwhile Knight, having read the missive through, took up the red pencil and begun shading in a corresponding patch along Edgware Road.

'Edgware Road, Notting Hill,' he said archly. 'Next stop, High Street Kensington.'

Pemberton let out an amused snort, appreciating the attempt at levity, though it did little to combat his growing sense of frustration. Why had these patches of Mist sprung up, and why now? Why had it taken so long for the first to start spreading, if that had been the intention all along? This wasn't his kind of warfare, for pity's sake! His men were trained to strike at an enemy swiftly and with impunity, not to stand by helpless, waiting for an invisible enemy to make the next move. It wasn't as if the Mist was following a set path either; cutting across buildings, parks, gardens and roads as if they weren't–

Wait.

What had Knight said? *Next stop, High Street Kensington…*

'Sir?' Knight queried, noticing that his superior had gone very quiet and very still.

Pemberton turned on his heel, heart hammering in his chest. 'I need a map of the Tube!' he barked at the room.

There was a frantic scrabbling among the assembled personnel, and after a moment a battered copy of the *London A to Z* was produced. Pemberton turned to the Underground map on the back cover, held it against the board, and traced along the shaded areas of Mist, connecting them.

'Sloane Square. South Kensington. Gloucester Road. Notting Hill Gate. Edgware Road...' He turned to Knight, his face alight with triumph. 'It's the Circle Line!' he exclaimed. 'It's following the Underground.'

The 18:22 Westbound Circle Line service out of Baker Street was hurtling along towards Edgware Road. The driver, Tony Singer, was counting down the stops until he could change over and take a break, and Edgware Road was the last one. He could hear the mug of tea and bacon sarnie calling him.

No sooner than he had thought it, though, than the headlights suddenly illuminated a great white wall across the tunnel in front of him. Singer's eyes bulged.

'What the hell!'

He slammed on the emergency brake, and the train came to a screeching, juddering halt about twenty yards short of the obstruction. Back along the train, he heard muffled screams and shouts as the passengers were thrown about the interior of the carriages. Trying to calm his breathing, Singer reached for the intercom.

'My apologies, ladies and gentlemen,' he said, in what he felt was a remarkably calm manner. 'An emergency stop was necessary due to an obstruction on the line. My apologies once again, and hopefully we can be on our way again very shortly.'

He lifted his finger off the button to signal the message had ended, then pressed it down again.

'Guard to contact driver, please.'

Almost immediately the voice of his conductor, Sid Billingham, crackled out of the speaker. 'What's the problem?'

'Get down here, Sid,' Singer said. 'You need to see this.'

While he waited for Billingham, Singer radioed in the incident in to Control. At least that would stop anybody running into them from behind.

'What's up?' Billingham said, arriving through the carriage door and locking it behind him. His eyes widened at the sight of the white mass filling the tunnel in front. 'Blimey! What is that stuff?'

'Gawd alone knows,' Singer said, getting up from the controls and releasing the manual catch to the cab. 'Stay with the train. I'll take a look.'

'Careful,' Billingham warned. 'Don't go touching it.'

Singer jumped down off the footplate onto the floor of the tunnel, and cast Billingham a despairing glance. 'Do I look like an idiot? Here, there's a pair of electrical gloves in the toolbox over there. Hand me those.'

Equipped with the gloves, Singer crept his way along the track, careful to keep as far away from the third rail as possible. Three yards short of the blockage he stopped, struck by a sudden feeling of dread. Singer had been a driver with the London Underground for twelve years, and in that time he had heard queer stories; ghost trains, haunted platforms, tribes of tunnel workers lost underground... This was something altogether new, but Singer felt its malevolence. It was evil. Pure evil.

'What is it?' Billingham called from the door of the cab.

Singer shook his head, trying to clear it. 'Don't know,' he called back. 'Looks like... some kind of fungus.'

'Can't be,' Billingham scoffed. 'Too bleedin' big!'

'Might be lots of small ones joined together,' Singer suggested. 'Can happen.'

Though how they could've grown so fast was beyond him. There were trains passing through there every three minutes. Anything growing across the tunnel would be obliterated.

Suddenly the white mass gave a huge, quivering shudder. The light it was emitting began to pulsate, growing brighter.

''Ere, what's that?' Billingham shouted.

But Singer didn't reply. He watched, horrified, as the fungus began to move, visibly growing and advancing along the tunnel. There was a high-pitched, singing noise, and Singer stumbled backwards, clapping his hands over his ears.

'Sid!' he cried out frantically. Willing his legs to move, he turned and ran back along the track. The fungus followed him, gaining rapidly. 'Sid, get 'em off! Get 'em all off the train!'

CHAPTER SEVEN
Ribbon of Darkness

A THICK PALL OF MIST SHROUDED THE SMALL STREET JUST off Kensington High Street. Bodies, swathed in fine filaments of Web, lay slumped across the pavements and in the road. Two cars sat collided, bonnets and windscreens smashed-in from when their drivers were overcome at the wheel; a third had swerved to avoid the first two and ploughed into the front of a bookshop. It was deathly quiet; no noise, no movement, no breath of wind stirred in this grey half-world.

Through the gloom, three figures approached. The first – a huge, hulking shape – was more animal than human. At seven feet tall, the closest thing it resembled was a large, shaggy bear walking on its hind legs, but there was nothing natural about the way this creature appeared or moved. By contrast, the two diminutive figures either side of it were clearly human; a middle-aged man and a teenage boy, their faces blank, their eyes empty of expression. On their backs they each carried three large burlap sacks, but though their burdens looked far too heavy for them, they did not seem to feel the weight. They did not seem to feel anything at all.

The Yeti shambled down the silent street, its headlamp-like eyes piercing the Mist with a malevolent glow. When it reached the entrance to the Underground station it stopped, the two men halting beside it. For a moment they stood there, silent and motionless among the bodies, as if waiting for something to happen.

Then a high-pitched electronic beeping began to come from the Yeti. As if a switch had been thrown, many of the web-covered shapes on the ground stirred and climbed to their feet; thirty in all, each one an able-bodied man or woman. Slowly they lined up in front of the Yeti, a silent army forming up for inspection. Seemingly satisfied with its troops, the Yeti gave a bubbling growl, rather like a lion with bronchitis, and moved off down a side street. The people followed mutely, like so many somnambulant rats after the Pied Piper.

Before long the small party came to a large factory yard. The name, painted in large white letters on the half-open gates, read *Bryden Industries Ltd.* The building beyond was dark and empty, the workers having fled shortly after the Mist began to spread. In front of the gates, the Yeti turned to its followers and growled again. One by one they filed through into the courtyard, the last man waiting as the Yeti and its bearers passed through, then the gates were closed and barred from the inside.

Deep within the factory, machinery rumbled into life.

Craftsman Steven Weams of the Royal Electrical and Mechanical Engineers climbed down from the ladder, dusted off his trousers and removed the screwdriver from between his teeth.

'Try that,' he said.

Corporal Lane flicked a switch on the control desk, and the indicator board depicting a map of the Underground tunnels lit up. 'Nice one, mate,' he said, by way of thanks. He turned and called over to Captain Knight. 'Board's up and running, sir.'

'Thank you, Lane,' Knight acknowledged, despite having witnessed the operation for himself. Things had to be done properly, after all.

They were in the old transit camp under Goodge

Street Station, one of many such 'secret' depots that had existed since the last war. Weams was impressed with how they had managed to get things set up down there so quickly. Being the Sparks of his workshop, it was his job to reconnect the power and ensure that everything was working properly. Astonishingly, there had actually been remarkably little for him to do to get the place back up and running; a couple of faulty junction boxes, several fuses that needed changing, a bit of replacement wiring thanks to rats and water damage, and that was really the worst of it. He was hearing far worse horror stories from his mates working on the other posts at Holborn, Embankment and Marble Arch. Whoever had been in charge of mothballing this place had certainly known their stuff.

Even so, Weams reflected as he unhooked the ladder, this was the strangest job he had been on to date; and 'strange' didn't cover half of what was going on down there, or up above, for that matter. Killer mist in the middle of London, glowing fungus choking up the Underground.

His Alice hadn't been happy about him being called away at such short notice, either – and neither had Weams, seeing as they'd only been married six months and the novelty had yet to wear off. Duty came first, of course, but it felt more than odd to be under deployment conditions here in the Smoke, knowing his wife was only a few miles away in Chatham.

As if Lane's flicking the switch had summoned him, the door from the main corridor opened and Colonel Pemberton stepped into the Ops Room. Weams didn't quite know what to make of 'Old Spence', as the lads of 1 Para called him. He seemed a decent enough sort, for a senior officer, though somewhat tight-lipped. The craftsman was more used to colonels who, on the rare occasions you did meet one in the wild, preferred to talk *at* a lad than to him. This colonel didn't strike him as the sort that was overly fond of the sound of his own voice.

Spotting that the board was working, Pemberton marched over and gave it a quick appraisal. 'Working now, is it?' he said, pre-empting the captain before he could state the obvious. 'Good show. How far has it got now?'

'The north section's still between Baker Street and Paddington,' Knight said, following the CO's example and cutting to the chase. Weams listened in as he tidied away his tools. 'The two southern sections have joined up and slowed almost to a standstill, holding just short of Victoria and Bayswater.'

'And above ground?'

'The Mist matches the path of the fungus precisely,' Knight confirmed.

'Proves the theory it's this stuff that's causing it,' Pemberton mused.

'Exactly.' Knight took a pen from his top pocket and pointed to a short illuminated section on the board. 'There's still this narrow gap between Bayswater and Paddington that's clear. Dawlish and his men are busy shoring up the tunnels either side so that we can keep it as our western access point.'

The colonel nodded. 'Buys us some time. With any luck that'll be as far as it goes. Are the sensors all in place?'

'I believe so,' Knight said, turning to look at Weams. 'Weams was on the party siting them, weren't you, Weams?'

'Sir.' Weams braced up, a little surprised to find himself on the receiving end of both officers' attention. That was the other thing the craftsman found peculiar; Pemberton and Knight seemed to form some sort of double act. Old Spence and Little Spence; one was never long without the other's company. 'Mr Dawlish ordered them laid twenty yards apart, so they'd only pick up if it was a significant advance.'

Pemberton nodded, tapping the board with his cane. 'And there's no risk of our men setting this off?'

'No, sir.' Weams knew enough to answer that query, at least. 'Each sensor's got to be covered for at least thirty seconds before it registers here. Us passing by won't show.'

They had been some pretty advanced pieces of kit too. Weams had never been on an operation that was so flush with kit and resources; but, then again, he had never dreamed he'd be on ops in the middle of London.

The main door slid open again and Corporal Blake arrived, throwing the colonel a salute and appearing a little flustered.

''Scuse me, sir,' he said. 'Um… *Doctor* Travers is here.'

'At last!' Pemberton remarked, the edge of exasperation in his voice all too plain. 'Now we might get somewhere. Wheel the chap in.'

'Yes, sir,' Blake said, though he didn't make an immediate move. 'But you ought to know–'

Before he could finish, an attractive young woman wearing a stylish trouser suit and sporting a pixie cut stepped into the room, carrying a large brown leather suitcase. She breezed past Blake, walked straight up to the astonished colonel and extended a hand.

'Colonel Pemberton, I presume?' she said. Her manner was brisk, business-like and utterly self-assured. 'I'm Anne Travers, your new scientific advisor.'

Blimey, Weams thought, grinning at the stunned looks on both the officers' faces. *This is going to be cosy, innit?*

Dame Anne felt her heart sink as she read the newspaper headline.

GAS EXPLOSION CAUSES TUBE CHAOS!

After two days of confusion and speculation, the Mist had started to expand and encircle the city; a development which Anne remembered also marked the first appearance of the web fungus in the Underground. If she remembered correctly, very soon she – that was, her younger self – would be called in by General Hamilton to advise on the situation underground. By the end of the week the first wave of Yeti would appear, and not long after that the wholesale evacuation of London would begin.

Knowing the truth of the matter as she did, the focus of the newspaper story seemed peculiarly cold to Anne. At this stage the general public still had no concept of the gravity of the situation – nor would they while the Army kept a tight rein on what information was being fed to the press. It would be days before it became known that there were casualties, and by then the death toll would have already risen significantly.

And to think it could have so easily been worse, Anne reflected bitterly.

She was sitting at the breakfast bar in the kitchenette of Rachel Ashcroft's flat in Parson's Green. It was part of a well-appointed Georgian terrace house, refurbished in the modern style in an effort to attract up-and-coming young professionals. Third-floor, granted, but even so... If that alone were not enough to confirm Anne's suspicion that Miss Ashcroft came from money, there was plenty of evidence to be had in the flat itself. Several framed photos recorded 'R. Ashcroft' as having attended the Benenden School for Young Ladies in Kent, including a couple that featured her as a member of the lacrosse team. A pile of envelopes on the coffee table stamped 'O.H.M.S.' from Hong Kong revealed 'daddy' was engaged in the diplomatic service – and the framed Bachelors' degree certificate in English Literature from Oxford University didn't do anything to raise Anne's estimation of her host, either.

Further investigation into the bedroom wardrobe had

turned up several garments with frankly eye-watering names attached to their labels. Neither was Rachel spoilt for choice when it came to the latest sounds. An HMV record player in a red leather case sat beside an impressive collection of vinyl LPs; Dusty Springfield, The Kinks, Bob Dylan, Cream, Nina Simone... and, of course, all of The Beatles albums. Anne was always too old to be a teeny-bopper, but even she couldn't help but be impressed by the pristine copy of *Sergeant Pepper's Lonely Hearts Club Band*. She didn't think she knew anyone who hadn't cut the paper cut-out pieces... well, out.

Though she was several miles outside of Central London, the Mist had risen to such a height that it was possible to see it from Rachel's living room window.

Anne walked over to take another look, newspaper still clutched in her hand. It was two days since she had left hospital, and in that time she had achieved frustratingly little. Granted, it had taken most of the first day to establish herself in her adopted surroundings, and things had not been made any easier with having to tread carefully as far as Malachi and her neighbours were concerned. It was very difficult to guard against 'unusual' behaviour when she didn't know what behaviour was normal.

The Mist cloud could clearly be seen over the tops of the interposing buildings, and at a rough estimate Anne thought it must now be at a height of about 150ft. It would continue to climb, she recalled, until it reached three hundred feet, after which it would form an effective barrier against radio waves and severely limit physical access by air, already beginning to isolate those who were left in Central London. Anne shivered involuntarily.

It was a horrible feeling, knowing so many more people would die and not being able to do a thing about it. If only she could–

In the hallway, the phone began to ring. Anne cursed

softly under her breath. Even without the innovation of Caller ID, she knew exactly who would be on the other end of the line; in the time she had been here she had only *had* one caller. She'd thought an 'It' girl would've had a bigger group of acquaintances.

Turning from the window, Anne marched into the hall and halted before the phone. It was one of those ultra-modern trim phones, all angles and smooth plastic, with the terribly insistent high-pitched electronic trill. Much as she wished she could ignore it, she couldn't; that would only make matters worse, in both the short and long term.

She took a deep breath and picked up the receiver. 'Hello?'

'Hello, darling.' Malachi's voiced sounded down the phone.

And she had been right. Anne closed her eyes, willing herself to patience. 'Oh, Malachi,' she said with false brightness, as if she were genuinely surprised it was him. 'I was wondering if it would be you.'

'Well, wonder no more,' Malachi replied jokingly, before carrying straight on. 'I'm afraid I don't have long to talk, though. I'm calling between clients. I just wanted to check to see how you're doing.'

'Oh.' Anne pretended to sound disappointed, but the quicker she could get off the phone the better. 'Well, I'm doing all right, really. You needn't fuss so much.'

'You can't blame a chap for worrying, darling,' Malachi pointed out gently, and utterly reasonably. Damn him.

'I'm sorry,' she said, though not sounding in the least apologetic. 'It just seems a lot of fuss over nothing.'

'You're hardly nothing, darling,' Malachi said warmly. When Anne failed to reply he gave an embarrassed cough and changed track. 'Um, been up to much today?'

'A little,' Anne said neutrally. She thanked her lucky stars that Bill had known better than to be so horribly sentimental when they were courting. Not unless he was *trying* to wind her up, anyway. 'Sitting, reading, listening to some music. Not very exciting, I'm afraid.'

'Really? I say, what if I come down this evening? Get us a spot of dinner at that little—'

'No, it's quite all right, I don't want to put you out,' Anne said hurriedly, stopping him before he could get any further. That was the last thing she needed. She gave an awkward little laugh. 'Besides, I don't think I'd be very good company at the moment. Still… thinking things over.'

'Oh. Oh, right.'

Anne cringed. Just going from his voice she could easily picture the mixture of confusion and disappointment on Malachi's face.

'I'll be fine, darling,' she said reassuringly, pretending not to have noticed his disappointment. 'Really. You have enough to worry about as it is.'

'Well, if you're certain.' Malachi's voice was reluctant, but Anne could tell she'd won her point. 'I'll come and see you soon, though, I promise.'

'Soon,' Anne agreed. *But not too soon.* 'I'll let you get back to your client. Goodbye.'

'Goodbye, darling.'

Anne put the receiver down quickly, and tried to dampen down the creeping feeling of guilt in her stomach. It was not Malachi's fault; none of this was. He was still living out of his hotel room, commuting to the office from there. He couldn't even go back home if he'd wanted to now, as yesterday the cordon around the Mist had widened to include the area around the Silverstein house. The poor man had just lost his father, was undoubtedly feeling horribly displaced and lonely, and the one person he would be expecting comfort from, his fiancée, was... *indisposed*. She could not push him away entirely – this was not her life and she had no right to do so – but she also had a job to do, and despite any personal guilt or regrets, she could not allow Malachi to derail her from her purpose.

Not for the first time, she found herself wishing that Bill was with her. The worst part about it was there was every possibility that he *might* be. If he and Alistair were also occupying the bodies of strangers, she would not recognise them even if they were standing right next to her. The odds against finding them were too great, and shortly after she had arrived at the flat, she had taken the decision not to spend time looking for them. Her time was limited; she could not look for the boys *and* save her father – and, right now, her father's future was the most important of the two.

Also, if Anne were to be completely honest with herself, there was another reason she had decided not to look for them. If by some chance she did find Bill and Alistair and they learned of her plan, she knew there was a risk that they would try and stop her. Bill she was not too worried about; he would protest, but she was confident she could persuade him around to her way of thinking. She would be a pretty poor wife, otherwise. But Alistair... He would not understand. He would only see the danger, and he would not let any sentiments of friendship get in the way of doing what he saw as the right thing.

No. Though it hurt to admit it, she was better off without them. The boys could look after themselves, and wherever Alistair and Bill were, *whoever* they were, she sincerely hoped they were having a better time of it than her.

Retracing her steps to the window, Anne began to review her plan of action. It had taken a while to formulate a practical way forward, things being made all the more difficult by having to operate within established events. Her first instinct was to find some way of contacting her younger self with a warning of what was to come, but she had dismissed that quickly enough. Even if she could convince her still-sceptical self that the message wasn't a hoax, there was a risk that she would act too early in an attempt to thwart the Yeti before the Intelligence's main assault began. If Dame Anne Bishop, seasoned operative and occasional time traveller, was having difficulty sitting by when she knew deaths might be prevented, then Doctor Anne Travers, reluctant scientific advisor to the military, was unlikely to stay her hand.

Returning to the here and now – her past, now the present – Anne crossed over to the coffee table where she had placed a notepad and pen. She had been busy scribbling down a timeline of events, remembering the dates as best as she could, though admittedly a few details seemed to be a little fuzzy here and there. One of the inevitabilities of old age, she supposed. Her aim was to somehow make sure that the Yeti could not break into Goodge Street and kidnap her father, preventing him from being possessed by the Intelligence, but otherwise to allow events to unfold in their predetermined course. The main problem overall was timing.

If she acted too early she risked others gaining foreknowledge and implementing drastic change, but too late and she would be swept up in the evacuation of the city, making intervention impossible.

Getting a message through remotely without the proper codes or authority would be nigh on impossible, though she was loathe to take any unnecessary physical risks. This wasn't her body, after all, and if possible she intended to return it in the condition she had found it, whenever that might prove to be. Somehow, she needed to avoid the evacuation and stay in London and then, when the time was right, she could get a message directly to her father.

Which sounded far simpler than it would actually prove. The Army had been thorough with their evacuation efforts, carrying out sweep after sweep of the city to make sure that nobody was left who shouldn't be there. People had escaped attention, certainly – looters, the homeless – but they had only done so by staying as far away from the soldiers as possible, which was the exact opposite of what Anne needed to do.

She frowned, tapping her pen against the pad in irritation as she carefully considered her options. Oh, for a digital camera and a half-decent laser printer! Ten minutes with her laptop and she could have knocked together an ID card and printed credentials that would have satisfied the most rigorous sentry in this era.

This was the sort of time where she could really do with some inside help, but from whom? Even if she could convince any of her friends from 1969 of her true identity – just the small matter of time travel and body-swapping – it was still well before she knew anyone with useful connections or experience when it came to alien incursions and the military. Who was there, now, that she could reach out to in this time and place?

Then she stopped, pen poised above the pad, as a thought suddenly struck her. She smiled.

Of course, there was always Ruby.

They were yet to formally meet, but in circumstances such as theirs that was only a minor detail. Yes, Ruby. Ruby would understand her. Ruby would know what to do.

Although, Anne thought as she headed out to the hallway to search through the Yellow Pages to find a number she had only ever used once before, it would still be a while before they started using the name Ruby...

CHAPTER EIGHT
Almost Persuaded

THE FOLLOWING AFTERNOON FOUND DAME ANNE SITTING in the office of Mr Rupert Slant, of *Morecombe & Slant Solicitors* on Mason Avenue in London's Square Mile. Slant's secretary had been reluctant to give her the appointment at such short notice, but Anne had put on such a sense of urgency that the woman had relented.

Anne took in the familiar heavy oak desk and bookcases stuffed with weighty tomes and pamphlets. On the book shelf behind the desk she saw her mother's much-loved first edition of *The Road to Oz*. In 2011, that same copy was kept in Anne's bedside cabinet, slightly more well-thumbed in appearance than it was now, but no less beloved.

It was, Anne reflected, a very peculiar case of déja-vu; remembering a past event that, as far as her 1969 self was concerned, had not yet occurred. In three months' time she would be sitting at this desk for the first time, having received a mysterious summons concerning a legacy from her mother's family, the Goffs. A letter attributed to one of her ancestors, Archibald Goff, would start her on a journey that would quite literally transport her back to 1823 – her first experience of time travel – where she and Archibald would guarantee her own future by securing her family's past.

Measured footsteps approached and the office door opened to admit the ancient, wizened form of Mr Rupert

Slant, senior partner in the firm of Morecombe and Slant, carrying a silver tea tray.

On the surface he looked to be in his seventies, though Anne knew that he was far older than that. In fact, Rupert had been solicitor to the Goff family for more generations than was humanly possible. Also, the last time Anne had seen Rupert *he* had been a luscious blonde in her forties, going by the name of Ruby.

This was because Rupert wasn't actually human, but rather a member of a shape-changing alien race. As far as Anne was aware, she was the only person alive who knew Rupert's true nature. She had steadfastly kept Rupert's secret for decades, making sure that he did not come to the attention of the wrong people. Or, perhaps more dangerously, the *right* people.

The china cups rattled unsteadily as Rupert placed the tray down on the desk. He turned to offer her a friendly smile, a vital spark in his pale blue eyes. Remembering her only previous visit there, Anne wondered if he was going to offer to be 'mother'.

'I chose Indian,' he said, picking up the heavy pot with deceptively frail hands. 'I always find it hits the spot on a winter's afternoon. Milk?'

'Please,' Anne said.

Rupert passed her a cup, before taking a seat behind his desk. 'Now, Miss Ashcroft,' he said, leaning back and steepling the tips of gnarled fingers. 'Mrs Simpkins said that you required advice on an urgent piece of litigation; an inheritance dispute, I understand. If you might start by laying out the main facts of the issue?'

Putting her cup down, Anne sat up and cleared her throat. *Well, here goes…*

'Actually, Mr Slant, I admit that I may have misled your secretary somewhat.'

Rupert frowned, clearly puzzled. 'Indeed?'

'I do need your help,' Anne assured him. 'But not in

the way described.'

'I see.' Rupert sighed wearily. 'I do not advise on criminal law, Miss Ashcroft. As it clearly states in the directory, Mr Morecombe and I deal exclusively with civil and–'

'No, nothing like that.' Anne took a deep breath. 'And I'm not really Rachel Ashcroft. It's me, Anne Travers.'

There was a beat of silence, then Rupert furnished her with a thin smile. 'Ah, there I must disagree with you, young lady. I am well acquainted with Doctor Anne Travers, and you are most certainly not her.'

'Physically,' Anne conceded. She could have approached that one better. 'My consciousness has been projected backwards from the future, and somehow I've ended up in this body.'

The smile slid from Rupert's face, to be replaced with wariness. 'I'm afraid, miss, that you are somewhat confused. If you will allow me...' He reached for the phone.

'Fang Rock,' Anne said flatly, deciding to take the bull by the horns. '1823. That was when we met.'

Rupert paused, hand hovering over the receiver, and regarded her with a studied blank expression. 'I beg your pardon?' he asked quietly, coldly.

'We *are* well acquainted,' Anne continued firmly. She certainly had his attention now. 'But though you have met me, I have not yet officially met you. You are not human.'

Rupert sat motionless, blue gaze fixed intently on her. Anne persevered, and explained the particulars of the first time he met her, of their adventure on Fang Rock and his decision to serve her family.

Once she'd finished, feeling she had said her bit, Anne folded her arms, sat back in her chair, and waited.

In the resulting silence, Rupert's expression remained unreadable. Then he reached across the desk, picked up his cup, took a delicate sip of tea, and then sighed.

'I think, Anne,' he said. 'You had better start from the beginning.'

Sir Alistair drummed his fingers on the edge of his desk in irritation. He was sitting in his office overlooking the compound's parade ground, working through the business of the day. Happily the Venetian-style blind kept out the worst of the sun's glare, while the open window and ceiling fan did a fair job of keeping the air moving. Nothing, however, could keep out Sergeant Palmer's powerful voice as he tore a strip off some unfortunate for Lord-knew-what-this-time, but it registered as nothing more than part of the background noise of military life.

It felt, quite honestly, as if he had never left. Forty-two years and he had gone straight in again, like a duck to water. He had just reached the weekly defaulters list in the course of his reading, and Alistair genuinely wondered how he had forgotten the average British soldier's sheer capacity to indulge in behaviour that was equally excruciating as it was entertaining. This week's star turn came courtesy of three lads from B Coy, who had decided to initiate a well-known party game involving a strategically-placed rolled-up piece of paper and a lighted match. Only, on this occasion, a misjudgement on their part had resulted in one charge of indecent exposure, and three of rendering oneself or another man unfit for duty. Captain Gill had let them off fairly lightly in Alistair's opinion, considering the charges he could have had them under. It was just a mercy there had been no civilian witnesses at the time.

There was a knock on the door.

'Come,' Alistair called, signing off the bottom of the page.

The door opened and Sanders walked in, clutching a

small bundle of envelopes. 'Mail from home, sir,' he said cheerfully. 'Sorted and handed out. Three for you.'

'Thank you, Sanders,' Alistair said, sparing the covers a brief glance before putting them to one side. He would take a proper look in a moment. 'My compliments to Captain Gill, and I should like to see him at 1600 hours.'

'Yes, sir.'

When Sanders did not make a move to leave, Alistair raised a querying eyebrow. 'Was there anything else?'

'Well, sir,' Sanders said, uncharacteristically hesitant. 'The Mess asked if you had received any further news about London?'

Ah. Alistair supposed he should have guessed. They had heard about the 'gas explosion' outside Edgware Road a couple of nights ago on the World Service, and details as yet were scarce. Follow-up reports only mentioned Tube closures, traffic disruptions and a temporary evacuation of the area.

'I'm afraid not,' he replied, and it was mostly true. Alistair did, of course, know better, but he certainly had not at the time. He had contacted the Embassy in Tripoli, along with Middle East Command, to try and obtain more details, but he was either given the run-around or everyone else was 'just as in the dark as you, old boy'. Which was, Alistair reflected, exactly how it needed to remain, but he recalled all too well his and his officers' frustration at the time. 'Please assure the men that I will let them know as soon as I hear anything further – which, hopefully, won't be too long.'

'Thank you, sir,' Sanders said, seemingly content. He smiled. 'Well, I'll leave you to your letters.'

'Yes, thank you. That will be all.'

The young captain departed, still grinning like a Cheshire cat, and Alistair frowned. Now what the devil was all that about?

Brushing the thought to one side, Alistair returned to

the papers in front of him, but his thoughts strayed elsewhere. His promise to pass on information was a fairly hollow one, seeing as he wouldn't be there to fulfil it. Pemberton and his men would soon engage the first of the Yeti, the full evacuation of the inner city would begin – and Alistair would be in the thick of it. In the next couple of days he would receive a phone call from Pemberton, summoning him to London to help with the evacuation.

Alistair had always secretly been touched at Old Spence's show of faith in him; it had been no mean feat for Hamilton to pull the necessary strings to temporarily release him from his duties here in Libya. Spence had only hinted at the sort of thing they were facing in that phone call, but nevertheless Alistair had leaped at the chance to be of use, favouring direct action over sitting on his hands in the desert, waiting for a revolution that may or may not happen.

He remembered the strong, driving feeling that had accompanied him all the way to London, as if he had somehow known that whatever was going on would have some profound impact on his life. In reality, he couldn't even imagine what he was letting himself in for.

Alistair recalled all too well the sight of hundreds of uniformed bodies smothered in web, lying across eerily empty roads and, later, lined up in hospital mortuaries. He remembered leading the raid on Covent Garden, after he'd taken over from Pemberton, his feeling of utter helplessness in the face of so... so *alien* an enemy.

Despite the heat, Alistair shivered. He had never wanted to feel that helpless again, and it was that which had driven him on his campaign to establish a permanent defence against such threats. They had been so raw back then, stumbling around in the darkness, not knowing what was around the corner or even how they would deal with it. It was almost embarrassing to remember the things they had got away with.

Giving up on the paperwork for now, Alistair picked up the first letter from the pile Sanders had brought in. Glancing over the direction, he received a shock as he recognised the handwriting.

Posted from Strategic Command, Fugglestone, addressed in a distinctly feminine hand.

Sally.

Alistair felt the bottom drop out of his stomach. Lance Corporal Sally Wright; the first woman he had thought he would spend the rest of his life with. No wonder Sanders had been grinning.

He sat back in his chair, feeling more than a little stunned. He had not thought about Sally in years; preferred, on the whole, not to. Women never really had been his strong point, but with Sally things had ended particularly badly. When he had asked her to marry him he had thought the both of them being in the Services would make things easier; in truth it had had the opposite effect. It turned out that while she had expected too much of him, he had expected too little of her.

At least with Fiona they had the chance to come to some accord; and when the truth had come out about aliens a few years ago, allowing him to tell her something about his real work, she had even forgiven him a little. Now he had Doris, and their finding each other again had introduced him to the son and grandchildren he would otherwise never have known. The past fifteen years had easily been some of Alistair's happiest, and in that he considered himself far more fortunate than he deserved.

Picking up the envelope again, Alistair turned it over to open it, but stayed his hand as he read the letters 'S.W.A.L.K.' marked on the back flap. 'Sealed With A Loving Kiss'. He had forgotten that she used to do that.

Oh, Sally… She really had deserved better than him.

Feeling like a traitor, Alistair put the letter to one side, unopened, and moved on to the next.

Rupert folded his hands neatly in his lap. 'Well, *Dame Anne*,' he said. 'It is a most extraordinary tale.'

'But true,' Anne said. She had been speaking for what seemed like hours, and felt utterly exhausted.

'Oh, undoubtedly,' Rupert agreed. 'It is too extraordinary to be otherwise. But, on a personal level, your mannerisms betray you. I spent enough time in your company in 1823 to see that it is you.'

Anne gave him a relieved smile. 'Thank you, Rupert. I don't know what I would have done had you not believed me.'

'You had me when you mentioned the translation matrix,' Rupert confided, returning his own thin smile.

Anne's face fell, a hollow feeling in her stomach at the mention of the matrix. 'I don't have access to it now. It was left behind with my own body in 2011.'

She had realised this on the bus journey there. Three seats in front of her, two men had been speaking Urdu, and it was with no small shock that she realised she could not understand a word of their conversation. It had made her feel suddenly very alone.

Rupert nodded his understanding. 'Regrettable, but not unexpected. Now we are on the same page, so to speak, how may I help you? The osmic projector is inoperable, so I do not think I can do anything for your physical predicament.'

'That's not why I've come to you for help,' Anne said quickly.

Rupert's feathery eyebrows lifted questioningly. 'Oh?'

'It's about events in the city.'

'Ah yes, the terror above and beneath,' Rupert said neutrally. Anne had explained hers and her father's connection to what was really occurring in the

Underground. 'It certainly explains all this fuss over a "gas leak". Though I still do not see how I could help. You are, at this time, assisting to defeat this menace – and it would seem you are successful.'

'But at a great cost,' Anne said darkly.

'You could have done no better,' Rupert said sympathetically, but Anne shook her head.

'Not then, but I can now. I need to get a message to my father.'

Rupert frowned, clearly uncertain of the idea. 'To what end?'

'In just over a week my father will be captured and, for a time, possessed by the Intelligence. In so doing it will leave a trace of itself in his mind, which will inadvertently lead to the decay of his mind and his death inside a year. If I can warn him, stop that happening–'

'You should not,' Rupert said shortly.

Anne halted, speechless. 'What?'

'It is tempting,' Rupert said. 'When you have foreknowledge, the urge to change things for the better is overwhelming. Believe me, I know. But you are from a future that relies on this past remaining as it is. You must not interfere.'

'But I have travelled to the past before, on more than one occasion, actually,' Anne argued. 'But on Fang Rock, we acted, we changed things. Over the past century you have done nothing but manipulate events so that I will return and interfere with the past!'

'That is a different scenario altogether. You and I are part of a self-sustaining paradox; one that must be allowed to continue in order to preserve our own futures. In this we are part of established events, but what you propose will change them. Hard as it may be, Professor Travers plays his part in this event for a reason.'

'I'm not going to stop him from going into the Underground,' Anne insisted. 'I will only change one small detail. The Intelligence doesn't need to take my father; if not him it will take someone else to be its messenger. Things will still work out as they did. If I can stay in London long enough, I can arrange to deliver a warning that will put him on his guard, and he will be safe.'

'You cannot be certain of that,' Rupert said stonily, blue eyes hard.

'Yes I can,' Anne insisted, leaning forward to labour her point. 'I've considered everything–'

'Have you really? Can you account for all the variables, all the possible outcomes? I can tell you now that you have not. There will be strands at work which even you, with all your knowledge and experience, will not realise are in play.'

Anne was livid. Of all possible people, she had never expected Rupert to question her competency or integrity.

'So, I am to sit back and let my father's mind be torn apart from the inside? Again?'

'I know it is hard, but–

'No!' she snapped. 'No, you don't. And if you will not help me, then I will just have to find a way on my own.'

She stood up, shaking with fury, and made for the door.

'Anne.' In the blink of an eye, Rupert was there next to her, his hand gently resting on her wrist. He had moved surprisingly quickly, belying the illusion of his physical frailty. 'A moment. I never said I would not help you.'

Anne blinked, anger giving way to confusion. 'But you said–'

'We must, in my profession, play devil's advocate,' Rupert said, inclining his head in acknowledgement. 'I had to be certain that you fully understood what you are undertaking. This is a dangerous task, and not one to assume so lightly.'

Anne held her breath, hope blossoming in her chest. 'Then you'll help me?'

Rupert nodded. 'I have safeguarded your family's interests for 146 years, Dame Anne, and I see it as my duty to continue to do so. Between us we shall be able to advance a plan that will protect your father, yet play to our known history.'

Anne's heart fluttered, almost giddy with joy. She clasped his hands in hers. 'Oh, thank you, Rupert! I knew I could rely on you.'

Rupert patted her hand affectionately, his thin lips curling into a thinner smile. 'You can always rely on me, my dear,' he said firmly. 'To do what is best.'

While Dame Anne was conferring with Rupert Slant, elsewhere Lieutenant Dawlish was leading an expedition along the Westbound Circle Line towards Sloane Square. Corporal Blake and Miss Travers followed on, with Privates Norris and O'Brien bringing up the rear. They were out to get a sample of the fungus, on the basis that a close examination might reveal how and why it was broadcasting, and indicate an effective way to combat it. So far it was proving as impervious to their efforts as the Mist.

For his part Dawlish was hugely relieved by this turn of events. While they waited for a real expert to arrive, Colonel Pemberton had cast him in the role of *de facto* boffin, and Dawlish was more than happy to give ground to Miss Travers. He was no scientist, never had been. Ask him to fortify a position or blow up a bridge, then he was your man, but all this… Well, thankfully nobody expected *him* to come up with the answers anymore.

'How much further, Lieutenant?' Miss Travers asked.

'Not far, ma'am,' Dawlish replied, keeping his voice low. He didn't like the way even the smallest sounds echoed through these tunnels. 'If you turn off your torch, you'll most likely see the glow.'

Following his lead, Miss Travers and Blake extinguished their torches. Sure enough a dim white glow filtered back through the tunnel, casting the party into soft relief.

'Remarkable,' Miss Travers murmured. There was just enough light to see the expression of wonder on her face. 'I've never seen anything like it!'

'I don't think anyone has, ma'am,' Dawlish said.

Blake raised his eyebrows suggestively in the lieutenant's direction, earning himself a disapproving glare. Admittedly Dawlish was over-compensating with the 'ma'am', but he wasn't going to risk antagonising her. He had been absent when she'd arrived at HQ, but he had heard plenty about it from Blake and Weams. Apparently, if looks could kill they would have been expecting a replacement CO and 2iC any day now.

'How do you want to proceed from here?' Dawlish asked.

Miss Travers indicated the camera bag she had slung over her left shoulder. 'I want to get a few shots in situ before taking a sample.'

Dawlish frowned. 'Will that work down here?'

'It's a particularly good camera,' she replied simply. 'And I have not a little skill when it comes to photography.'

She smiled, and Dawlish observed it was a very pretty smile. He had hitherto believed all female scientists were dowdy, spectacle-wearing spinsters, possessed of figures similar to that of a test tube; Anne Travers, though, was surprisingly easy on the eyes. Dawlish wouldn't have minded trying his luck, only it seemed Knight had staked his claim as far as that was concerned, despite the rocky start. Typical Para really, calling first dibs on the best crumpet.

Dawlish smirked, imagining what Miss Travers

would do if she ever heard anyone refer to her as 'crumpet'. He wished the captain luck; he was certainly going to need it.

Suddenly, out of nowhere, a low rumbling reverberated down the tunnel. The soldiers and Miss Travers exchanged uncertain glances.

'S'at a train?' Norris asked, directing a nervous glance back along the tracks.

'Can't be,' Dawlish murmured. There was an uneasy feeling growing in the pit of his stomach. 'Power's off.'

'Look, sir!'

The others turned to where Blake was pointing. From the darkness ahead, two large figures were approaching. There were four bright points of light where their eyes should have been, like headlamps.

'Halt!' Dawlish shouted, drawing his Browning as the men readied their weapons. The bad feeling was growing stronger. 'Identify yourselves!'

A menacing, bubbling roar came in reply. Switching his torch back on, Dawlish was astonished as the light revealed two huge, shaggy beasts advancing towards them with a powerful, shambling gait.

Dawlish heard Miss Travers gasp, and he turned to see her face pale in the torchlight, eyes wide with disbelief and fear.

'Yeti!'

'What?' Dawlish didn't believe his ears.

'They're Yeti!' she cried. 'But it's not possible… There was only one of them!'

At that moment Blake and the others opened fire. The Yeti roared, but continued to advance, muzzle-flashes reflecting off long sharp claws.

'Stop!' Miss Travers shouted, trying to make herself heard above the gunfire and roaring. She clutched at Dawlish's arm. 'Stop, you can't harm them. They're robots!'

'They're what?'

'Robots! Machines!'

Robot Yeti in the London Underground. Dawlish would have laughed at the absurdity of it, had he not been staring two of the creatures in the face.

A scream from Norris drew Dawlish's attention back to the fray. The Yeti had halted, but one brandished some kind of gun. It fired Mist at Norris, who had taken up position a couple of yards in front of the others. The private fell to the floor, shrouded in web-like filaments of fungus, and stayed there; still and silent. Dawlish's eyes widened in horror.

Then the Yeti began to advance again.

'Fall back!' Dawlish cried out to Blake and O'Brien, moving to cover Miss Travers, who was fumbling with the straps of her camera bag. Uttering a curse, the lieutenant raised his pistol and aimed between one set of headlamp-like eyes. 'Fall back!'

CHAPTER NINE
Seven Lonely Days

A WEEK. A WEEK, AND STILL NO NEWS.

Sir Alistair paced the floor of his quarters, his brow creased with unaccustomed anxiety. It was the early hours of the morning, somewhere around four o'clock, he estimated, as the sun was yet to rise. He had not been to bed that night, knowing instinctively that sleep would utterly evade him.

Something was deeply wrong.

Yesterday, at about 15:00hrs, he should have received his call from Pemberton summoning him to London. Instead he had finished up the day's reports, gone over the plans for next week's manoeuvres in southern Cyrenaica, dropped in for a spot check of the armoury, and cheered on an impromptu football match between A and C Coys. But there had been no call; no word from London, and no indication that there would be.

Why was he still here?

Eight paces between the door and the window. Eight back, passing the somewhat Spartan camp bed, small wash basin, and beaten-up desk. About-turn, repeat.

The latest news they had heard on the radio was that Central London was to be completely evacuated of all civilians, with the government officially moving north to reconvene at St Albans. The men were getting increasingly restless with the continued absence of detailed reports, especially as repeated requests for information through official channels only returned evasive platitudes; and Alistair was becoming increasingly frustrated at his having to play along. At this moment he had no other choice.

He should have left that very morning. In two hours he should be flying from El-Adem to RAF Akrotiri in Cyprus, where he would have a layover of about an hour before boarding a flight back to England.

Another two sets of sixteen to add to the total. Had there been a carpet in here, he would have been well on his way to wearing a groove in it, as Doris would say.

There was, of course, the possibility that he could be mistaken. Years did creep up on a fellow, and old age struck when least expected. He couldn't possibly remember *every* detail from forty-two years ago... But in that Alistair knew he was clutching at straws. He remembered the day, the time, and the circumstances perfectly. He was not mistaken.

He glanced over at the desk as he continued to pace. Propped up behind his shaving kit was a rectangle of heavy, cream laid cardboard, printed and embossed with a gold edge; an invitation to a drinks do at the consulate in Benghazi. A common enough event, just a courtesy really, but Alistair knew for a fact that he had never received the invitation. Somewhere – he had no idea how or when – something had occurred to change events.

Could this somehow be down to the gnome? Alistair would lay money on that being it. Potentially, if what he had gathered about the theory of time travel was correct, the act of his transportation back to this present alone could be enough to have upset some small but vital occurrence; those tended to be deadlier agents of change than direct action, in Alistair's experience. Whatever had happened, events had altered so that, for some reason, Pemberton had either been prevented or decided not to recall Alistair, and now his immediate future was in jeopardy. Before now he had not appreciated just how much had hinged on that one phone call. Without it he could not go to London, he would not be there to take over from Pemberton, he would not be there to confront the Intelligence in Piccadilly Circus... and he would never meet the Doctor in the Underground.

Before his mind's eye, Alistair saw the threads of his life begin to unravel. Without him being a part of the London Event, none of it would happen; Anne, Bill, Professor Travers, Chorley... He would not meet any of them. Nor would he be there to instigate the activation of the Fifth Operational Corps, nor push for the formation of UNIT. Every invasion he had thwarted, every Earth-bound conspiracy toppled; he would never have been there to help stop it.

He'd always tried to remain humble about his role in history, despite his knighthood, calling it arrogance to think he was that important. But what if he was wrong? Was that why he was reliving 1969 - to teach him his place in history? After all history, this present, was changing around him. He could genuinely feel it; a tangible sensation. There was no one single future in front of him anymore, but many. Was *he* the fracture point?

Temporarily overwhelmed, Alistair stopped his pacing and leaned against the desk. Seeking something to ground himself with, he picked up his glengarry and turned it over in his hands. His fingers brushed over the heavy woollen cloth, the red, white and royal blue diced headband, the black ribbons at the back. He and it had seen some interesting times together; happy and sad occasions, and a few more close calls than he would care to admit.

It was a peculiarity of history that had the Scots alone of the Guards regiments wearing the glengarry instead of berets. One very senior officer had decided to take particular pride in their northern origins before the Great

War, and just like that a tradition was born. Funny to think it could so easily have been otherwise.

The London Event was one of the last times he would wear his in action. Soon after its formation, the Fifth would be issued with a variation – dark green wool, hatbands in the hunting Stewart colours. A personal joke on the part of General Hamilton. Four years down the line he would exchange it for an entirely different headdress altogether.

But I don't have to.

Realisation dawned on him suddenly, out of nowhere, and stuck fast. He could turn his back on it all, and be none the wiser. He could stay with the Scots; marry Sally and start a family, maybe seek out Doris and be a proper father to Albert. He could remain an ordinary Army officer; take the life of minor notoriety he had imagined for himself when he put his name down for Sandhurst all those years ago. Perhaps he would obtain a general officer rank before retirement, write a memoir or two about the wilder parts of his career, advise on a few committees, then fade away into dignified obscurity, occasionally stirring himself for the odd reunion or garden party. History would find someone else to fill his shoes.

Alistair's heart hammered in his chest. He could do it as well, and quite easily. All he had to do was finish the tour and return home as the battalion's CO. The revolution would not come in these next few months; the Scots would be long gone before Colonel Qaddafi and his Free Officers Movement staged their *coup d'etat* in September. Alistair briefly toyed with the thought of tipping the authorities the wink, before dismissing it outright. It was bad enough that he was considering rewriting his own history, let alone world events, however noble his intentions.

What, if he was honest with himself, had duty ever

done for him? It had certainly not made him happy. Duty had robbed him of his father, had seen Sally and Fiona leave him, left him estranged with his daughter for many long years – had seen him witness far too many young men die by cruel and unusual means, more often than not robbing them of their humanity before the end.

Still holding the glengarry, Alistair turned to gaze out of the open window. The first thin grey light of dawn was beginning to show on the horizon.

Nothing was set in stone anymore. At this point in time, all things were possible. He did not even have to stay in the Army; on his return he could resign his commission, go back to his original plan of being a Maths teacher. Why not cut to the chase?

No aliens, no monstrous deaths, no broken home.

But there was no guaranteeing it would be so. History may find someone else to fill his shoes, but would they have devoted their life to making sure this planet was defended? Would anyone else have given a scruffy little man in his ill-fitted coat and chequered trousers the benefit of the doubt? They might so easily fail where he might otherwise have succeeded.

But then he would never have met Fiona, never have found Doris again. Would he know any of his grandchildren? They may never have existed! He might regain the memories of his brother, never becoming a target for 'Maha' and so have James to himself as it was always meant to be – but then he would not have met Owain. He would never have known either of his nephews.

This was never about him, not really. He was just a part; a cog in a mechanism, but if he should fail in his function, the whole system would be warped out of shape; maybe stop working altogether. He may have started the fight, but he would not be the one to finish it; he recognised, now, that it would never be finished.

119

Humanity would need protecting for generations to come, and Anne, Bill, Kate – they had all taken up his mantle. That was his real legacy.

Duty may not have made him happy, but it had given his life meaning, and meant that others could carry on living theirs in peace and security. Which was all anyone could hope for, really.

Decision made, Alistair placed the cap on his head and stepped into the corridor. Time was tight, and he needed to make his move now. He headed for the stairs, and from thence to the Comms room, his sudden arrival startling the poor signalman on duty.

It was time, as the old proverb said, to make his own destiny.

The small Italian restaurant just off Novello Road was surprisingly busy. Dame Anne could not decide which she found more bizarre; that anyone could think of dining out of an evening during the current crisis, or that the restaurant had decided to remain open for business.

The full evacuation of Central London had been underway for almost a week. The official story now being circulated by the press and local authorities was one of widespread bomb damage to the city's Victorian gas pipe network, hitherto unnoticed but exacerbated by the heavy build-up of road traffic over the past twenty years. It was, they said, impossible as yet to estimate how extensive the damage might be, and now there was talk of a 'buffer zone' being put in place throughout Greater London to be on the safe side. And, on a side note, some bears had escaped from London Zoo, any sightings of which were to be reported immediately to the police.

And yet here people were still going out for dinner, clinging on to their normal routines as long as they could in the face of impending danger.

Being in the thick of it, isolated underground at

Goodge Street the first time around, Anne had not been in a position to appreciate just what effect the evacuation had on the citizenry. Oh, she had heard about the objections, the questions raised on the radio about whether the Gas Board was guilty of gross neglect, residents bleating the line, 'If Hitler hadn't made us go, why should we now?'

Anne had been irritated on behalf of the soldiers at the time, imagining such people idiots for wanting to stay in the face of danger. But it was only now, sitting among them here, that it became clear just how little sense of urgency there had been. Many of these people had lived through bombs falling out of the sky night after night, yet carried on their daily lives among the wreckage; the remote possibility that they *might* get blown up by a gas explosion didn't cut much ice.

But what else could the authorities do? The truth, that London was under siege by an alien menace, would cause mass hysteria, if anyone believed it at all – and between a slow but ordered evacuation, or panicked crowds, Anne knew which was preferable.

Just two more days, Anne had reminded herself as she got ready. Two more days in which she had to keep up the pretence, then she and Rupert would put their plan into operation, and she could end this dreadful limbo.

Anne had not wanted to go out for dinner that evening, but she had put Malachi off enough times over the past week that, in all good conscience, when he had phoned earlier she could not say no.

For the occasion she had chosen an emerald green Mary Quant mini dress from Rachel's wardrobe, being the only thing remotely suitable that didn't sport too low a neckline and had long sleeves. She'd also been more than happy to find that Rachel also possessed some thicker tights than the flimsy hosiery she had been wearing on her arrival; those, and a nice black wool Dior coat would keep out most of the cold – and help discourage Malachi from getting any ideas about prolonging the evening. With that in mind she had gone minimal with the make-up again, only short wing tips and a little coloured eyeshadow. And even that felt like too much.

It was odd, having to consider after all this time how she dressed. She hadn't had to bother with that nonsense for years; she wore something that was smart, comfortable, and practical, and that was that. In fact, the last time she had fussed so much over an outfit was back in 1999 when she had met the Queen to receive her DBE for three decades of service to the advancement of science in the UK and abroad. It had been a moment of honour and excitement, but one person had been absent. Oh, a *version* of him had attended, but that Edward Travers wasn't her *father*, not really. Her father, the man she had known since birth, not the time traveller who had turned up mysteriously in 1973, had not been there to share the moment with her. To see her become a Dame Commander of the Most Excellent Order of the British Empire. This time, if everything went according to plan, he would.

On arrival at the restaurant, the Maître d' had greeted them like old friends ('*Signor* Silverstein, happy to see you again, and your so-lovely young lady.'), and Malachi had booked them 'their' table, which turned out to be a small, secluded booth just over from the bar. It was quite a nice place, though a little on the clichéd side with the chequered tablecloths and candles stuck in wine bottles; although, to be fair, it was technically not yet a cliché. Odd, too, to think that Italian food at this point was still regarded as an exotic luxury and, from some quarters, viewed with mild suspicion. Coming from a time when hard pressed-students routinely lived off economy sized bags of dried pasta and takeaway pizza, it was quite jarring to realise how much they took an international diet for granted, when only decades before they'd had so little. It might be fun, once she'd returned to the future, to come back and see if the place was still there; though hopefully the lone accordion player in gypsy garb wouldn't be.

Anne had picked her way through her starter awkwardly, letting Malachi do most of the talking, dropping in an occasional vague response to give the impression she was listening while she turned the rest of her mind to the preparations for hers and Rupert's upcoming expedition into Central London. It wasn't all that difficult.

Forced to quit his Chelsea hotel some days ago and now lodging at a guest house in Battersea, Malachi had an awful lot to say.

'Honestly, darling, it really is too bad. Couldn't give me any idea as to how long the work would take. Not that any of those jackbooted oafs would have the least clue, of course. And as for this story about animals escaped from London Zoo... Utter rot if you ask me! Probably spotted by some tramp off his head on something. You know what those types are like.'

'I suppose so,' Anne said distractedly.

Finally catching on to something in her voice, Malachi looked at her apologetically. 'I'm boring you, aren't I?'

'No, no, not in the slightest,' Anne lied, though it didn't sound particularly convincing even to her.

Malachi gave a rueful smile and shook his head. 'I am. Listen to me; London falling apart at the seams, government paralysed, and all I can do is complain! Dashed lucky to have a roof over my head at all, the way things are.'

He broke off as their waiter brought out the main course. She had decided to play it safe and go for the ravioli, simply because she had long ago come to the conclusion that she should never be allowed to eat spaghetti in public, and was unwilling to expose herself to that level of ridicule. It was a fairly moot point, though, as now she was feeling anything but hungry.

But Malachi didn't seem all that interested in eating, either. He was watching her intently, his dark eyes filled with warm adoration, and Anne began again to feel that dreadful, creeping sensation of guilt.

'Do you remember when we came here last?' he asked gently. 'You made me the happiest man alive that night.'

He reached across the table and took her left hand in his, his thumb brushing the engagement ring, making the diamond sparkle in the candlelight.

Anne felt her stomach plummet through the floor. *Oh no...*

'I know it's difficult to think past all this chaos,' he continued softly. 'Everything's such a mess at the moment, but we'll get through it. Together. I promise, after the funeral–'

'Malachi!' Anne snatched her hand away quickly. She could feel herself trembling. 'Please stop. Just stop.'

Malachi blinked in surprise. 'Stop what?'

'This.' She gestured at the distance between them and the restaurant. 'I... I can't cope with this right now.'

'Whatever do you mean?'

Anne's emotions were in a state of turmoil, and she wondered how much of it had to do with the battle between her consciousness and her host body. Emotional states, after all, were chemical reactions, not mind. *Two more days,* her inner voice insisted loudly. *Just two more days!* But she couldn't maintain the pretence any longer. It was just too cruel; to her as well as to him.

'I need some time apart,' she said firmly. 'Alone. To think things through.'

People at the other tables were beginning to stare, and Malachi quickly adopted the self-conscious half-whisper of someone desperate not to make a scene. 'But why?' he hissed.

'It's difficult to explain.'

Malachi went as white as a sheet. 'Oh no. You're not pregnant, are you?'

'No!' Anne gasped, horrified at the thought. She hastily lowered her voice again. 'No. Of course not.'

'Thank goodness for that.' Malachi couldn't have looked more relieved, and let out a shaky breath. 'Though, you know, if you *had* been... I would have forgiven you, even though it wasn't mine.'

'Malachi Silverstein, how dare you!' she hissed, scandalised. It did answer one question she had not wanted to consider, and knowing certainly didn't make it any better.

'No, no, I didn't mean to suggest you would,' Malachi said, hurriedly back-peddling. 'Just, if it ever did come to that, well. You know.'

'Please, Malachi,' Anne said firmly, willing herself to be calm. She risked losing control of the exchange, and that could not be allowed to happen. 'I need you to listen. You are dear to me, more than I can say, and I am deeply, deeply sorry for everything you have been through recently – but I just can't be who you need me to be. Not now.'

It was possible that Malachi could not have looked more shell-shocked had she slapped him, and Anne had to drop her gaze to the table. She heard him take a deep breath and steel himself.

'All right,' he said quietly, earnestly. 'So not now. And after that?'

But Anne could only shake her head. 'Maybe, I don't know. But for now...' She slipped the ring off her finger, and placed it gently, deliberately on the table. 'I'm sorry.'

Malachi didn't reply. His eyes were fixed on the ring, the diamonds glittering coldly in the candlelight.

Mutely, Anne rose from the table, and one of the waiters came over to help her on with her coat; clearly the staff had clocked the way things were going and anticipated her move. She managed to brush off the embarrassment at that, whispering a 'thank you'.

The waiter returned a sympathetic expression, and conducted her to the door, holding it open and bidding her a quiet 'Goodnight, *signorina*,' as she stepped into the street.

She did not look back until she had walked a good few paces, at which point she risked a glance through the restaurant's window. She could just about see Malachi, tucked away in the back corner behind the other diners. He was still sitting there, staring desolately at where she had left the ring on the table.

An overwhelming sense of shame welled up in her chest, and she turned away. She'd had no right; this wasn't her life. But what else could she have done? It wasn't as if she had *asked* to come back in this body – she hadn't asked for anything at all! Like it or not she had a task to complete, and Malachi had become a liability. She simply didn't have the luxury of taking his feelings into account.

Anne pulled the collar of her coat close about her face, and quickly crossed the road. Besides, it would be for Malachi's own good in the long run; if she had not disappointed him now, she would only have done so later. And who was to say that he and Rachel would not get back together again after she'd left?

It was all a dreadful mistake.

Anne shivered, Malachi's words from Julius' funeral coming back to haunt her. She quickened her pace, footsteps echoing briskly in the cool night air as the heels of her shoes clicked against the paving slabs.

Rachel and Malachi's engagement had broken off

around the time of the London Event; this much was an established fact. Had her actions tonight altered history? Maybe so, maybe not; there was no definite way of telling from here. Perhaps, then, history had already changed to accommodate her presence? Perhaps she had always been the reason that Malachi had never married?

And could that mean that she had already failed?

CHAPTER TEN
Communication Breakdown

'I'VE GOT YOUR SECURE LINE THROUGH TO LONDON, SIR,' Sanders said, indicating the phone on Sir Alistair's desk. 'You should be able to use it now.'

'Thank you, Sanders.' Alistair waited until the door to the ante-office was shut again before he picked up the receiver.

It had taken most of the day to schedule the call. In his time, the youth were certainly spoiled when it came to instant communication, when all you had to do was tap a button to be able to speak to someone on the other side of the globe at no cost. In recent years Alistair had found himself looking back and wondering how they had ever managed to cope, and the answer, as illustrated by this call, was inevitably 'with minor to great inconvenience'.

Although, being on the cutting edge of military technology had often provided certain advantages. He smiled as he remembered when Con, only a teenager at the time, had decided to introduce him to Skype. 'Oh, video calls. We had those back in the '70s.' The poor lad had looked as astonished as he was crestfallen.

In a way, Alistair was somewhat disappointed in himself that he had not figured things out sooner. Coming to the end of his life, Alistair had imagined that his past was an open and shut book; but the gnome was all about proving otherwise. Both times now he had been transported back to points in his life where choice played a part; one where his memory was hazy, the other where he remembered things all too well. In 1981 he had acted as he had always acted, despite not knowing the outcome, and had managed to preserve the future. Here, he had been offered the chance to take his life down another path – one which, in his darkest hours, he sometimes wished he had travelled – but he had resisted the temptation. His future self, here and now, would guide him to where he needed to be in 1969; the instigator of his own destiny, because he already knew it was meant to be.

It was a mind-boggling thought, but it made a round-about sense. Alistair was also starting to wonder whether he was wrong in assuming whatever force controlled the gnome was inherently malign. Something bigger was taking place here; something which, as yet, he could only see a part. Whatever the gnome was, and whatever its end-game, he would have to wait a little longer to find out.

In the meantime, having made his choice, he needed to get himself to London; a feat which required diplomacy, a little low cunning, and faith in a very dear friend.

Alistair placed the receiver to his ear. 'Hello?'

The operator's voice sounded at the other end of the line. 'Yes, sir, how may I help you?'

'CO 2 Scots here,' he said shortly. It would save her asking who was calling. 'Put me through to Colonel Pemberton at the HQ post at Goodge Street.'

'One moment, sir.'

The line went quiet as she hunted down the connection, and Alistair waited patiently. The Yeti had not yet started attacking the communications lines, so there would be no question of his being unable to get through. And Pemberton would be there to answer.

'Putting you through now, sir.'

There was another brief silence, and then a different voice came on the line.

'Pemberton.'

Old Spence. Alistair swallowed in an attempt to banish the sudden dryness in his throat. He had expected that hearing Spence's voice would rake up old feelings of guilt and regret, but he had not anticipated how strong those feelings would be, even after all this time. Memories of Spence's funeral, and more recently Joan's, flooded through his head. Spence's death had nearly been the breaking of him, and in a short time from now he was about to live it all again.

Steady now, he told himself. He had to keep his nerve. Taking a shallow breath, he ran to meet the problem head on.

'Lethbridge-Stewart, sir,' he said quickly.

'Alistair?' Pemberton's surprise was clear to hear. 'So, it really is you. I thought you were in Libya?'

'I am. Damn difficult to get a line through to you, I can tell you.'

'How did you even know where to phone?' Pemberton asked, somewhat baffled.

'Don't ask questions you won't like the answer to,' Alistair said bluntly. Enough bluff; he was running to a schedule. 'Spence, just what is happening over there? The Embassy's giving me the run around and I can't get a straight answer from anyone in Middle East Command.'

'You phoned to ask me that?' There was an edge of distaste to Pemberton's voice now. 'I thought you knew better than that.'

He did know better, of course, and the Lethbridge-Stewart of forty-two years ago would never have dreamed of pushing his nose into an operation like this. But there was, however, a certain audacity that only came with age, and Sir Alistair Lethbridge-Stewart had that in spades.

'The men are worried,' he said seriously. He could play the altruistic line, especially as it was a genuine concern. 'We're getting no news from home, they can't contact their families, and now they hear that the Palace and Whitehall have cleared out entirely. You're in the thick of it; I owe it to them to find out what I can.'

'Gas leak,' Pemberton answered woodenly. 'Whole network's in danger of rupturing and it's completely swamped the City.'

The official line. Alistair hadn't expected anything else at this stage. 'And the "bears" people have reported seeing?' he asked archly.

'Escaped from London Zoo, along with some of the other animals. Still trying to recapture them.'

'Rot,' Alistair scoffed into the receiver.

There was a brief silence on the other end of the line. 'I'm sorry?' Pemberton asked, and Alistair detected the warning edge to his voice. He ignored it.

'I said "rot",' he repeated, enunciating every word clearly. This was the tricky part. Friends or no, Pemberton was still his senior, and Alistair knew he was dangerously close to overstepping the mark. If Spence took it the wrong way, Alistair could very well lose his commission over this. 'Special Forces to deal with a gas leak? Even on that scale, you would hardly make the decision to evacuate the entire city. I know a cover-up when I see one.'

'Colonel–'

'Eight million people, Spence,' Alistair growled into the phone. 'What the hell's going on?'

An ominous silence lapsed over the line, and Alistair judged that they had reached the tipping point. Time to give things a last gentle nudge.

'I've called in pretty much every favour I'm owed to get through to you,' he said quietly, softening his tone.

131

An outright lie, but it served. 'Please, Spence, don't let it have been in vain.'

And Alistair waited, offering up a silent prayer. None of this was his business; he had no right to any information whatsoever, and Pemberton owed him nothing outside of friendship. But Alistair knew his man, knew that in one reality, at least, Spence had considered bringing him into the fold. With any luck, it would not take much to sway his decision.

'This line is secure?' Pemberton asked, after what seemed like an age.

'You know it is,' Alistair replied.

'This operation is classified as Top Secret,' Pemberton said, after only the briefest hesitation. 'And you're right, it isn't a gas leak. Not any sort of gas we've seen, anyway. We thought it was some kind of nerve agent, but it doesn't disperse; just hangs static in the air, like a great wall of mist, and it's growing. We've tried everything to neutralise it, but nothing seems to touch it.'

'Where's it coming from?'

'Somewhere in the Underground. Two days after the Mist appeared they discovered a sort of luminous fungus that is growing along the Circle Line, blocking up the tunnels. It corresponds exactly with the path of the Mist above.'

'Is it the Russians?' Alistair asked, doing his best to sound confused. He had been pretty confused when Pemberton had explained it the first time.

'No, not that we know of, but we believe it to be the work of a hostile force. Those "bears"...? Unknown agents guarding the fungus from anyone who tries to get near it. But so far no one's claiming responsibility – or seems to have the least idea of what the real situation is. Our allies are starting to get suspicious, however, and are starting to demand answers. Outside of the city, only Strategic Command and a few at Cabinet level know the full story.'

'And now I know,' Alistair murmured.

'Yes, you do,' Pemberton replied archly. 'Though what you can do with it beats me.'

The other colonel's tone held something of a challenge, and that was certainly encouraging. Time to give things another push.

'Bring us back over there,' Alistair said.

'Impossible.'

'Eight million people to evacuate?' Alistair said dryly. 'Sounds like you need all the help you can get.'

'As far as that's concerned we're all right. We've reactivated the Civil Defence Corps, and as it's only been a year since they disbanded there's plenty of them. Quite a few still had their old kit. They're working with the police to temporarily rehouse people outside the danger zone.'

'And what about the city itself, those "bear-agent" things? You can't expect us to sit on our hands over here when there's a battle at home.'

'I can't bring the battalion back,' Pemberton said shortly. 'And even if I did have that sort of pull, you know I wouldn't. The world needs to believe we have this under control, and pulling your lot out without replacements would send exactly the wrong message. Your battalion stays in Libya.'

'But–'

'However,' Pemberton continued, cutting over him. 'I can bring you back.'

Alistair breathed a mental sigh of relief. He had done it; he had manoeuvred Pemberton to exactly where he wanted him. Now to clinch it.

'Me?' he said, feigning confusion. On the other end of the phone he heard Pemberton let out a sigh; which alone was a measure of how much strain his friend was under.

'I'll be straight with you, Al. The Brass have been expecting an attack like this for months, and they've had me assembling a taskforce.'

'It's a targeted attack?'

'No doubt about it. But now it's happened, we didn't predict anything on this scale, and I'm spread too damn thin. I need another safe pair of hands here on the ground; someone I know I can trust to keep things moving on the outside whilst I'm down here attacking the root.'

'Surely you have a 2iC?'

'Not senior enough to deal with this,' Pemberton said, and Alistair immediately pictured Ben Knight. A solid fellow, cut down in his prime, but far too junior for such a job. 'This whole thing's grown too big, too fast. Besides, I don't know who they'll send me from here, and I'd rather I have someone who'll work with me, not against me. I need a man I know will keep his head and adapt quickly to the situation, and you're one of the best there is.'

'Can you swing it?' Alistair asked dubiously, despite knowing the answer.

'Yes, General Hamilton's co-ordinating the whole thing. He won't say no if I ask for you, golden boy.'

Even at this end of the phone, Alistair couldn't help but wince at that old barb. It was true that several of his early career appointments owed a lot to the patronage of General Hamilton, though he had never actively sought it out. Even now Alistair was mystified as to what he had done to earn the general's particular favour.

'It's all quiet here,' he said aloud pretending to consider the idea. 'The battalion can do without me for a while, and both my majors are competent.'

'Good,' Pemberton said gruffly. 'So, do you want the bloody job or not?'

Alistair smiled to himself down the receiver. *Success.* 'Do you even need to ask?' he asked warmly.

'Capital. Be at El-Adem for 06:00hrs tomorrow. You'll be briefed once you touch down here.' Pemberton gave a dry chuckle. 'Odd, really. I had been planning on co-opting you for my team once you finished your tour out there, but events overtook us. Felt you'd be perfect for the job. And now, you phoning me... Well, nice to know a chap gets it right every now and then.'

'Thank you, sir.'

'Don't thank me,' Pemberton said wryly. 'You don't know what you've just talked yourself into.'

Oh, but I do, Spence, Alistair thought grimly, as he replaced the receiver on the cradle.

And now, in one form or another, it seemed that he had always known.

'Can you pass me those pliers, Weams?'

Weams put the requested tool into Miss Travers' outstretched hand. They were in the base workshop, which had been given over to Miss Travers as her workspace for the duration. She currently had the back panel off an impressive-looking piece of kit he had been informed was some sort of signal measuring device. It had only arrived yesterday as a special requisition item, complete with armed guard, only to discover somewhere along the way it hadn't travelled too well.

Weams had been detailed off to 'assist' Miss Travers when she first arrived, though so far that had mainly consisted of his standing by and watching her work, passing her tools, hunting down stray components, and fetching her tea. Not that he minded in the least; Steve Weams was certainly the envy of many a squaddie at the moment, which made a nice change. Blake had called him a 'right jammy beggar' only that morning. Out of his league, mind, even if he wasn't married, but that didn't stop him from admiring the view.

'So these Yeti are the real thing, then?' he asked,

picking up their conversation from where they'd left off a few minutes ago.

'I suppose you could say that.' Miss Travers let out a soft grunt as she wrestled with some unseen element within the machine. 'Just as real as you or I. So they must be.'

'Crikey,' Weams murmured. 'Must have pretty thick skin, way bullets keep bouncin' off 'em. Blake says they're going through grenades like nobody's business.'

He hadn't seen one in person, thankfully, but he had seen the picture Miss Travers had managed to snap on their first encounter, and received the follow-up briefing from the colonel along with the others. More to the point he had heard Blake's and O'Brien's story of what had happened to Norris on the expedition, and that was chilling enough. What was even worse was that, with those hairy monsters in the way, there was no chance of going back to recover the body.

'Well, it's not the skin that's the problem,' Miss Travers said. She stood up straight and admired her handiwork. 'You see, under the fur–'

The door opened, and a small man in a velour jacket, glasses and bow-tie walked in. Weams felt his spirits sink. Oh yes, and this was the newest development; they'd picked up a passenger. The Brass had caved to pressure from the Press, the whole pack baying for blood, and agreed to let one journalist down to cover the operation – much good it would do them, in Weams' opinion. Anyway, the rumour was that they'd be getting Larry Greene, which Weams wouldn't have minded. His mum liked Greene, and she would've been thrilled if he'd managed to get his autograph for her. The bloke who had turned up *looked* like Larry Greene, but he was definitely not Larry Greene.

Harold Chorley was nothing short of a first-class tick in Weams' opinion. He had only arrived a couple of hours ago, and already he had managed to put nearly everybody's backs up. Colonel Pemberton had managed some small revenge, though. On the pretext that space was short down here, he had told Chorley that he had no option but to bunk with the SNCOs – which had ruffled the man's feathers no end. He had probably imagined he'd get his own room, or something ridiculous like that; he was a man clearly accustomed to soft living.

Unfortunately for Chorley he had made a particular enemy of Anne Travers – and thus earned the ill-will of the entire Fortress. When she had first arrived, admittedly they were surprised to have been sent a female scientist, but there was no denying she knew her stuff, and they'd got used to the idea PDQ. Chorley, however, had laughed and asked who the 'real' scientist was.

He was now doing everything possible to wheedle his way into her good books, but that was nothing short of a lost cause.

'Ah, Miss Travers,' he said, giving her what he doubtless thought was a charming smile. 'Glad I caught you. I really could do with that interview, so if I could–'

'I'm afraid now's not a good time, Mr Chorley,' Miss Travers said curtly. 'I'm just on my way to see about some electronic supplies. Weams, could you please put this panel back on? Thank you.'

She breezed past him, ignoring Chorley's half-uttered protests, and shut the door firmly behind her with a *snap*.

The two men left together, Chorley sighed and rolled his eyes in what was meant to be a conspiratorial way.

'Women, eh?' he said, the greasy smile returning.

Weams chose not to comment, turning away to get on with reassembling the equipment. He was not in the mood for banter; not with this twit, and certainly not about Miss Travers.

Realising that he was failing to ingratiate himself,

Chorley tried another tack. 'Sorry, I haven't introduced myself properly,' he said smoothly. 'Been finding my way about the place. Harold Chorley, London Television. You've probably seen me on the box.'

He offered his hand, but Weams didn't take it. He wasn't sure he'd get his back.

'Weams, sir,' he said stiffly, by way of response.

'Ah, Private Weams.' Chorley dropped the hand, but retained the smile. 'Good to meet you.'

Weams felt his hackles rise. It seemed Chorley was one of *those* civvies. 'Craftsman.'

Chorley's brow crumpled in confusion. 'I'm sorry?'

'Craftsman,' Weams repeated coldly. 'My rank. I'm REME. I'm the Sparks 'round 'ere.'

'Ah, yes. REME, you say?' Chorley said, though he still didn't seem all that enlightened. 'Electrician, then. Jolly good. So you're the chap I see if my tape recorder needs fixing, eh?'

'I s'pose, sir,' Weams admitted grudgingly. Damned if he'd be doing odd-jobs for this clueless civvie, though. 'Military work's priority.'

'Oh of course, of course,' Chorley said quickly, apparently in an attempt to show Weams he understood the gravity of the situation. 'I promise not to take up too much of your valuable time.'

'No, sir,' Weams replied shortly, in a tone that very much suggested he wouldn't let the journalist take up any of his time at all if he could help it.

Chorley made an awkward noise in his throat, and straightened his bow-tie. Moving away from the workbench, he started to take a look around the room, casting his glance over the various electronic gadgets, blueprints and tools Miss Travers had laid out. Weams stopped what he was doing, and stared at Chorley mutely. He didn't think for a moment that Chorley would steal anything – twit wouldn't have the first clue about any of this gear, for a start – but the craftie was determined to make the man feel as unwelcome as possible.

It seemed to be working. Chorley soon started to squirm under the unwelcome attention, coughed awkwardly again and came to rest next to the Geiger counter, which was currently switched off. He tapped the glass of the dial like that of a barometer, as if he was hoping to see the needle move.

'Summat I can help you with, sir?' Weams asked pointedly.

Chorley's face immediately took on an eager expression. It seemed this was the opening he had been waiting for.

'Yes,' he said enthusiastically, crossing back to the workbench in a few quick strides. 'Yes, there is, actually. You've been here since the set-up, haven't you?'

Weams was a little surprised by that. Either Chorley had made a very shrewd guess or he was quite a bit more perceptive than he seemed.

'Yes, sir,' he said dubiously, wondering what Chorley was after. 'Was one of the first ones down here. My workshop had to get it all up and running again.'

'Quite. So, you've seen things develop down here quite a bit, haven't you? I mean re-opening the place, all this equipment moved in, personnel coming and going night and day, the colonel co-ordinating everything… I expect you've seen it all.'

'Wouldn't say "all", sir,' Weams said reluctantly. Chorley wasn't far off the mark, though, and the journalist sensed it, like a shark homing in on blood in the water.

'Oh, come now,' Chorley said, his smooth self-assured air returning. 'Everyone knows it's you chaps that really run the place. Brass hats give the orders, but it's fellows like you that make it all work. Bet you could tell tale or two about what's really been going on down here.'

'There you are, Mr Chorley.'

Both Weams and Chorley started, turning to see Staff Arnold standing in the open doorway. His face was set in a stern expression, directing a particularly withering glare at the journalist.

'CO's compliments,' Arnold said brusquely. 'And he's ready to brief you on the situation down here. He's waiting in the Common Room.'

'Right, yes.' Chorley straightened his glasses, regaining something of his composure. He gave a lopsided grin. 'Thank you, Sergeant. Mustn't keep the colonel waiting, must we?'

And he very quickly left, but not without having to squeeze past Arnold to get through the door, from which the staff sergeant very deliberately didn't move. Once Chorley had gone, Weams puffed out his cheeks in relief and leaned against the workbench.

'Thanks, Staff.'

'Don't mention it, lad,' Arnold said gruffly. He jerked his head in the direction Chorley had gone. 'Got to watch that one. He's sharper than he looks.'

'Yeah, should've known better,' Weams admitted. He still didn't quite believe how quickly Chorley had managed to turn the tables on him.

Arnold nodded. 'Well you do now; journalists are slippery customers at the best of times. Now, he's got full access down here whilst he's with us, but he'll also be digging for dirt. He tries anything like that again, you keep schtum and send him on to me or one of the officers. You've got better things to do than bandy words with the likes of him, you hear me?'

'Yes, Staff,' Weams said, grateful to be given the out. If the craftsman had his way, he wouldn't go within five yards of the fellow.

'Good,' Arnold said curtly, switching seamlessly to a

disapproving tone. 'So, you'd better straighten yourself up and get to it before Miss Travers comes back, 'stead of slopping 'round like a scarecrow with the straw hanging out.'

Weams grinned even as he stood abruptly to attention and made a show of tidying his uniform.

'Yes, Staff. Sorry, Staff. Won't happen again, Staff!'

'See that it doesn't,' Arnold said crisply, jutting out his chin imperiously. 'Mind you, why she'd want a bleedin' spanner monkey 'bout the place instead of a proper engineer escapes me.'

Weams smirked as Arnold left, then bent back to his task at the workbench.

He was a decent sort really, was Staff Arnold – for a wedgehead. *Spanner monkey.* The craftsman snorted as he aligned up the panel. Considering the right mix of regiments and corps down here, there had been, and would continue to be, plenty of that flying around between the blokes. He'd already heard most of the alternative acronyms for REME, particularly 'Royal Engineering Made Easy' from Mr Dawlish's lot.

Of course, that wasn't what REME stood for at all. *That* was really 'Royal Engineers Minus Ego'.

CHAPTER ELEVEN
Time Is Tight

A COLD BLAST OF AIR HIT ALISTAIR SQUARE ON AS HE hurried to disembark the aircraft, and despite his best attempts at appearing stoical, he could not help but shiver. He had made relatively good time, managing to catch a prescheduled flight from RAF Dhekelia and touching down at RAF Brize Norton in the late afternoon. Usual practice was to allow returning personnel a period to re-acclimatise before heading back into action, only there was nothing usual about these circumstances. The pilot had assured Alistair on the way back that the weather was not particularly cold for February, but having just spent three months under the Saharan sun, he might as well be in the Arctic for all the difference it made.

At the bottom of the ramp a smartly-uniformed captain waited to meet him. An Army Land Rover stood just beyond the shadow of the plane, driver in place, doors open and engine running.

The captain saluted as Alistair's foot touched the ground. 'Fairbodie, sir, on General Hamilton's staff. This way, if you please.'

Alistair acknowledged the salute with an indistinct wave, and followed Fairbodie to the Land Rover. A corporal wearing the insignia of the RAF Regiment jumped out of the passenger seat to take his kitbag, stowing it in the back of the vehicle. Fairbodie indicated that Alistair should get into the back seat, taking the seat next to him. As soon as the doors were shut they moved off. Alistair certainly couldn't fault their efficiency.

Now underway, Fairbodie leaned forward into the foot-well in front of him and produced a thermos and small package wrapped in tinfoil.

'Compliments of the NAAFI, sir,' he said ruefully. 'Coffee and a bacon sandwich. Best we could get between meals, but they're still hot.'

Alistair took both gratefully, unscrewing the lid of the thermos and carefully pouring himself some coffee – which in a Land Rover of dubious suspension was a skill and a half – downing it quickly. Standard NATO instant; white with two sugars. Foul stuff, but hot, as Fairbodie had said, and right now that was all that mattered.

'I'm sorry about the tight turn-around, sir,' Fairbodie said in his clipped accent, raising his voice above the noise of the motor. 'Orders have come through to step up the evacuation, and we need you in place to take the lead.'

Alistair nodded, appreciating the sense of urgency. He was a day behind schedule as it was – not that anyone knew he knew that – and he would have to move fast to make up for lost time. Changes to the timeline was still in evidence; most particularly the first time around he had flown from RAF Akrotiri to RAF Lyneham, from whence he had been whisked down the A3602 to Fugglestone and his briefing with General Hamilton.

'Are we driving directly to Strategic Command then?' he asked, raising his voice in turn as he unwrapped the tinfoil to investigate the sandwich.

'No, sir!' Fairbodie replied. 'The general wants you there on the ground ASAP, so he's come up to give you your briefing here. After that, you will go straight on to London to take up your command.'

Lethbridge-Stewart arched his eyebrows; another

143

new element. He just hoped they were all adding together to play to his advantage.

'Well,' he said philosophically. 'At least I'll be able to get my head down for a couple of hours before then.'

Fairbodie shot him an apologetic glance. 'I'm afraid there won't be the opportunity, sir. Have about an hour to change and freshen up, then you attend your briefing and you're off to London. You're to be dropped by parachute.'

Lethbridge-Stewart hastily swallowed the bite of some sandwich he had just taken. 'I'm to be what?'

'All the roads to the capital are chock-a-block with traffic from the evacuation, and we need to keep the routes as clear as possible. General Hamilton says you have parachute insertion experience.'

'Yes I do,' Alistair admitted distractedly. That part was true to form; he *had* been dropped into London instead of fighting through the organised chaos on the roads – but that had been in the daylight. Surely they couldn't get a plane up before dark? 'I'm not exactly keen on it, though.'

Fairbodie laughed. 'With you there, sir! Never catch me leaving a perfectly serviceable aircraft mid-flight.'

'But tonight?' Alistair pressed.

The captain nodded. 'Orders were given for the pre-flight checks to start as soon as you touch down. Colonel Pemberton told the general that you've done a night drop before.'

'One,' Alistair said pointedly. 'And a very long time ago.'

Over fifty years ago was a very long time. He had been a lot younger and a lot stupider then, an eager second lieutenant fresh from Sandhurst, and the whole experience had been Spence's fault for taking that bet, anyway.

'It will come back to you, sir,' Fairbodie said

encouragingly, and Alistair wished he could share his confidence. 'Just like riding a bike.'

Hardly. 'Remind me to thank Colonel Pemberton when I next speak to him,' he said acidly.

He spent what was left of the ride back focused on demolishing the sandwich as quickly as possible. Cardboard-consistency white bread and thick, greasy bacon; just about as horrible as the coffee, but much-needed fuel. He remembered his briefing with Hamilton very well from the first time around. He had sat there, incredulous, as the general had finally revealed the true nature of the matter; the Yeti, the Mist, fungus - even the 'alien intelligence' theory. Though at that point Alistair had not been concerned with the scientific aspect of the problem, Hamilton had told him about Edward and Anne Travers.

'We've got a boffin chap here, Professor Edward Travers,' Hamilton had said. 'He knows more about these Yeti than anyone else; made them his life's work. He is working on some schemes to combat them from here, whilst his daughter, Miss Travers, is with Pemberton trying to implement them.'

Alistair had struggled to take it all in, and he suspected that had he heard it from anyone else but Hamilton, he would never have believed them. Hamilton must have been of the same opinion, seeing as he had left Strategic Command to brief him in person.

It would be odd, this time, to sit through the briefing, knowing now what he hadn't known then; that Hamilton had been heavily concerned with extra-terrestrial threats to Earth for years. It's still amazed Alistair just how much the general had played him in those early days; informing him of the Special Forces Support Group as it stood, but not indicating that it had ever been formed with anything other than terrestrial threats in mind; no inkling of Hamilton's true agenda, no foreshadowing in the least of what was to come. In hindsight it was clear that Hamilton had been auditioning him for a part he'd never known even existed, but Alistair had been clueless; so completely clueless at the time, and for quite a few months after.

The Land Rover pulled up in front of the admin block, the driver throwing on the handbrake with a little too much enthusiasm, him and his mate jumping out and immediately doubling around to open the doors. *Too keen*, Alistair thought with irritation as he straightened his glengarry which had been knocked sideways.

He stepped out, dignity intact, accepted his kit bag from the corporal and followed Fairbodie up the front steps.

The main block was certainly a much nicer set-up than most Army bases, but then that was the RAF for you. Alistair was looking forward to taking advantage of the accommodation, if only briefly, as this was probably one of the few places in this timeline where he could guarantee himself a piping hot shower.

'Your briefing will be in there, sir, one hour from now,' Fairbodie said, indicating a set of impressive mahogany double doors with brass handles. 'That's the library. The officer's guest accommodation is off to the right and upstairs. If you follow me–'

'Alistair!'

Alistair turned on the spot in astonishment, to be greeted by a vision in WRAC blue, walking purposefully towards him.

'Sally?' he asked, slightly stunned.

She smiled, an amused twinkle in her eyes. 'In the flesh. I hoped to catch you before they shipped you out again.'

His throat had gone dry. With all the changes, he had not expected Sally to be here. She should have been back at Fugglestone, safely away from danger. What on earth was Hamilton thinking bringing her here?

'Well, they certainly are keen enough to get rid of me,' he said, making an attempt at a joke.

The corners of Sally's mouth twitched in appreciation. 'He's really sorry to push you like this, but at the moment every minute counts. Trying to steal a march on these things is proving trickier by the hour.'

And this, Alistair remembered gloomily, was why their relationship had been doomed to failure. He had never straightened out in his mind when to treat her as his fiancée or as his subordinate. His younger self, from this present, would have given her a very stern talking to for calling him 'Alistair' in a professional setting, especially with an audience – a very uncomfortable-looking audience too, judging by the embarrassed expression that Fairbodie was wearing.

'Well, needs must, Lance Corporal,' he muttered vaguely. He gave an awkward cough. 'I suppose I'll see you afterwards.'

Sally's smile faltered a little. He was doing it again. 'Yes, I suppose you will, Colonel.'

He heard the false cheerfulness in her voice, and confound it! He was doing it again, wasn't he? He had side-lined her in favour of duty too many times, and even at a moment like this – when they hadn't seen each other for three months, when he was about to go into danger – he couldn't bring himself to give her a proper goodbye. If nothing else, it would be by way of an apology. Problem was the Services as a whole frowned upon PDAs, even between man and wife, and though his and Sally's relationship wasn't exactly discouraged…

Oh, to hell with it. He had spent too much of his life worrying about 'shoulds' and 'shouldn'ts'.

'Captain Fairbodie,' he said crisply, making the young man jump. 'About turn and ten paces forward, if you please.'

Fairbodie looked at him, utterly baffled. 'Sir?'

'At once, if you please.'

Seeing he was serious, but still none the wiser, Fairbodie turned smartly 180 degrees on his heels and marched ten paces across the foyer, where he came to rest in front of a potted plant. Alistair turned his attention back to Sally, who was looking up at him questioningly.

'Now then,' he said. And he wrapped his arms around her waist and kissed her.

It was not a snog by any means; no need to go in for that exhibitionist rubbish. Besides, he was a married man. Long enough to leave her in no doubt of his feelings, though. When they broke apart, Sally looked up at him in wonder, her eyes bright; surprised and confused, but undeniably happy.

Alistair raised a hand and brushed his thumb over her cheek. 'Take care of yourself,' he said softly.

'And you,' she whispered by way of response.

Smiling again, Alistair planted another brief kiss on her forehead, then picked up his kit bag and went to put Fairbodie out of his misery.

'Stand easy, Captain. Lead on.'

Dame Anne pressed herself against the wall and held her breath as the Yeti approached. There were three of them advancing ponderously along the street towards her. Beneath her coat she felt the letter crinkling faintly against her chest. The words appeared before her mind's eye, black ink stark against the white paper, the shape of her neat handwriting. She didn't need to see it. She had been through so many drafts that the words were etched into her memory.

Dear Father,

I am not sure how this letter will reach you yet, but please, be assured that it's me, Anne.

*What I am about to tell you will seem far-fetched, but follow
me, please. You told me before about your mysterious friend
who helped save Det-Sen Monastery from the Yeti. Well I've
met him, and he is just as extraordinary as you say – and he
really does have a time machine!*

*I myself have travelled back in time to bring you this letter.
I am from 2011; quite a bit older, but not that much wiser. So
strange to find myself back in 1969, watching the Mist grow
from afar, at the same time remembering what I was – am –
doing in the Underground.*

*Soon you will be called from Fugglestone to join us at
Goodge Street, and it is in this instance I must deliver a
warning. In a few days' time, there will be a point where you
and I – this present's me – will be left alone in the Fortress with
only four soldiers to protect us, whilst the others mount a raid
on the tunnels. Whilst they're gone Yeti will attach HQ and
attempt to capture you. Promise me this: When you hear the
soldiers' screams in the corridors, hide. Hide us away and make
sure we stay hidden until re-enforcements arrive to repel the
Yeti. I know you are not a coward, and never one to run from
danger, but I beg you to do as I ask. The future depends upon
it.*

*Don't tell the present me about this letter until after the
event. Even if I did see it, I don't think I would believe it.*

*I am an old woman now, and it has been many years since
I last saw you last; but know that I treasure every memory that
I have of you dearly.*

Take care of our future.
With all my love,
Anne.

The Yeti were drawing level with the mouth of the
alleyway in which she was hiding. They were close now,
so close that she could almost reach out and touch them.
She had forgotten what they were like. Not what they
looked like, of course, but she had forgotten what it was
to be in their presence; that air of silent menace, the dirty,

greasy animal stink of their fur, the sensation of dread that formed in the pit of her stomach...

This had not been the plan. The plan she and Rupert had devised for getting into Central London was a good plan; a sensible plan. Rupert would take the form of a soldier, they would travel together, and when they got to Goodge Street he would be able to bluff his way past the sentries posing as an official messenger, and deliver the letter to her father. They had calculated the timing exactly against the professor's scheduled arrival, plotting the distances they needed to cover, factoring in potential delays and detours.

But Anne had grown impatient; again the chemical reactions of Rachel's body overriding her good sense. She had waited an excruciatingly long time as it was; trapped in another person's life for nearly two weeks, in which she had watched her every word, step and gesture, in case a wrong move endangered her mission. She had spent the past two days gathering together what supplies she would need, purchasing a sturdy rucksack and a pair of decent boots that would stand up to long distance walking. Fortunately, Rachel did own some practical winter clothes, so she hadn't needed to worry about that. This morning she had done everything she could to prepare, and the prospect of waiting another day had seemed unbearable in the extreme...

And then she had realised they need not go into Central London at all. The letter need not be delivered to her father directly, only left somewhere he would definitely find it and read it. And she knew exactly where.

When Professor Travers returned to their home in St James' Gardens to gather up his things to take to Goodge Street, he would place them in the old red carpetbag he always kept in the cellar workshop; the bag she sometimes used to leave notes in if she wanted to guarantee his attention for something while he was working.

It was more than feasible. The house was only three miles from Parson's Green, outside the Mist barrier and almost directly north. It was empty now, her father having been whisked away to Fugglestone as soon as the Yeti were sighted, while her younger self worked away in the Underground. The streets would be deserted, the district one of the first to be evacuated; no one would see her go in or out. Her father would get the letter, read it – and do so with no further risk to Rupert's or Rachel's lives. It was a perfect plan.

So she had set off immediately for their house in St James' Gardens, the letter safely tucked away inside her coat pocket. Unfortunately, she had only managed to get as far as Earls Court when she very nearly ran straight into the Yeti.

They were past her now, heading south. Anne slowly breathed out, feeling slightly dizzy. *Stupid, stupid!* Being stuck in the Underground she had just not appreciated how many Yeti were roaming the surface; both inside and outside the barrier. It was a foolish risk to take. Over-cautious Rupert's plan might be, but over-caution was better than winding up dead.

Still berating herself, Anne moved to the other end of the alleyway, turning to the next road and making her way back towards Fulham.

From now on, she would stick to the plan.

In Whitechapel, Alistair was running for his life. Behind him, the gurgling howl of the Yeti was too close for comfort.

'Keep up, Welby!' he shouted to the lieutenant beside him.

Lieutenant Welby was breathing hard, but somehow managed to put on an extra turn of speed. He was a short, skinny young chap, and was already having to make double the effort to keep up with his superior's stride.

Bad form, Alistair thought absently, as they rounded the corner and broke out of the side-street and onto a wider road. *Not keeping up with his fitness. Must mention it to his CO.*

That was if they lived long enough to get out of this.

Alistair's mind had been so focused on straightening out the chaos in Greater London and his eventual arrival in the Underground, that he'd forgotten about this part; his first encounter with a Yeti. Welby and he had been driving him back from visiting the secondary command post at Highbury and Islington, when they had run into two Yeti blocking their way. Before Alistair could tell him to stop, Welby had put his foot down and tried to ram his way through the beasts. Unfortunately, the Land Rover had come off worse, and now they were running from the Yeti that was not embedded in two tons of corrugated Army-green steel.

As far as initiative was concerned, Alistair was very happy for Welby never to use his own again.

Fortunately, all was not lost. If Alistair had remembered correctly, then around this next corner there should be–

Bingo! One military roadblock, complete with makeshift barricade and fully-armed squaddies.

'Yeti!' he bellowed, charging towards the sandbags.

'Grenade!' came the immediate response.

Alistair instinctively grabbed Welby and made a dive to the side, hitting the dirt and covering his head with his arms. A few seconds later there was an explosion mixed with a furious roar, followed by a crash of something heavy hitting the floor. Then silence.

Alistair risked lifting his head to gaze back along the street. The wreck of the Yeti lay smouldering in the middle of the road, electronics fizzing, headlamp-like eyes dark.

'You all right, sirs?'

Alistair looked up at the soldier standing over him; a corporal, Royal Anglian Regiment. One of the local boys.

'Perfectly, thank you,' he grunted. He accepted the offered hand-up, straightening his glengarry. 'Jolly good shot.'

'That was Tovey,' the corporal said, indicating a young private over the other side of the sandbag wall. 'Bowled for Basildon before he signed up.'

Tovey gave an embarrassed salute, which Alistair acknowledged as Welby picked himself up off the floor.

Meanwhile the corporal had taken a speculative glance at Alistair's uniform.

'Bit lost aren't you, sir?' he asked. 'I thought your lot was in Windsor?'

Which, Alistair had to acknowledge, 1 Scots were, along with several other regiments of the Guards, although the comment was verging on the impertinent.

'I'm taking over the Greater London command,' he said stiffly. 'Just arrived.'

Truth be told he was still a little thrown by last night's hair-raising parachute drop. On arrival at the Elm Park command post he had immediately phoned Pemberton, ostensibly to report in, but also to tell his friend that it would be a very long time before he was forgiven.

Although, that was before Alistair had found the bottle of Johnnie Walker Red Label in the bottom drawer of the desk in the tiny station manager's office; now, by virtue of succession, his office. Not the best stuff, but by no means the worst either. There had been a note taped to it in Pemberton's handwriting: *You'll need it.*

The corporal nodded, understanding the message. 'First Yeti, sir?' he queried.

'Yes,' Alistair answered, distractedly. Depending on perspective, it wasn't a lie.

The man pulled a face. 'Ugly brutes. You'll get used to them, sir.'

'I daresay I shall,' Alistair said neutrally.

He finished straightening his uniform, then turned to face the still somewhat red-faced lieutenant.

'See about getting us some more transport, Welby,' he said coldly. 'And this time, I'll drive.'

As beginnings went, it was not the most auspicious start.

Pemberton considered his personal map of the Underground carefully. He was sitting in the small room that doubled as his office and quarters; in reality a card table and two chairs in one corner, and a camp bed in the other, with just enough room to manoeuvre between the two without bashing his shins. It was about as good as it got down there, but the colonel was more than used to roughing it. Indeed, compared to some of the 'rough' in his career, this was practically civilised.

Above ground the Yeti continued to advance, pushing their cordons ever further back, spreading their hellish Web with those guns – and each day they seemed to be growing in number.

Just where were they coming from, though? Pemberton studied the map, which he had heavily annotated with all the locations and directions of attacks to date. This had all started with just one Yeti, Miss Travers had said. One Yeti, which her father had accidentally reactivated with a restored control sphere. So, where had the others come from? They had secured one co-opted factory in Kensington, and saw something of the construction methods. But more Yeti continued to advance – no doubt from other similar factories. But who was controlling them, guiding them? According to Professor Travers they were not autonomous, but guided by one individual controlling mind. Like drones working for a queen bee. Pemberton was still intensely sceptical about the professor's claim that this 'Intelligence', as he called it, was an invader from another world; that sort of rot was fodder for the B-movie buffs and tinfoil hat brigade.

What had he said last week, that this wasn't 'his' kind of warfare? Well, it damn well was now; the enemy was out there in the open for all to see, but it was fast becoming clear that he was heavily outgunned. The small arms were having little to no effect on the creatures, even with armour piercing rounds, although Dawlish's lucky shot on their first encounter had revealed a potential weak spot between the eyes, but that irritatingly didn't seem to be consistent between Yeti. Miss Travers had been able to explain that one; the professor's studies of Yeti remains from the Det-Sen incident in 1935 had revealed that no two Yeti were built to exactly the same design. Numerous small variations in construction meant that what might be a weak point in one model was as likely heavily reinforced in another. Because, of course, Pemberton thought bitterly, it couldn't be that simple. Otherwise all their problems could have been solved with a few well-placed snipers.

The only thing that seemed to do any real damage were the grenades, and they were in increasingly short supply. Bringing artillery in was out of the question, of course, as they were liable to cause too much damage to infrastructure, and their use would draw 'unwanted attention' – but he had today received authorisation to use bazookas. Typical, really. Here he was, fighting a desperate battle for the future of his country, and all the government were concerned with was that he keep the noise down!

It was, despite their best efforts, a battle they were losing. They were holding the Underground, but above ground each day the Yeti were advancing a little further east, and in each encounter lives were lost. Not many; one or two, but with multiple contacts a day, every day... It was a rate of casualties that they could not sustain. Already Pemberton was having to get support army troops to make up some of the numbers. That day alone he'd had to send Corporal Lane, a signalman, out on tunnel patrol. If their luck didn't turn soon, and he prayed to God it would, he was going to need reinforcements. And fast.

At least he didn't have to worry about the city limits anymore. He was lucky to have Lethbridge-Stewart on side; there were very few officers who were just as skilled with logistics as they were with tactics, and Alistair was one of the best.

A knock on the half-open door made Pemberton look up sharply, but his expression softened several shades when he saw Anne Travers poke her head around the door.

'Miss Travers,' he said pleasantly, setting down his pencil. 'What can I do for you?'

'Colonel Pemberton, may I please have a word?'

'Of course.' Pemberton gestured that she should come in and take a seat, and he closed the door behind her. She only waited until he had sat back down again to begin.

'I've been considering our next moves as far as the Yeti are concerned,' she said. She insisted that her father be brought in to help her, him being the one who knew most about them. 'A phone call only serves up to a point, but it's difficult to keep him focused. The last two times I called him he's had more questions than answers. It would be so much more efficient if he were here on the ground.'

'I thought you know everything about the Yeti that he does?'

'I know the nuts and bolts of it,' Miss Travers admitted. 'The circumstances of their creation – assuming the stories of a mysterious Tibetan toy-maker are real, of course. My father is never quite clear on that point; one day it's just a story, the next he talks as if he actually met this mysterious figure. Either way, it's my father who's really got the experience of combatting these creatures. I've only studied them in isolation, as inert objects. He's made them his life's work. I think we would stand a much better chance of coming up with a solution were we able to work together down here.'

Pemberton nodded, thinking it over. On a personal level he was not overly keen on the idea. He had not met Professor Travers in the flesh, but he had plenty of irate telephone calls with him, trying to get some sense out of his bluster and half the time failing miserably; he was highly unlikely to be any pleasanter in person. However, they were in desperate need of effective counter-measures, and if the only way to get them was to have Travers working here with his daughter, then that was what needed to happen

'And you consider it vital to get him here?' Pemberton asked.

'Absolutely!' Miss Travers agreed fervently. 'I'm working on a way to try and block the control signal from the controlling intelligence to the Yeti, but I'm working on principles of an entirely alien logic that I only half-understand at best. Please, Colonel, I really think it's our only real chance of success.'

Pemberton paused for a moment longer, then he nodded his assent. 'Very well, then. I'll get on to Strategic Command and persuade them to release Professor Travers to us.'

Miss Travers smiled, relieved. It was the happiest Pemberton recalled seeing her all week. 'Thank you, Colonel. We'll start making progress now; I just know it.'

CHAPTER TWELVE
Which Way You Goin', Billy?

IT WAS EARLY EVENING WHEN THE FIRST BEDFORD LORRY swept out onto the Tooting Bec Road, leaving the remaining residents of Wheatlands and Netherfield Roads climbing into the backs of the remaining two. The planned route would take them across the southern edge of the Common, down the Streatham High Road, and from then on further south and clear of Greater London.

Sir Alistair scanned the rows of Victorian semi-detached houses with a keen eye, watching for any sign of web, mist or Yeti. They had not been able to give the residents of Tooting Bec any meaningful warning. The area had been scheduled for clearance the day after tomorrow, but a sighting of 'bears' by the railway sidings at the north end of the Common had been reported an hour ago, bumping it up the list to 'immediate priority'. As things stood, most were having to leave with little more than what they had on their backs. Fortunately, the CDA had done a sterling job in setting-up and supplying the numerous refugee depots outside of the capital, aided enthusiastically by the local communities. No one would end up going without.

Now they were much further into the crisis, the reality of evacuation was a familiar concept to London's citizenry; hardly anyone was refusing to leave anymore. Some would inevitably slip through the net at this stage, either by accident or by design; most would be found and rescued in the second, even third sweeps, but for some it would already be too late.

They needed to get moving. Alistair turned back to chivvy things along, when he became aware that a small altercation was taking place over by the lorry furthest away from him. Frowning, he went over to find out what was going on.

One of the men seemed to be doing his best to calm a woman in a floral pinafore, who was holding a toddler by the hand. He was urging her to get into the lorry, but she kept shaking her head violently, glancing anxiously around the street.

'Everything all right, Kipps?' Alistair asked crisply, drawing level with them.

Private Kipps opened his mouth to reply, but the woman got there first.

'It's my eldest,' she said quickly, her brown eyes wide with worry. 'Jonathan – John. He's not here!'

Alistair felt his heart sink. A lost child. That was all they needed...

'Where did you last see him?' he asked calmly, clearly. In all likelihood the boy wouldn't have gone far, so they might still get going without much of a delay.

'At home,' she said, reassured a little by the cool authority in his voice. 'I went over the road with my Danny to see Jane, but he was watching his favourite programme on the telly, and I was only going to be gone a minute–'

'Won't he still be in the house, then?' Alistair suggested reasonably.

The woman's brow wrinkled, having apparently not considered this. She pulled the toddler closer, probably the afore-mentioned 'Danny', who was industriously sucking his thumb, uncomprehending of the confusion around him.

'Maybe,' she said, but clearly dismissive of the idea.

'But I called and there was no answer, and with all this noise and people... How could he miss all this?'

Quite easily, Alistair thought scornfully. He knew very well just how oblivious children could be when sat in front of the idiot box. His mind turned briefly to his five grandchildren over the years, and he suppressed a smile.

And then all the street lights went out, plunging the road into darkness, save for the headlights of the lorries. Alistair had not scheduled a power outage at this time, and his hand moved on his pistol holster. He sensed trouble was not far off.

And then he remembered why this all seemed so familiar. *Oh no.* And there was he thinking of his grandchildren... If he didn't rescue John, one of them wouldn't even be born!

'Which is your house?' he asked quickly.

The woman – Mrs James, he now realised – was quite frightened, and pointed to a house with a green door on the opposite side of the street. 'That one.'

'Get in the lorry,' Alistair said firmly, his tone brokering no argument. 'I'll look for your son.'

The woman nodded mutely, realising that things had somehow taken a sinister turn, and did as she was told, handing her other child up into waiting arms before climbing aboard herself.

Alistair turned to Kipps. 'Tell Pearson to get going. We'll all meet at the rendezvous in Croydon.'

'Sir.' Kipps saluted, then went to pass the message onto the driver of the other lorry.

Alistair was already halfway up the garden path when he heard the second Bedford's engine start and pull away. *And then there was one.*

He didn't bother looking in the house, knowing the boy would not be there, but headed straight for the side passage which led to the garden, unholstering his pistol as he did so. He rounded the side of the house and he heard the hideous, gurgling roar of a Yeti.

He arrived not a moment too soon. Bursting through the garden gate, Alistair was met by the sight of a boy, eight years old, lying sprawled on the grass, transfixed as a Yeti towered over him; arms raised and ready to strike.

The boy, John... A face he'd almost forgotten. And, for a moment, Alistair saw the boy as an adult, and their meeting at Brendon in 1989. It was like time was playing games with him. The first time around he had simply rescued the boy because that was his duty, but now... Now he knew the consequences if little John hadn't been rescued. Now Alistair had even more reason than duty.

Alistair fired. The bullet struck home and the Yeti reeled backwards, knocked to the ground. It wasn't damaged, not by a long chalk, but it would buy them time.

Surfacing from whatever trance he had fallen into, John turned his head to stare at his rescuer, wide-eyed with astonishment. Alistair quickly closed the distance, his still-smoking gun trained on the Yeti which was struggling to right itself, and stretched out a hand.

'Come on, John, let's get you out of here.'

The boy shook his head, whether out of disbelief or refusal Alistair couldn't tell, but he took the offered hand.

'Where's my-?' he began, but blinked in surprise as Alistair hauled him up off the grass.

Alistair looked around briefly, making sure their exit was still clear. 'Safe.'

Another bubbling growl drew his attention back to the Yeti, which was rising to its feet again. Alistair stepped protectively in front of John, waiting for the moment he could get a clear shot between its eyes.

The boy looked up at him in awe. 'What's going on? You're-'

'Colonel Lethbridge-Stewart,' Alistair said briskly. The Yeti was back up, and he raised his gun, taking aim. 'Now cover your ears.'

John did so, an excited grin plastered across his young face, and Alistair pulled the trigger.

For a split-second he could have sworn he heard a shot from behind him, along with the strangest impression that his gun had both fired and not fired in the same instance. Then the sensation was gone. The bullet struck home, and the Yeti staggered back.

'Come on!' Alistair grabbed the boy, who all at once looked as if he had seen a ghost, and bundled him into his arms. Taking to his heels, he made for the garden gate.

But John started wriggling and shouting, trying to break free. 'Sir! Brigadier, don't! Please, put me down!'

Hearing a roar behind him Alistair tightened his grip. The boy clearly didn't grasp what was going on, and though he could commend the boy's desire to escape on his own two feet, now was not the time for bravado. John, however, continued to struggle, and Alistair uttered a curse. He didn't remember him making a fuss like this before!

'Hang on!' he barked. 'We're nearly there!'

He rounded the corner of the house at a sprint, his burden clamped tightly to his chest, and made a dash across the road to the waiting lorry.

'Move out!' he bellowed, handing the boy up to a soldier, before jumping up himself. 'Make ready – we've got company!'

The lorry motor gunned as Alistair and two of the soldiers knelt at the back, rifles to the shoulder, pistol at the ready. As they pulled away, the Yeti lumbered around the corner of the house and into the road, roaring and brandishing its claws.

'Fire!'

The soldiers loosed off several shots, a few hitting

home, but more went wide as the distance increased between them. Alistair squeezed the trigger of his pistol, but was met only with an ominous *click*.

Feeling his blood run cold, Alistair looked at the gun, breaking it apart to inspect the chambers. It hadn't fired; something was stopping the mechanism. He had meant to have it serviced in Libya before he returned, but there had simply not been time. He had been lucky. If the mechanism had failed in the garden just now…

He glanced at John, who was sitting further back in the truck with his mother, her arms wrapped tightly around him; head bent to one side, and refusing to meet anyone's eyes. Alistair only hoped he was not ashamed at having to be rescued.

Another life saved where it could so easily have been otherwise. Once again, his future seemed to be heading in the right direction.

Somewhere a church bell chimed eleven o'clock as Dame Anne hurried down the eerily empty Chelverton Road. She felt to all the world like a cat burglar; slipping through the night, keeping to the shadows, ever watchful for prying eyes. The streets were in total darkness, as was the case in all the evacuated boroughs of London; Pemberton's policy, shutting down the Grid section by section as the houses emptied. It was a sensible move, reducing the risk of fire raging through abandoned boroughs unchecked, while at the same time denying the enemy of a vital resource. Quite literally a case of last one to leave, turn off the lights.

Anne felt a chill creep down her spine as she glanced at the vacant houses either side of her. Again, having spent her time underground, the sheer emptiness of the streets was another aspect of the Event she had missed. This complete darkness, this sense of desolation, was something altogether different and unsettling. She imagined it would only get worse the further into the city they went.

Counting down the houses, she stopped outside number fifteen; a neatly-proportioned Victorian villa with white gingerbread decorating the upper storey, and two large lime trees framing the gateway. In all, Anne had not been surprised to learn of Rupert's address in Putney. The area had a long-standing connection with the legal profession, and she could well imagine Rupert as one of the original residents to have started that association. He'd certainly been around long enough.

Opening the gate as quietly as she could, she hurried down the tiled path, tucked herself into the porch and rang the doorbell. From the outside the house appeared just as lifeless as the rest, so Anne was very gratified when barely ten seconds later she heard the rattle of curtain rings, and the door opened a crack. A narrow stream of light spilled out onto the path.

'Anne?' Rupert's voice whispered from inside.

'It's me,' Anne confirmed. The door opened wider, just enough for her and her rucksack to slip through, and Rupert closed it swiftly behind her.

Inside, Anne was momentarily dazzled by the brightness of the hall lights. She blinked in amazement, and Rupert gave her one of his customary thin smiles.

'I have my own little contrivance set up in the cellar,' he explained. 'Much quieter and far more economical than a petrol generator.'

'I was afraid I'd got the wrong house,' Anne said, glancing around the neat and uncluttered hallway. 'There wasn't the least sign of life from outside.'

Rupert indicated the heavy curtain over the door. 'Blackouts. I kept them handy after the last war, and I admit they have proved quite useful on more than one occasion.'

Anne suspected she'd better not ask for details of said

164

'occasions'. Rupert gestured to a doorway off to her left. 'Shall we?'

Anne walked into what appeared to be the sitting room. Rupert's taste in décor seemed to run to Edwardian elegance; the only jarring note being the L1A1 SLR lying prominently on the table. As interior design features went, it was a little outré. Out of the corner of her eye Anne saw a bright green glow of light, and turned to look at Rupert. He had been replaced with a young soldier in full combat gear; a private, about eighteen or nineteen, ginger hair and freckles. His beret sported the cap badge of the Queen's Own Regiment – a distinction Anne only knew thanks to almost forty years of marriage to a career officer.

Seeing the young face though, Anne felt a creeping sensation of regret. She remembered Rupert once telling her about his 'infiltration' techniques, and how he had taken the form of Jacob Travers after his death. Anne had seen too many young soldiers cut down before their prime that she would rather not know, yet she found she could not help but ask.

'That young man,' she ventured. 'Is he dead?'

Rupert shook his head. 'No, Anne. He is real, but very much alive; although, at present he probably wishes he had never been born.'

Anne's eyes immediately narrowed with suspicion. 'And why would that be?'

'Careless really,' Rupert said airily. Anne noted the slight trace of a Kentish accent in his new voice. 'Poor fellow was part of a patrol that stopped off at Fulham Broadway. He put his weapon down momentarily for a smoke, turned his back…' Rupert patted the butt of the rifle. 'Last I heard of it, I'm afraid he was headed for a court martial.'

Anne winced, imagining how that scene must have played out. In a way it served the soldier right for being so dreadfully negligent, but even so…

'Do we really need it?'

Rupert raised his eyebrows. 'I would draw more attention to myself as a soldier *without* a rifle.'

Anne had to admit he had a point. Besides, if they met any Yeti it would be nice to have the option of *trying* to defend themselves.

'Are we ready to move?' she asked, moving on to the matter in hand. 'We're cutting it fine as it is. Word came around last night that they're going to clear Parson's Green today. Fortunately, with so many people already leaving no one paid the least bit of attention to me.'

'Fortunate,' Rupert agreed, picking up the rifle and slinging it across his shoulders. 'And yes, I have everything I need.' He regarded her seriously, the sombre expression in his eyes belying the youth of his new face. 'I must ask though, Anne; are you certain you want to do this? You need not go. It's much less of a risk for me; I can go alone.'

Anne shook her head. 'I appreciate the offer, Rupert, but I'm going. You don't know the situation on the ground as I do – or under it, for that matter – and you'll need that knowledge if you run into trouble. Besides, I need to do this. This is for my father, my future; I should be there to see it through.'

Rupert looked at her sadly, but nodded his understanding. 'Very well,' he said. Then he smiled. 'I imagine your Brigadier will have arrived in London by now?'

'Yes,' Anne said, a small smile curling at the corners of her own mouth. 'Although at the moment he's plain old "colonel". He will have parachuted in the day before yesterday.'

She recalled that her first impressions of him in the Underground had not been favourable, striking her as a typical military stuffed-shirt type. Ben Knight had certainly bridled at his cut-glass accent and easy superiority, made all the more abrasive in the face of Pemberton's death. She had soon learned, however, that behind the affable exterior there lurked a keen intelligence and a certain ruthlessness, which anyone underestimated at their peril, along with a very real sense of compassion.

'Another legacy in the making,' Rupert murmured thoughtfully. 'So many futures anchored to this moment in time. I hope, one day, that I might be able to meet Lethbridge-Stewart, if only for curiosity's sake.'

Their plan was to drop down and move east in the shadow of the South Circular Road, striking north again when they reached Vauxhall and crossing into the city at Waterloo Bridge. Anne had questioned the sense of going so far out only to head back in again, but Rupert had pointed out that first they had to get around the Mist barrier, and the closer they were to the centre, the greater the likelihood they would run into Yeti or patrols sweeping for stragglers. Better to do their easting further out, then head for Goodge Street on a direct trajectory. There was a certain logic to it, so Anne had conceded; although she had made Rupert promise to see if he could commandeer a Land Rover, seeing as the journey would take the best part of a day. Young legs or no, her feet were going to ache after this.

They had just made it down to the junction of the South Circular when they heard the roar of a motor engine.

'Get down!' Rupert hissed.

There was a low wall in front of a shop, and they both crouched down behind that. Anne peered carefully over the top, trying her best to see and not be seen.

'Military patrol,' she whispered, taking in the Land Rover and its occupants as they drew nearer.

Rupert checked his watch again, and nodded. 'They come by approximately every half hour. How many of them are there?'

Anne felt a stab of irritation even as she peered out from behind the doorframe. Why had Rupert not thought to mention the patrols before, or at least timed their departure around them? They really couldn't afford any further delays.

'Six of them,' she said, after the briefest of hesitations. 'Long wheel base Land Rover, tarpaulin down. Two in the cab, four in the back; definitely armed.' She squinted, trying to make out the two hunched figures that were sitting between the soldiers in the back. 'Looks like they're arresting stragglers.'

'How far away?' Rupert asked.

Anne felt him inch closer, doubtless eager to see for himself. She hoped he wasn't planning to be foolish enough as to try and commandeer *this* vehicle. Even if they could overpower the soldiers, that would be too many witnesses.

'Fifty yards, and closing,' she reported. 'They're not going fast, but they'll be up with us in a moment.'

Next to her, Rupert breathed a sigh of relief. 'Good.'

There was something off in his voice, and Anne turned to see what was wrong. Rupert was not looking at the oncoming patrol, but at her. There was an air of sadness about him, but the expression in his eyes was one of resolution.

'Rupert?' she asked warily. Something in the back of her mind was shouting a warning.

Rupert shook his head. 'I'm sorry, Anne,' he said. 'Forgive me.'

Then he grabbed her and dragged her out of the shadows, moving them both into the open, and in full sight of the soldiers.

'Oi, over here!' he bellowed, waving an arm

frantically in the air to attract their attention. 'Got another one!'

'What are you doing?' Anne gasped. She tried to pull away, but Rupert's grip was like steel – as was the expression in his pale eyes.

'This is for your own good,' he hissed. 'I won't allow you to jeopardise everything.'

And then Anne realised. Rupert had never intended to help her at all. All this time, all this waiting, all this hoping... when all along there was no plan, save to betray her.

The world came crumbling down around her. She felt sick. She had forgotten how to breathe. Her head was spinning, her mind refusing to take it in.

'No!' she moaned hoarsely. She fought off the giddiness, tried to free herself from his grip. 'No, you can't do this! Rupert, please!'

The patrol had seen them. The Land Rover pulled up and two soldiers jumped out of the back, jogging over to meet them.

'What's this then?' one of them demanded. He had a corporal's stripes on his arm.

'Hiding behind the wall, Corp,' Rupert said, pinning Anne's hands behind her back as she struggled. 'Wouldn't come quietly.'

'No!' Anne cried, turning to the corporal, desperate for him to see the truth. 'No, don't listen! He's not a real soldier!'

The corporal and his mate looked at Rupert questioningly. 'Where're you from?'

'Parson's Green evacuation party,' Rupert said, without missing a beat. 'Was told to keep a watch on the bridge, and I saw her running over here. So I followed.'

'He's lying!' Anne insisted, but she could already tell that they believed his word over hers.

'Look, miss, we won't hurt you,' the corporal said

firmly, moving forward to take her from Rupert. 'But you need to come with us, right now!'

No, no, this could not be happening. Abandoning all sense of decorum or sanity, Anne kicked out and screamed, all the rage and frustration of the past two weeks venting itself on her would-be captors. She had to escape, she had to get the message through!

More soldiers rushed to help, more hands trying to grab her. Somewhere else she heard the sound of another motor vehicle pulling up, but it just blended in with the noise and shouting around her. Then suddenly she was grabbed from behind – another soldier; taller than the others – his hands clamped securely over her wrists, pinning her arms to the side and pulling her backwards off balance. Nevertheless she continued to struggle, twisting in his grip and blindly kicking out for all she was worth, hoping to catch him either on the knees or the shins. It was no good though; he was sensible enough to keep both of them moving, knew how to use both his height and weight to his advantage.

'Miss!' A voice – cultured and imperious – sounded loudly in her ear. 'Miss, please, we're here to help. We need to get you to safety.'

At the sound of that voice, Anne froze. She looked up, and was met by a pair of sharp hazel eyes, a jet black military moustache, a glengarry. She gasped, cold air filling her lungs.

'Alistair!'

CHAPTER THIRTEEN
Put Yourself In My Place

HAD ANYONE ASKED HIM UNDER NORMAL circumstances, Sir Alistair would have said that he'd be thrilled to have his name called out by an attractive young blonde. However, as these were not normal circumstances, and the attractive blonde was in the middle of causing an affray, his reaction was one of shock, confusion, and deep suspicion.

The young woman in his arms looked no less shocked than he felt, and there was definite fear in her eyes – but there was also a sense of recognition. She knew him, or at least thought she did. Alistair's grip relaxed, frowning as he riffled through his memory, trying to put a name to the face, or at least place her. This was certainly not part of his original timeline – yet another variation – but neither could he remember meeting her at any other point in his life. And he was damn certain he would have remembered *her*.

The woman ran.

Blast it!

'Get after her!' Alistair bellowed. As the soldiers set off in pursuit he hissed in a furious breath between his teeth.

'Shall we stay, sir?' Lieutenant Welby asked from over by their Land Rover.

Alistair and Welby had been driving back from the depot at Croydon when they'd caught sight of the altercation. He turned to Welby. Lord knew what the lieutenant made of all this; probably that she was some sort of old girlfriend of his. Either way, he was tired, hungry, fed up, and wanted nothing more than to distance himself from this embarrassment.

'You'll stay here, Lieutenant,' he growled. 'I'll drive myself. See that they find her. And when they get back, take those men's names.'

He held out his hand for the Land Rover keys. Welby looked utterly dismayed, but reluctantly handed them over.

'Should you be on your own, sir? The Yeti–'

'–had better ruddy-well steer clear!' Alistair snapped. And he slammed the door, turned the key in the ignition, and floored the pedal, leaving the whole sorry problem with a wretched-looking Welby.

That had been priggish of him, Alistair knew, fury still bubbling in his chest as he sped along the empty road towards Wandsworth High Street. But it was a senior officer's prerogative to delegate, and he had. In spades.

He swerved to avoid an urban fox, cursing under his breath. He thought back over the two strange encounters he'd had today. First the boy, now this mystery woman. When did everyone become so damned reluctant to be rescued?

Dame Anne ran. She ran, and ran, and she didn't look back.

Oh God, Alistair!

Her heart was pounding, her ears ringing, and there were tears streaming from her eyes. It had been him. Him from all those years ago; young, sharp and imposing. She had not meant to meet him – *couldn't* meet him – and yet he had been there. She had failed.

She ran, but not in a straight line. She was confused,

distraught and despairing, but she wasn't stupid. She hadn't gone straight down the main road across Putney Bridge, but back into the residential streets, twisting this way and that way with no thought for direction, save away from the voices that were chasing her. Taking turnings at random, cutting through gardens, running through alleyways, until she was just as lost as her pursuers.

When she could no longer hear voices, she stopped; panting for breath, her legs on fire, sweat pouring from her brow and prickling beneath her thick jumper and coat. Leaning against a brick wall for support, she waited for the world to stop spinning, then looked to see where she was.

She was in an alleyway – no name or signs of course – behind the back of what looked like it might be a restaurant. There were two large steel industrial bins next to her, reeking of well-rotted food. The smell made her gag, nausea and dizziness overcoming her as she sank to the floor. Arms wrapped around her legs, exhausted and defeated, she curled up and began to sob.

Her thoughts were so loud that she thought they might split her head. She could not contain it all; the anger, the frustration, the fear, the regret, and the pain. She was full to the brim, and she felt she might burst.

She thought back to what Rupert had said when she first told him her intent, how against the idea he was. Of course he wasn't going to help. He never intended to – she could see that now. All to protect the timeline, never mind her loss. She was expected to make a sacrifice. Live through it all over again.

Nobody talked to Lethbridge-Stewart of making 'sacrifices', only congratulated him on his 'legacy'. Her father had died; his mind unravelled from within, nothing more than 'collateral damage' in this great fight of theirs. Alistair's father had returned from the grave, a war hero on an alien world to which he had returned of his own free will. This conflict had taken her family away from her, while in that respect Alistair had only gained; a father back from the dead, two nephews, and a brother of sorts. She wasn't asking for half as much. After all she'd lost, everything she'd done for this miserable universe, why couldn't time and space grant her this one, precious happiness?

Stuff legacies. Stuff sacrifices. Stuff this whole bloody stupid game of soldiers! She was finished playing by the rules.

In her heart, she felt a new emotion taking hold; something hard, something cold, something clinical. She was never a soldier; she was a doctor. So, she was going to play doctor.

She was going to destroy the Intelligence.

'You're where?' Colonel Pemberton thundered down the phone.

It was Miss Travers that had alerted him to the fact that her father had not yet arrived at Goodge Street. Pemberton would have thought one of his men – just one! – would have considered it important to mention to him that their new expert was meant to have been with them an hour ago.

Just one, Pemberton thought darkly. But that 'one' was not here at the moment; was out doing some proper soldiering, instead of skulking down here playing 'peek-a-boo' with monsters and acting as nursemaid to a whinging journalist.

'At his house,' the soldier on the other end of the line repeated, his voice coming over the loudspeaker. 'Passenger insisted on going to his laboratory to fetch additional equipment. Been here two hours and he's still gathering things.'

Pemberton cast Miss Travers a questioning glance.

She was standing next to him, listening in on the conversation with an expression that was equal parts fury and concern.

'Eighteen St James' Gardens,' she clarified. 'W11, just north of Holland Park Avenue. Outside the Mist barrier.'

With the Mist making all radio communication within the city centre impossible, they potentially might never have found out what had happened to the professor's party, had not the soldiers of the escort managed to get a connection using the phone at the Travers' house.

Over to the west. Pemberton felt a knot of anger forming in his stomach, wondering why on earth the patrol had let themselves be diverted into such dangerous territory. Inside or outside the Mist, the whole place was crawling with Yeti, and the chances of the party getting to them in one piece were significantly reduced every minute they stayed there.

'Hello, Charlie Five,' Pemberton said, using the patrol's designation. 'What's your ETA with Passenger?'

'Hard to say, Sunray,' the soldier replied. 'He won't talk to us.'

Miss Travers made a noise of frustration, and Pemberton clenched his jaw.

'Tell him to get a move on,' he growled. 'We need him here. ASAP.'

'We've tried, Sunray.' Charlie Five sounded desperate. 'Won't listen to a word either of us say.'

'Get him to the phone!' Miss Travers snapped. 'I'll talk to him.'

'Hello, Charlie Five, get him to come to the phone,' Pemberton ordered, but this seemed to bring no joy either.

'Negative, Sunray. He's down in the basement, won't come up. Short of threatening to shoot him, there's nothing we can do.'

Pemberton willed himself to calm, resisting the urge to scream at the man down the phone. Really, this was too much!

'What the devil's he gone back for?' he demanded, rounding on Miss Travers. 'What's there that's so important he risks his and my men's lives to get it?'

'I don't know!' she snapped, meeting his steel with her own. 'There's some pieces of a control sphere, other Yeti parts and his notes... But he must have gathered those by now!'

Supressing a growl, Pemberton turned to Lane. 'What's the latest from Captain Knight?' he demanded.

'Corporal Buscombe reported in ten minutes ago.' Lane responded promptly and precisely, clearly desperate not to be the one that copped the colonel's temper. 'They'd done Covent Garden and were moving on to Soho.'

No use sending Knight, then.

Miss Travers stepped forward, the expression in her dark eyes like flint. 'Colonel, let me go out with a patrol,' she said firmly. 'I'll get him back.'

Lane made a choking noise, and Pemberton frowned.

'Out of the question, Miss Travers,' he said bluntly. What a damn-fool thing to suggest!

She bridled, hands on hips. 'Colonel, I really–'

'Whilst the professor is in transit you are our only expert,' Pemberton cut over her, engaging the voice only used when giving particularly obtuse privates an ear-bashing. 'And, as such, I need you here on the ground. Understood?'

Miss Travers' face went red, but she didn't argue back. Pemberton would take that as acquiescence. He turned to the lieutenant over by the sensor board. 'Whittaker?'

'Sir?'

'Get a squad together. I'll go after him myself.'

'Sir!'

There was still the gap in the Mist curtain between

Notting Hill and Bayswater. Convenient. They could lead a rescue party through the Central Line…

'Hello, Sunray?' Charlie Five's voice came out of the speaker, temporarily forgotten in the heat of the moment. 'What are your orders?'

Pemberton raised the receiver to his mouth again. 'Hello, Charlie Five. Stay where you are. Barricade yourselves in if necessary. We're coming…'

'…to get you. Over and out.'

The line clicked off at the other end as the colonel hung up. Arkwright put the receiver down, letting out a sigh of relief as he did so. Moses, but he'd been quaking in his boots! He had heard the undercurrent of rage in the colonel's voice all through the conversation. Arkwright imagined it must have been something akin to sitting on a volcano; hearing the rumbling, but not knowing when it was going to blow its top.

All-in-all the private had discovered he was not a fan of Professor Travers, of scientific and murder mystery notoriety, and was firmly of the opinion that he and Griggs had definitely drawn the short straw, escorting the blasted boffin. Having demanded a detour to his house to get 'vital equipment', he had vanished into the basement and spent two hours crashing around, loading up a large carpet bag with all kinds of odds and sods, grumbling to himself and occasionally shouting for someone called 'Anne'. He had not responded to any of their cajoling, verbal or otherwise; and despite being an old duffer, Travers was built like a beast of burden and twice as stubborn. Arkwright only hoped Travers proved to be worth all this trouble. Potty, if you asked him!

'Noah!' From his station by the hall window, Griggs motioned at him. Arkwright doubled over to join him.

'What's the matter?' he asked.

Griggs nodded out of the window, twitching the net

curtain aside with the muzzle of his rifle. 'Two o'clock, over by the lamppost. Thought I saw something move.'

Arkwright felt his guts knot together with anticipation, and squeezed next to the other man to take a look.

The street outside appeared grey and empty. They were only a few hundred yards from the Mist here, and it was possible to see it over the tops of the neighbouring buildings, eerily still in the cold winter sky. Arkwright had heard plenty about the Yeti, but he had never actually seen one yet. Could the bushes over the other side of the road be concealing one?

'Stay here,' he murmured, unslinging his rifle from his shoulder. 'I'll take a look outside. Lock the doors behind me. If there's trouble, barricade yourself and the prof in the cellar. There's a relief party on the way.'

Griggs, himself not much older than Arkwright, nodded and took up position by the front door. At the given signal, he pulled it open and Arkwright stepped out into the street. He heard the door click shut behind him.

Across the street, the bushes were definitely moving. His heart hammering in his chest, Arkwright brought his rifle to the shoulder and advanced cautiously, waiting for whatever was in there to break cover. His first real action – and against an abominable snowman, no less!

He was so focused on the bushes in front, however, that he didn't hear Griggs' warning cry until it was too late. There was a gurgling roar from behind him, and as he turned a huge furry paw swung down at him, sharp claws ripping open his throat and knocking him to the ground.

From his vantage point on the tarmac, Arkwright watched as half a dozen Yeti emerged from the bushes, shuffling slowly past him and making for the Travers' house.

Strange, he thought muzzily, a grey fog beginning to crowd his vision. *And I always thought they'd be white...*

Dame Anne shut the front door behind her and jogged up the staircase to Rachel's flat, taking the steps two at a time.

On leaving the alleyway in Putney, Anne had discovered that she was down next to an embankment by Putney Pier. From there she had crept along the foreshore, it being low tide, and crossed back over to Parson's Green via the railway bridge, the steel girders providing ample cover.

It was coming up to dawn, and she needed to move fast. Happily she still had everything she'd packed in her rucksack – the soldiers had failed to get that off her – but there were a few more things she could stand to take, especially now that she had abandoned the subtle approach.

Rupert had thought that it was too late for her to act, but in this he had been sorely mistaken. Because Anne had a plan. She would cut into the centre via Victoria, then make her way up to Green Park, breaking into the Tube via the old Dover Street station. She remembered reading about it in the files; Churchill's 'secret station' from the war, but it had been gutted to a degree that it had not been considered for use in the current crisis. From there she would access the Piccadilly Line, make her way east to Piccadilly Circus, and destroy the Intelligence before it got even anywhere near her father.

It sounded simple. And it was simple. No pussy-footing around roadblocks on the other side of the river, just straight to the point; plain and simple.

She caught herself thinking that Alistair would be proud of her, but reminded herself that no; no, he wouldn't be. And that was the whole point, wasn't it?

Starting to make a mental list of things she would

need, Anne let herself into Rachel's flat. Crossing the dark hallway, the first thing she needed to do was light some candles...

And then she saw that there were already candles alight in the living room.

Anne froze, a lump rising in her throat. Had Rupert changed his mind and come to try and arrest her again? An excited thought bubbled up in her chest. Maybe it was Bill? Maybe, whoever he was in, he had worked out who she was and had come to find her?

Her heart beating in anticipation, Anne advanced cautiously into the living room. There were six or seven candles burning on the coffee table and on the windowsill, where a man was standing with his back to the room. He was wearing a long black coat, his head bowed and his shoulders hunched.

'Bill?' Anne asked breathlessly.

The man turned, but it was not the face of a stranger. Malachi Silverstein stared back at her, eyes red from lack of sleep, his usually so neat shirt and tie awry under his coat. His short dark hair was an uncombed mess, and it didn't look as if he had shaved in a couple of days.

Heart plummeting into her boots, Anne was about to demand what he was doing here, when she noticed that he was clutching a sheaf of papers in his hand. Her mouth went dry. They were her notes on the London Event, and on the top was her sketch of the Yeti.

Malachi stared at her, framed in the doorway. The expression on his face was thunderous; his eyes, until now nothing but sad or loving, were hard and accusing.

Slowly, he held up the sketch of the Yeti for her to see. 'Would you mind explaining to me,' he asked frigidly. 'Just what you think you're doing?'

CHAPTER FOURTEEN
It's Me That You Need

DAME ANNE STOOD STOCK-STILL IN THE DOORWAY. Something in that furious expression, that demanding tone struck a chord, prompting a horrifying thought. No, it couldn't be! Not now, not after everything she had been through already; it just *couldn't*.

'Alistair?' she asked, her eyes widening in disbelief. 'Is that you?'

Malachi's righteous indignation instantly crumpled into bafflement. 'What? I– No! No, it's me, Malachi. You can see it's me!'

No, it wasn't Alistair. Along with the relief this news brought, Anne began berating herself for having thought something so stupid. Of course it wasn't Alistair; he wouldn't be here. He'd be off elsewhere on some terribly important mission to save the universe from, oh, from invisible squid-people attempting world domination while everybody else was distracted by the Intelligence. That was how these things usually worked, wasn't it? Admittedly she was glad; cold fury had carried her thus far, but deep down she knew the one thing that could stop her would be if Alistair were to turn up now. She couldn't face him; not when she had just decided to rewrite the entirety of their lives.

Besides, the thought of being romantically involved with Malachi was bad enough, but had he proved to be Alistair as well... Some things were just too appalling to contemplate.

'What are you doing here, Malachi?' she asked, more irritated now than anything else. She had thought that she'd taken him safely out of the equation, but here he was again; like the proverbial bad penny.

Malachi, however, wasn't paying attention. 'Who's Bill?' he demanded. 'Who's Alistair?'

'No one important,' she said stiffly.

Malachi gave a disbelieving snort in answer to that, and at that moment Anne caught the faint whiff of spirits. Come to think of that, there was a deliberate, careful edge to his speech. She scowled.

'Malachi Silverstein, are you drunk?'

'Yes. Possibly,' he admitted grudgingly, ducking his head a little. 'Took a couple for Dutch courage, seeing as I came here to ask you back. Wanted us to leave together, go to the country place for a bit to work things out. But you weren't here. But these were.' Now that he remembered them, he brandished the papers at her again. 'For pity's sake, Rachel, just what is all this?'

Anne berated herself for her carelessness. She should have hidden those papers away, or better yet, destroyed them.

'It's none of your business,' she said curtly.

Malachi's mouth hung open in disbelief. 'Not any of my...? You've taken my father's murder and turned it into some sort of... Some kind of science fiction pantomime! And you say it's none of my business? After everything he's done for us, for you... It's grotesque. Utterly grotesque.'

'Please, Malachi,' Anne said firmly, calmly. She was trying her utmost to keep her frustration from showing. 'It's not what you think it is.'

'Then what is it?' he demanded sarcastically. 'Go on, tell me. What else could this possibly be?'

Anne hesitated, then she gave up. What did it matter

now what he did or didn't know? Hadn't she decided to throw the rulebook out of the window, anyway? She crossed her arms over her chest, and levelled a defiant gaze at him.

'The truth,' she said.

Malachi scoffed, then sobered very quickly as the expression on her face registered. 'Dear God, you believe it,' he said, wonderingly. 'You actually do believe it.'

'Of course I do!' she snapped impatiently, crossing the room and heading into the kitchenette.

Time was pressing on, and she had already been delayed enough. Without a 'soldier' to help bluff her way past any patrols, Anne had to allow for a longer journey time to accommodate further details. Extra rations would not be a bad idea.

Malachi shook his head. 'You're sick,' he murmured faintly. 'Rachel, do you hear me? You need help.'

'No, I don't.' There were a couple of tins spare she could probably make use of.

'Yes, you do,' Malachi insisted, moving closer to the kitchenette. 'It's the shock; Farleigh said this might happen.'

Anne stopped, her hand halfway to opening a cupboard, thinking she had misheard. 'What did you say?'

'Farleigh,' Malachi repeated bitterly. 'The doctor at the hospital. Said that you could get hysterical again and that you wouldn't want to...' He made an obscene gesture. 'But he was right in a way, wasn't he? It all makes sense now. The shock was too much, so you've fixated on it and linked two horrific events together to make some sort of story. But we can fix this, darling, I know we can. We can make you better. Everything will be all right again!'

Anne felt like screaming. Just what, what had she done to deserve this? She had tried so hard to play by the rules, and now it was all being thrown back in her face.

'I don't have time for this!' She extracted the stray tins from the cupboard – one spam, two corned beef – and packed them into the rucksack, which she had opened on the kitchen counter.

'Where are you going?' Malachi asked from the doorway.

'None of your concern,' she said over her shoulder.

She had the nagging feeling that she was still missing something, though. What could it be? Tin opener, water bottle, torch, spare batteries, matches, candles... Ah, yes; a girl's best friend. She reached under the sink and pulled out the crowbar she had bought last week at a hardware shop on Fulham Road. Slant had insisted she wouldn't need it, but now finding herself without an accomplice Anne was more than glad she had made the investment.

At the sight of the crowbar Malachi recoiled slightly, jaw slack, but held his ground in the doorway. 'Damn it, Rachel, you can't just walk out like this. This is our future!'

'Your future,' she said. 'Not mine. I thought I made that abundantly clear the other night.'

He remained standing there dumbly, blocking the doorway. Anne gave a small growl of frustration, adding the crowbar to the sack and securing the buckles.

'Just go, Malachi,' she said, wearily. 'Or stay here. I don't care. Just know that I'm leaving, and there's no point in your following me – not now, not ever again. I have things to do, which you won't understand. And I have to go. Now.'

She snatched up the rucksack, and in two quick steps reached the door. Surprised at the sudden movement, Malachi took a step back and she passed him, crossing the sitting room and heading for the hallway.

'Please, Rachel,' he begged. 'I love you.'

But Anne kept going, let the plea slide off her like water from a duck's back, opened the flat door, stepped out and slammed it behind her.

Please, no more, she begged the universe, as she crossed the landing and headed down the stairs. No more, or she thought she might break.

But the universe, time and again, seemed to have other ideas when it came to Anne Bishop.

'Come on, you lads. Pick up your feet!'

The sappers grumbled, but nonetheless responded to Arnold's chivvying, hitching up the large drum of cable between them and paying out the line as they went.

On the whole, Dawlish was quite pleased with how they were bearing up. Already they had travelled most of the westbound section of the Piccadilly Line, joining as they had from Leicester Square, and were now approaching Knightsbridge. They still had the return journey, of course, but by then their load would be much lighter.

They wouldn't be bringing back the explosive charges, for a start.

Their job down there was twofold. First, they were laying the cables to rig up lighting in the tunnels that were still clear of fungus and Yeti, meaning their patrols didn't have to keep taking torches with them, and also reducing the chance of the enemy getting the jump on them. Secondly, they were heading to all the points where the other lines intersected the Circle and District Lines, where they were to place charges and bring down the tunnels, hopefully halting the spread of the fungus and cutting off key access points for the Yeti; Pemberton's idea to buy them some more time. Dawlish knew there would be teams in Greater London doing exactly the same, but from the opposite direction, in an attempt to prevent the fungus advancing outwards.

It was hard to keep up with events as a whole when stuck down there, but as Dawlish understood it there had as yet been no indication of the fungus or Mist heading further outwards; and save for a few stray Yeti, they seemed to be staying close to the barrier. Whatever those creatures wanted, Dawlish felt, was very definitely in Central London.

And whatever it was, they were about to seal themselves in with it – along with the enemy.

Much good it may do us, Dawlish thought gloomily.

To look at a Yeti, anyone would be forgiven in thinking that it would be impossible for such a hulking great thing to get the 'jump' on anyone; but therein lay one of their most frightening abilities. One minute they were there in front of you, lumbering along *en masse*, the next there would be one behind you, looming large in a previously empty tunnel, having not made the least sound. At times their movement was practically ghost-like, as if they could move through walls. What a few tons of rubble might do against such creatures was anyone's guess, but at this stage anything was worth a shot.

The lieutenant glanced briefly back over his shoulder at the men following him. They were a party of six in all; himself, Arnold, Collins, Naylor, Jones and Clarke. Almost half of what was left of his original troop. Their casualties had been just as high as the Para's – proportionally higher, as there had been fewer Engineers to start with – and the latest series of reversals had done little to boost morale. Fortunately, there was plenty of work down there to keep them busy, especially since the Yeti had started cutting the phone lines where they were exposed. Dawlish sincerely hoped Miss Travers would get the breakthrough she needed once her father was there. He wasn't laying any bets as to how much longer they would last otherwise.

Up ahead Dawlish could see the tunnel opening out to the platform of Knightsbridge Station. Not far now;

only one more stop to journey's end at South Kensington, where they would meet the Circle Line. Funny, really, to think that was where all this started…

Something caught at the edge of his hearing, and he stopped, listening intently. Behind him the rest of the party halted, questioning and confused, but Dawlish waved them to silence, his other hand inching towards the holster on his belt.

Arnold edged forward to join the lieutenant, rifle raised and scanning the tunnel around them. 'What is it, sir?' he whispered.

'I… thought I heard…' Dawlish began, but then it was gone. He frowned, shaking his head. 'Forget it. Imagining things.'

Arnold gave him a look that could be called 'sceptical' at best. 'Are you sure, sir?'

Dawlish felt a stab of irritation at Arnold's questioning him in front of the men. He prided himself on being less priggish about that than some, but there were limits.

'Of course I'm sure!' he said sharply, raising his voice back to normal levels again. 'Come along, Staff; get these men moving.'

'Yes, sir,' Arnold acknowledged, getting the message, before turning to the others. 'You heard the officer. Get yer skates on, you bunch of idle layabouts!'

The encouragement wasn't strictly necessary, as the men were already getting back to their task, but there were certain expectations. Things needed to be done properly, and all that. Satisfied that he'd put the staff back in his place, Dawlish once again led the advance along the track.

Imagining things. Must have been it.

Somewhere, just at the edge of his hearing, he thought he'd heard someone whispering.

*

Croydon was undeniably one of the busiest of the refugee hubs south of the city. What seemed like an almost constant flow of Army lorries had arrived out of London for almost a week now, full to the brim of tired, confused, angry and displaced people, several of whom had little enough possessions to last them a couple of days, never mind start an onward journey.

Co-ordinating it all was exhausting work, and Sergeant Fred 'Freddy' Nevill of the Queen's Regiment was fairly glad in this instance that this side of things was largely down to the civil authorities. Thanks to the threat of the Bomb, plans to deal with a large-scale disaster had been in place for a good twenty years, and members of the recently disbanded Civil Defence Corps had turned out in their droves to assist. It was heartening, in such a crisis, to see that it all actually worked.

With so many people coming and going, it was inevitable that friends and families would become separated, and one particularly pressing role of the hub was to help reunite them as quickly as possible. So, when Nevill, having helped his patrol's latest load of 'passengers' disembark from their Bedford and now on his way back to Streatham, spotted the lone boy heading determinedly north on London Road half a mile out of Croydon, he immediately stopped and ran over to intercept him.

'Here, lad, you're going the wrong way.'

The boy, about nine years old, Nevill reckoned, glared up at him in frustration. 'Leave me alone!'

Nevill frowned. Whatever reaction he'd been expecting, it wasn't that. 'Where's your mum and dad?'

The boy ducked his head and looked away sullenly. 'Don't know,' he said reluctantly.

Ah, so that's it, Nevill thought as Corporal Knook came over to join him. Poor kid had probably got separated from his folks on the way out of the city and, thinking they might still be there, had got it into his head to look for them. Understandable; the sergeant remembered how headstrong he had been at that age. It was a good thing the street lights were still on here, or they might have missed him completely in the dark.

'Well, they won't be out here, will they? Come on, we'll get you back to the hub and we'll look for them there.'

But the boy only hunched his shoulders further, glowering at the pavement. Nevill shared a look of despair with Knook. *Kids.* He was grateful his son Martin hadn't hit the awkward stage early.

'What's your name, sonny?' Nevill asked, hoping to break the ice that way.

'None of your business!' the boy snapped, raising his head to glare at them.

'Don't you give the sergeant any lip,' Knook warned.

The boy seemed to relent a little. 'My name's Wi- *John,* Jonathan James!'

'Well, then, John Jonathan James, 'snot our fault you've gawn and got yourself lost, is it?'

'I'm not lost,' John protested. He pointed in the direction he was travelling; towards London. 'I know those creatures. I can help!'

Again, Nevill and Knook exchanged glances. So, young Master James had seen one of the Yeti, which meant that his evac party must have had a pretty close call. Commendable of the boy for wanting to help, but hopelessly misguided.

'Not much you can do 'gainst bears that we can't, is there?' Nevill said reasonably.

John frowned, angrily. 'They're not bears, and you know it! They're Yeti, and bullets can't stop them.'

Nevill laughed dismissively, Knook joining in to show a united front.

'Hark at 'im!' Knook said. 'Been reading too many

comics, you have. What you going to do? Blast them with your Dan Dare cardboard space-gun?'

John fumed, and Nevill decided that this had gone on long enough. That last bit about the space gun had been a bit unfair, too.

'Well whatever you think they are, they're dangerous and you're not going anywhere near them,' the sergeant said firmly. 'And you belong with your parents, who're probably going spare right now. You're coming back with us.'

He nodded to Knook, who went to take John's shoulders and steer him back towards the lorry, from where the rest of the men had been watching the scene unfold with mild amusement. But the boy had other ideas; kicked the corporal smartly in the shin and legged it.

'Agh! Come back here, you little 'orror!' Knook bellowed, running after him.

The lads whooped and cheered John on, making disappointed noises when all too soon the corporal caught up with him and grabbed him by the scruff of the neck.

Nevill sighed and rubbed his temple in despair as Knook returned with the wriggling boy and dumped him unceremoniously in the back of the truck.

Kids these days!

Dame Anne woke up, shivering. Outside the bedroom window the sky was dark, and she checked her watch; four o'clock in the afternoon.

She had spent the middle of the day sleeping in an abandoned converted house in Pimlico, thinking it best to move under the cover of darkness. It would make no difference to the Yeti, but it would make it easier for her to slip past any humans she might encounter. Having almost been taken into custody once, she was determined not to get caught again.

With the Mist pressed so close to the edge of the river, her choices of shelter were quite limited. The house had been fairly snug and safer than sleeping in the open, but as it had been without heating for nearly two weeks it was not much warmer inside than it was outside. The bed had been comfortable though, if a little damp, and she had found some additional quilts and blankets to put over the top. A pity she couldn't risk lighting even one candle, but that would be asking for trouble.

Kicking off the blankets, she shivered again as the cold air hit her, and she pulled on her coat and boots as quickly as she could; grateful that she had been thoughtful enough to take them off beforehand so that there would be an extra layer of warmth to put on when she woke. Her knitted hat quickly followed.

She made a quick snack of a caramel wafer biscuit, pulled on her gloves, and made her way downstairs. She headed back through the hallway into the kitchen, where she had broken in early in the morning, the back door and garden offering far more cover in which to come and go.

Cautiously she stepped outside into the lane that ran between the houses. She stopped, orientated herself, and then headed east towards the Embankment.

Her journey last night had gone relatively smoothly. She had only seen a couple of Yeti in the distance, but they had not seen her, and the few soldiers she had encountered were in a Bedford lorry driving at speed, and so not engaged in looking for stray civilians. She expected things would only begin to heat up significantly once she was inside the barrier.

There was a small *A to Z* concealed in her pocket, but on the whole Anne was fairly confident she would not need it. She had always known London pretty well, and even if she hadn't, the past two weeks had provided more than enough time for her to commit most of Central London to memory. Embankment was the furthest east the Mist and fungus had reached, and once past Cleopatra's Needle there were enough side roads and back alleys for her to sneak around the roadblock she knew was at Charing Cross. She would continue north from there, skirting Piccadilly and approach Dover Street from that angle; frustrating to have to go back on herself, but a frontal assault on Piccadilly Circus from above ground would be nothing but suicidal.

Turning her way onto Millbank, Anne caught sight of the unmistakable outline of the Houses of Parliament, stark against the white backdrop of the Mist. Something about seeing the familiar silhouette brought the reality of it all home to her then. Fury and the cold determination that went with it had carried her so far, but underneath it all she was a being of logic, of sense.

Was she really going to do this? Was she really going to rewrite human history just to get her father back?

She fought the doubt down, telling herself firmly that she mustn't falter. Who was to say that theirs had been the best or the only possible future? Her actions, her intervention would save lives, spare thousands from future suffering; who was to say her way would not be better? And whatever she had done, *would* do, was on whoever or whatever had brought her here. History would just have to face the consequences.

Head bent down against the wind, she quickened her pace towards Parliament Square.

CHAPTER FIFTEEN
Ticket to Ride

AT THE CORNER OF WARWICK AND GLASSHOUSE STREET, Dame Anne hugged the side of the buildings, pressing herself back against the stonework, steadying her breathing and trying to make her profile as small as possible.

Yeti; five of them. They moved together as a pack, lumbering down Glasshouse Street towards Piccadilly Circus with slow deliberation. In an effort to keep herself grounded, Anne forced herself to recall what she knew about the Yeti as machines; reducing them to the mundane, taking them apart piece by piece.

One thing she had never been able to discover was the exact nature and function of their sensory inputs. The Yeti had been made to resemble an idea of a creature by Jemba-Wa, the Tibetan toymaker, and so they had eyes, mouths (and fangs!), hands and feet (both with dangerously sharp claws!); but none of these things seemed to provide any function beyond the superficial. And yet they clearly were able to pick up and process both sound and movement, along with receiving signals from the Intelligence via the control spheres and converting that information into actions, but she had never found any satisfactory explanation as to a technological way for the Yeti to gather and transmit information *back*. Still, they did.

The Yeti were the Intelligence's eyes and ears when

it did not resort to using human spies, and Anne could only conclude that the process was a strange hybrid of technology and mental projection techniques; almost as if the robots were being remote controlled and possessed at the same time.

The distraction was working. The explanation had always frustrated Anne – too much flimsy guesswork, yet at the same time grounded in hard fact – and by the time she had finished mentally reviewing her notes on the problem, the Yeti had safely passed her by.

Breathing in a shallow sigh of relief, Anne began to move again, keeping to the shadows and making for the junction with Regent Street.

The sense of desolation was, as she had suspected, so much worse inside the Mist. On her way up from Embankment, Anne had been treated to the site of empty street after empty street; cars abandoned, buildings deserted, streets that were usually cheerful with bright artificial light now dark and unwelcoming. While she was happy that she had managed to escape detection so far, it was starting to worry her that she had not actually seen any more soldiers since Charing Cross. Nor had she heard any other sounds of military life; no motors, no voices, not even any gunfire. Just oppressive, all-encompassing silence. Surely she should have heard something by now?

The old Down Street tube station was on the other side of Piccadilly, almost as far as Hyde Park Corner, which meant she had another mile or so to go before she reached her destination. Again, Anne was thankful for the youthful (and fit!) body she was occupying; trying to do this in her seventy-year-old frame would have been impossible. It was so easy to forget just how much of a pain London was to get around when the direct routes and public transport were not accessible.

Between her stopping and starting to avoid Yeti, and

forced to take a round-about route, she must have covered about six miles already. The final stretch of the journey would take her parallel to Green Park, but first she needed to cross Regent Street. While it was possible to bypass most of the city's major thoroughfares, there was, quite literally, no getting around Regent's Street – not unless she wanted to add yet another two miles to her journey, and with time pressing that was something she could not afford. She would just have to risk it.

Covering the final ten yards to the end of Glasshouse Street, Anne made it to the junction and cautiously peered around the corner of the building – and could not supress a gasp.

The sight of Regent's Street, usually bustling with shoppers and tourists day and night, completely devoid of life would have been unsettling enough, but on turning the corner Anne was also confronted by the dreadful scene of an Army Land Rover covered in web and marooned in the middle of the street; its doors open, a dark shape slumped against the drivers' side wheel. Around it were further corpses – eight in all – some wrapped in web, some bloodied and broken. All were wearing uniforms.

By the look of things, they had not been long-dead. Anne put a hand to her mouth to stifle the sob that threatened to escape.

Further down the street she caught sight of more bodies; these in a pile, slumped behind some sort of makeshift barricade constructed from department store furniture, and behind them...

Anne bit into the back of her glove, supporting herself against the wall.

She had been spared this the last time around. After the Event she had been whisked away to the Vault to start work on the Web, but she had heard something of it from Alistair, who had been left to deal with the aftermath. He had once commented darkly, when reflecting on the number of corpses, that he'd been grateful it wasn't summer.

Anne now finally grasped the full implications, felt sick at the idea; but once again the scientific part of her brain took off on its own. Bodies kept better in winter, and the web-fungus itself was found to have some low-level preservation properties. It was one of the things she had discovered while working at the Vault.

She closed her eyes against the memory, and the old shame. So awful, the things that had taken place under the Cheviot Hills, the things she had been a part of before she had known the full horror of what was going on – and all facilitated by General Gore, Alistair's not-brother from a parallel reality.

If she was successful today, Alistair would not be on a plane to Cyprus in April, so he would not get struck by a capsule and knocked into that parallel reality, alerting Gore to the possibility of escaping to their world. The Vault would not exist at all! More lives and more suffering spared.

But Gore had not come alone; there was Dylan, Alistair's other 'nephew'. He would remain trapped, raised in a world of fascist brutality, never knowing the joy of a family that truly loved him.

She may not have been able to save the men before her, but there were others; Knight, Lane, Blake, Weams, Dawlish, O'Brien... even Arnold, maybe, if it was not too late for him. Them, and more besides. She could save them all; she just had to be strong.

Steeling herself with that thought, Anne focused back on the next stage of her journey. She fixed her target; Vigo Street, almost directly opposite her, a distance of barely twenty yards. No cover whatsoever; best take it at a run, corner to corner, than to try and take it slow and be caught in the open.

Anne readied herself, took a deep breath, and ran.

Colonel Pemberton slotted the new magazine home, and looked back at his squad. There were fewer than when he'd started out, and the fact prompted a spike of anger directed towards Professor Edward Travers. The man that they shouldn't have had to rescue in the first place.

The old fool was lucky to be alive. They all were.

The squad had arrived to find the Travers' house under siege, the professor and what remained of his original escort only still clinging on thanks to their having barricaded themselves in the cellar laboratory. They'd managed to drive the Yeti back long enough to extract them, and then they'd headed back through the gap in the Mist between Notting Hill and Bayswater.

Only this gap, which had remained mysteriously open, had been a ruse on the part of the Intelligence all along. Instead of the safe route the soldiers had been lured into believing it to be, it was in fact a bottleneck that had closed up as soon as Pemberton had brought Travers back through into the city centre. Caught on the back foot, they had been hard-pressed all the way on their retreat into the Underground.

They'd managed to get as far as Charing Cross Station before they had run into fresh difficulties and been forced above ground. Until now it had been safer to travel on foot through the Underground tunnels, but the Yeti had started advancing there too.

If Pemberton was angry at Travers, then he was just as furious with himself. If he had his way, he would have simply left the man to die, but they needed him. According to Anne Travers, her father was the one man who might possibly turn the tables on these creatures and the intelligence that controlled them, and so they needed to get him back safely. Whatever the cost.

And at least Miss Travers would be able to keep a rein

on her father, though she was probably the only one who would be happy to see him. And maybe Knight, by extension. Poor Ben, he had certainly fallen hard there.

'Right, lads,' Pemberton said decisively. 'We're going to need to move over ground. But keep sharp. Who knows what the state of play is up there.' He directed a glare at Travers. 'And you, Professor, you keep close to my men. I'm not risking any more for you.'

He ignored whatever Travers grumbled in reply, and gave the signal to advance.

It was, Pemberton knew, a sight he'd never forget. Emerging from the subway they were presented with Trafalgar Square completely devoid of life. No traffic, no tourists, no pigeons… just abandoned cars, rubbish and the statues in lonely, bleak isolation. It was utterly chilling.

Shaking off the feeling, Pemberton addressed the squad.

'Okay, men, we—'

'Sir, over there.'

Pemberton looked to where Whittaker was pointing, and saw a horde of Yeti arriving from the Strand, armed with web guns.

Damn!

There were more of them too, emerging from the National Gallery and from the direction of Cockspur Street.

They were surrounded.

So many, far too many. Pemberton's mind reeled at the sheer number of Yeti. Where had they all come from? There could only be one reason they were here, though; they had come for Travers. And they could not be allowed to have him.

Damn the man.

Pemberton ordered a third of the troops to form a rearguard at the top of the steps. 'Keep them at bay, Whittaker,' he instructed. 'They're after Travers.'

He followed the rest of the troops down back into the subway, pushing Travers along in front of them and back towards the station. They would have to try the exit at the other end of the Strand, which with any luck they could reach before the Yeti realised their plan and doubled back. For this, though, the rearguard needed to buy them as much time as possible to get away. And there was only one way to do that, seeing as they'd had to use all their grenades at Travers' house.

There was a strange inevitability to it, Pemberton thought bitterly, but then he supposed that was as it should be. He turned to the corporal next to him. Kelly, the man's name was.

'Give me your rifle,' he ordered stonily.

Wide-eyed, Kelly complied, and was even more surprised when the colonel gave him his own gun.

'See the professor safely back,' Pemberton said. 'And get this to my son.'

The words 'if I don't make it' did not need to be said. Kelly nodded, and Pemberton ran back up the steps to rejoin Whittaker.

He took up position next to the lieutenant, slinging the rifle over his neck and bringing the weapon to the shoulder. They waited steadily, the Yeti converging on their position, and unbidden a verse rose to his mind. Pemberton had always been fond of a good quote. A good quote could get you through the toughest of times, but over this last week he'd found that his words had deserted him. Until now.

That was no place,
Or time for chivalry or for grace.
The fury had him on his back.

Edwin Muir. How appropriate.

Spencer Pemberton knew that few, if asked, would have said he was a naturally violent man, but in this they were wrong. He knew with absolutely certainty as he stood in the shadow of Underground sign, as he pulled back the cocking hammer of the SLR and prepared to deliver death to these unnatural beasts, that he was a violent man. Any second now the madness of that violence would rise up like a great wave and possess him, body and soul. It would drive him on; drive him to kill, to scream and roar, to kill and kill until the enemy were dead or he himself was killed.

And as he bellowed the order to fire, he felt glad to be carried away in that madness. For once he welcomed the hate, the simple primeval bloodlust that sent all of his rage and desire for revenge spinning along with the bullets to embed themselves between the Yeti's eyes. In this battle there would be no quarter, for the Intelligence would show them no mercy.

On and on the Yeti came, closing in on them, roaring and howling like the wild animals they weren't, intent on cocooning his men or tearing them limb from limb. Too many, far too many. All too soon his magazine was empty, and Pemberton let out a battle cry, charging the nearest Yeti and swinging the rifle butt hard into its face, thinking only to smash in those burning, hellish eyes.

'Sir!' someone screamed from behind him.

A warning.

Pemberton started to turn, but a massive blow struck him across the face and knocked him flying. He heard an explosive, sickening *crack*.

And then there was nothing.

As Naylor and Jones finished laying the last few charges at the tunnel mouth, Dawlish stood watch, keeping an eye on the platform area, but not venturing any further forward.

They were below the Circle Line, and the tunnels above them were filled to bursting with fungus. Dawlish could feel it; that low sense of dread, the desire to curl up in fear or run as fast as he could in the opposite direction. They all could. Dawlish kept telling himself that it was just the effect of the infrasound, but for a while now he had not been quite so sure.

Much earlier attempts to breach the barrier had revealed that the influence of the fungus extended down through the earth, as well as manifesting as the Mist above. 1 Para had lost several good men in an attempt to break through using the Bakerloo Line beneath Paddington. Rumour had it the bodies were still there, lying on the tracks where they had fallen.

Dawlish shook his head, trying to banish the ghoulish thought from his mind. Enough of that; he had a job to do, and letting himself go to pieces was not in any way going to help him or his men.

'Are we all set, Jones?' he asked, as much to bring himself to order as anyone else.

'Yes, sir,' Jones said, looking up from where he had just attached the final wire. 'Detonator's in place and all set to bring this lot down.'

'Good, let's get on with it.'

On that cue, the two sappers got up and began following the wire back along the tunnel to where the others had set up the control switch. Dawlish remained a moment, waiting for them to get ahead, then followed on, conducting a last check of the cables as he went. It was always risky, conducting demolition in a confined space. He had studied the schematics for both the station and this tunnel section thoroughly before they left, checking and rechecking that he had made the right calculations. For a start, the blast–

His train of thought ground to a halt at the same time as his feet. There it was again; the whispering just at the edge of his hearing. Definitely a voice this time, but still too faint, too indistinct for him to make it out. Dawlish looked up and around, fear beginning to mingle with irritation. Where on earth was it coming from?

'Sir?'

Dawlish started, heart hammering in his chest, and turned to see Arnold standing next to him, looking at him with a wary expression.

'Staff?' Dawlish blinked. How had Arnold got there so quickly? 'Why aren't you with the others?'

'I were, sir,' Arnold said carefully, still giving Dawlish that questioning look. 'Only Naylor and Jones came back, and you didn't follow... You were just standing here, distant-like. Are you sure you're all right, sir?'

Dawlish shook his head, angry and embarrassed. What the hell was he thinking, letting himself zone out like that, and so close to the charges?

'I'm fine,' he lied. Lord, but he wanted a cigarette! 'Just–'

'–hearing things again, sir?' Arnold asked carefully.

Dawlish bristled, angry at Arnold for calling his bluff. Concerned or not, the staff was dangerously close to insubordination with that remark, and Dawlish was in no mood to let that slide.

'Staff Sergeant, I've just about had enough of–'

But Arnold wasn't listening. He was looking over Dawlish's shoulder, his eyes wide with alarm. 'Look, sir!'

Dawlish turned on his heel and saw that where the tracks had been previously empty, two Yeti were approaching the charges, web guns in their claws. They raised them to fire.

'Run!' Dawlish bellowed.

He and Arnold took to their heels, sprinting back towards the rest of the men. After a few seconds Dawlish stopped, looked back over his shoulder. The Yeti weren't chasing them, but had stopped by the charges. What on earth were they doing? It looked for all the world as if they were thinking of a way to sabotage the set-up – which, Dawlish realised as they aimed their web guns at the charges, was exactly what they were about to do.

'Detonate!' he bellowed, resuming his mad dash to join the others. 'Do it – now! Fire!'

Then something ran across his feet, tripping him and flinging him down between the rails. Somewhere up ahead he heard a wordless shout from the men.

The world around him rocked. A blast of hot air hit his back, and with a mighty thunderclap the sky fell in on his head.

Dame Anne gave a small grunt as she levered open the entrance door to the ticket hall of what used to be Down Street Station. The site had been converted into a corner shop, and from the exterior there was little to suggest its previous role. Luckily there was an access door to one side, kept to provide workmen access to the running tunnels beneath. Skills gained during a misspent adulthood meant she had been able to pick the padlock, but the door itself had seized up somewhat, either due to the weather or lack of recent use. Happily, a well-applied crowbar and a little brute force went a long way.

When she had created enough of a gap, she took a quick glance over her shoulder and slipped through into the gloom beyond. Once inside she pushed the door to, cringing as the sound of the metal door meeting the frame boomed in the space beyond. She waited breathlessly for the echo to die down, and when she was certain that no one had heard, she switched on the torch and turned to look at her surroundings.

The narrow corridor beyond was not as much of a mess as she had imagined it would be. The hallway was clear of obstruction and rubbish, though the trail of bright white boot-prints through the decades upon decades of dust and soot served as a much starker illustration of neglect. She followed the trail, careful to keep clear of the filthy walls either side, and very soon found herself at the top of a wide spiral staircase. The torch beam glinted off familiar brown and cream glazed tiles.

Here she hesitated. Poised on the edge, staring down into the darkness, she felt that she was standing at a crossroads. Memories came flooding back; the damp warmth of the tunnels, the stale soot-filled air, Yeti eyes glowing in the shadows, the creeping sense of entrapment, bestial roars and screams of fear...

She saw before her faces, companions of ages past; Ben Knight, her father, Colonel Lethbridge-Stewart, Gwynfor Evans, Victoria, Jamie, and the Doctor, whose eyes twinkled with a mischief but betrayed a fierce intelligence. They were still there, all of them. She could sense that future; so familiar, so tangible that she almost felt she could reach out and touch it. It could still happen; all she need do was turn and walk away.

But that wasn't *her* future; not anymore.

Courage now, she told herself. *You can do this.*

She only wished she didn't have to do it alone.

Taking a breath, torch pointed down to light her way, Anne began her descent into darkness.

Dawlish woke to the feeling of something heavy being moved off him, and the dulcet tones of Staff Arnold hollering in his ear.

'Sir? Sir, can you hear me? Sir! So help me, Collins, if you've killed 'im–'

'Hang fire, Staff,' he murmured indistinctly. 'I'm still here.'

Above him he heard sighs of relief, and he coughed. His throat was filled with dust, making it hard to breathe, his chest feeling as if it was on fire from the inside out. Two pairs of hands helped him to sit up, and a canteen was thrust under his nose.

'Clear it out, sir,' Arnold said firmly.

Dawlish obediently took a mouthful of water,

spluttered but managed to wash it around and spat onto the tunnel floor. He thought he tasted blood. Another, an actual drink this time, and he was beginning to feel something resembling human again; albeit a human that felt as if he had been hit by a bus.

'What happened?' he asked hoarsely, finding his voice.

'Section of the roof came down, sir,' Arnold explained. 'Fell right on top of you. Must have been a fault there no one knew about.' He gave a humourless chuckle. 'Thought you was a goner, but the tracks must have taken most of the fall. Bloody lucky.'

Dawlish didn't feel lucky. But then, that he was feeling anything at all proved otherwise.

'Reckon you can stand, sir?' the staff prompted. 'Because if you can we'd best get a move on. Don't know how long that'll hold 'em.'

Dawlish squinted back down the tunnel, the light from their overhead rig illuminated the chaos where the entrance to the station had once been. The charges had all fired by the looks of it; the section of the tunnel roof had collapsed in on itself, completely blocking the way. In the distance he could just make out the arm of a Yeti protruding from beneath a large block of concrete. It wasn't moving.

'Did we get them?' he asked in wonder. He sounded a little dazed even to his ears.

'Looks like it, sir,' Naylor said. 'Though, them things being robots... *Can* they die?'

One of the long claws twitched. The soldiers stared at it.

'Get this lot packed away, Staff,' Dawlish said quickly. 'At the double.'

'Yes, sir,' Arnold replied. The men didn't need to be told twice.

*

In his small office at the Elm Park command post, Sir Alistair sat contemplating the thin slip of paper that was lying on the desk in front of him. It had been handed to him by the signals operator over two hours ago, and bore only a short message scribbled down in haste:

Sunray is down.

It had been the last message to come out of the Fortress at Goodge Street, shortly before enemy action had rendered their phone lines inoperable. In those two hours since, the paper had become somewhat crumpled, having been folded, smoothed out, only to be folded once again. Repeat.

Alistair had known it was coming, of course; knew it had to happen, knew the date and time to the minute, etched as it was into the fabric of his memory. It didn't make it any easier, though, when it had come. After a moment, he leaned back and pulled open the bottom drawer of the desk, taking out the bottle that Pemberton had given him on his arrival. His friend had been right, of course; Alistair did need it, just not in the way Pemberton had intended.

Fetching his enamel mug, Alistair wiped out the last remains of the tea with his handkerchief, broke the seal on the bottle and poured himself a dram. He raised the mug in a solemn salute.

'Godspeed, Old Spence,' he murmured to the air, and drank.

The time to mourn Pemberton properly was yet to come, and mourn he would – already had, in fact, but the world did not stop turning just for one death; even that of a very dear friend. It would not be long now before Alistair was back where he needed to be in the Underground. How long he may yet stay here, as his younger self, was anybody's guess. What if the variations he had noticed continued and, in order to negate their affects, he would have to relive the whole of the London

Event again?

Alistair felt a tremor run through his hand at the thought, and balled it into a fist to make it stop. Up until now he had coped, been on the outside looking in; but there were so many more deaths to come. Could he stand among them, look them in the eyes and lead them into mortal danger, knowing that he alone would survive?

He couldn't do it.

Alistair closed his eyes, and prayed it would not come to that. His other concern was that going into the Underground would mean his coming into contact with Anne. If she were in the same predicament, as he suspected, then he would be dealing with the version of her from 2011; not the stranger he had first met in 1969. The possible implications of that made Alistair's head spin, and he rubbed at his temples wearily. Would they even be able to acknowledge each other? Would they end up tiptoeing around, him knowing that she knew, and she knowing that he suspected, but acting like strangers? Even if Anne did decide to play along, how long could they possibly keep a farce like that going? On a military base where there was space and more personnel, maybe, but in close confines...

Alistair halted down that train of thought, before it vanished in ever-decreasing circles. Whatever happened from hereon would happen; he would just have to make the best go at it. Either way, his journey to the Underground was very nearly over. There was just one more act to come; one more hoop he needed to jump through.

There was a knock at the door.

And this will be it, Alistair thought archly, refilling his mug.

'Come!' he called, setting the bottle down next to the note with deliberate care.

The door opened and Welby stepped through the

door. Alistair waited with detached interest as the lieutenant clocked the whisky bottle, the mug, and the paper in quick succession. He could guess what the man was thinking – Alistair had been a junior officer himself once upon a time – and what conclusions he might jump to, yet Welby also knew that Pemberton had been a close friend. The lieutenant may not be particularly gifted when it came to initiative, but he was not stupid.

'Yes, Welby?' Alistair asked impatiently.

Welby, his face carefully blank, handed him a large brown sealed envelope. 'Special dispatch from Strategic Command, sir. In light of Colonel Pemberton's death, you're to proceed to Goodge Street and take over command there.'

Alistair took the envelope and unsealed it, extracted the contents and scanned through the papers. It was all here; operational brief specific to HQ, letter of authorisation to the OC at Goodge Street, personal note of condolence from General Hamilton – all sending him back to where he started.

'Very well,' he said curtly. 'I'll leave within the hour. Inform Major Simmons at Highbury that he's to take over here until Strategic Command decide whether to appoint another officer.'

The likelihood of the Brass appointing a brand-new commander from outside at this point was slim, but it would be best to prepare for every eventuality.

Welby nodded his understanding. 'Very good, sir. I'll arrange for an escort to take you to Goodge Street.'

But Alistair shook his head. He knew what was meant to happen next, and it wasn't that. Besides, for better or worse, somebody *else* needed to enter the tunnels with him, and Alistair was damned if he was going to let him slide out of it.

'No,' he said shortly. 'You're short enough on manpower as it is without sending out extra patrols.

Haven't we got a supply party already scheduled to go in that direction?'

He waited patiently while Welby ran through the schedule in his head, knowing full well what the answer would be before he voiced it.

'There's an ammunition delivery, sir. Though it's only going as far as Holborn.'

'Capital, that's close enough. I'll catch a lift with them.'

'If you're certain, sir,' Welby said somewhat dubiously, and with good reason.

Holborn may not be far from Goodge Street, but it was still enough of a distance for something to happen. Unfortunately, this was precisely what Alistair was relying on.

'I am. Make the arrangements, Lieutenant.'

'Sir.' Welby came to attention, then left to carry out his orders.

Alistair sat in silence for a moment, staring into the middle-distance, thoughts of every variety racing through his head. Then he downed what was left of his whisky, put the bottle back in the drawer, and rose to his feet.

Once more unto the breach. Or, perhaps, more suitably in laymen's terms: *Well, here we go again.*

CHAPTER SIXTEEN
Stand!

DOWN AND DOWN SHE WENT, EACH STEP CAREFUL AND measured, the torchlight only penetrating a short way into the gloom. Through the thick wool of her gloves, Dame Anne could feel the layers of grime and grit scraping along the handrail, but with the staircase so dark and slippery with dust and debris she daren't let go for fear of falling. It did not stop her from wrinkling her nose in disgust, though. She'd only been below ground five minutes and already felt as if she needed a shower.

And then she was around the last corner, down the last step, and the staircase opened out into a wide, low passageway. Directly opposite her the torch beam caught the outline of a large, long metal object attached to the wall on the other side of the passageway. Curiosity getting the better of her, Anne stepped over to investigate.

It was a tin bath. A big, old-fashioned, badly-corroded tin bath.

Anne couldn't help it. She laughed. Well, she had thought about needing a wash…

When she had control of herself again, she moved the torch around to take in more of her surroundings. After the Event, and learning of the Vault's citadel beneath Shoreditch, Anne had made it her business to find out all she could about the various 'hidden citadels' that lay beneath London. Some still being active, it had taken a while to gain the proper clearance – or more accurately, to learn whom to badger until they relented and gave her the files. Mark Lane had been her personal favourite, with its barnacled walls and scorched platform.

Down Street, on the other hand, was one of the 'open secrets'; a station closed just before the last war due to lack of use, appropriated by Churchill as a temporary base of operations while the Cabinet War Rooms were being constructed. The tunnel in which she was standing, the one that connected the stairs to the platforms, had been accidentally built to the scale of the running tunnels, providing plenty of space to partition off for offices and living quarters – hence the remains of the bathroom.

She remembered the Fortress at Goodge Street, of their own cramped set-up where space had been at a premium and men were practically sleeping on top of each other. It had caused the soldiers some degree of consternation and embarrassment when she'd turned up, though Knight had been quick enough to surrender his room for her use, bunking down with Lieutenant Dawlish. The men had adapted to her presence soon enough, yet Anne had never shaken the sense that they were perpetually in fear of her walking in on them in one of the bathrooms. Considering the reputation soldiers had and some of the language on offer, they could be peculiarly bashful at times.

Advancing carefully along the tunnel, Anne directed the torch at the floor, listening intently for the least indication that she might not be alone. Her footsteps echoed faintly on the tiles, her breathing seeming strangely loud in the subterranean stillness. It had taken her a while to want to use the Underground after the Event; and in this she knew she had not been alone. She needn't have worried. When she had finally braved it again, one Sunday afternoon in July, it had seemed like a different world; alive with the bustle, noise and light of everyday existence. Against such a backdrop it was impossible for monsters to exist. But here, alone, in the silence and the darkness it was all coming back to her.

Anne remembered her initial surprise and suspicion when she had received General Hamilton's summons to investigate the fungus. Until that point she'd had very little to do with the Ministry of Defence or any projects they had funded, yet Hamilton confided that he'd had his eye on her work 'for quite a while'. Though the general's interest was not in the least sinister – and a million miles away from that of another 'general' – Anne had still felt uncomfortable at the prospect, as if she had been somehow manipulated.

They all had been, to a greater or lesser degree; Pemberton, her father, Alistair, even Bill.

It was strange to think that at first Hamilton had groomed Pemberton for the job that would ultimately become Alistair's. Anne had only known Pemberton for a short time, but he had struck her as a competent and professional officer; careful of his men and his responsibilities, but not opposed to taking risks when needed. Yet Anne knew without a doubt that, had Pemberton lived and stayed in the Underground, he would not have been able to carry the day. He had lacked Alistair's sheer tenacity and vision, his innate belief in people, and willingness to take a leap of faith.

Alistair had never claimed to be anything special; in fact, quite the opposite ('Wrong place, wrong time!'), but it seemed in that opinion he was fairly outnumbered. After all, as Bill had once pointed out, Sir Alistair Lethbridge-Stewart would be remembered in history as the man who went to the United Nations to ask for money to hunt aliens, *and they gave it to him*. For all his natural scepticism, Alistair had never failed to appreciate the scale of the threats they faced and, once provided with a just reason to act, had never held back in rushing to meet them head-on. With the hindsight of years, it seemed impossible to think of anyone but Alistair in the role. It was just who he *was*.

Anne shivered, though it could not be from the cold. One of the things people often presumed about the Underground was that they thought it would be cold, when it was actually quite the opposite. The air down below was close, warmed by the city above, the many electrical lights and cables, and in some places even by the underground rivers.

Now her initial fury had faded she was beginning to feel guilt creeping up on her again. She had been wrong to be angry at Alistair; he had been just as much a victim of circumstance over the years as she. After that fateful meeting and her initial distrust, he had never proved himself to be anything less than a valued colleague and the most loyal of friends.

But it would not change her actions in the here and now. Fury had been replaced with grim determination, and she pushed all thoughts of Alistair to one side, focusing again on her purpose. Others may or may not be spared in the process, but this was her one chance to save her father from a fate worse than death, and she was going to take it.

Pressing on through the darkness, she passed a raised dais bordered by metal railings, before turning a corner and finding herself next to the remains of a large bank of telephone terminating blocks; the clearest indication so far of the station's wartime use. One of the main complaints made while the station was still open concerned the unusually long distance from the bottom of the stairs to the platforms. If memory served correctly, the phone blocks indicated that she was at last nearing the tunnels – and a few further paces revealed she was right.

In order for the station's wartime operations to be kept secret, false walls had been built to disguise the edges of the platforms from passing trains, which meant that access was by two metal gates dropping straight down onto the trackside.

Approaching the eastbound side, Anne heaved on the gate and was happily surprised at how easily it moved, albeit with a little more squeaking of hinges than sounded healthy. The tunnel beyond loomed ominously, but it was not pitch dark; a string of overhead lights broke the gloom enough to clearly make out the tracks, so Anne turned off her torch and dropped down onto the rail bed.

The landing was not quite as soft as she expected, and she stumbled, the sound of her scuffling and half-whispered curse carrying further than she would have liked – but a quick glance eastbound showed no sign of Yeti. Now, Piccadilly Circus was only two stops back towards--

'Halt! Hands in the air!'

Anne gasped, turning on the spot, eyes widening with disbelief.

Standing in front of her, rifle aimed at her heart, was Staff Sergeant Arnold.

She slowly raised her hands above her head, her mind racing. *Arnold.* What was he doing here? How had she not seen him? Did the Intelligence already know her plan and had sent him to kill her?

Further back along the tracks she could see more soldiers approaching; six of them in total, five of which were armed, including Arnold. The sixth looked in a bad way and was being supported by another. The sight of other soldiers served to calm her a little. If Arnold was not on his own, then he was at least pretending to be on their side, and that meant he would not kill her outright. What explanation to give them, though, when they asked what she was doing down here?

And then the answer was handed to her on a plate.

'What is it, Staff?'

The rest of the soldiers had caught up with them, and it was the injured one who had spoken. Hard to see under the dust and grime; but with that accent and attitude, definitely an officer. As he came closer, the dim light fell across his face, and Anne choked out a laugh of relief.

'Civvie, sir,' Arnold said. 'Young woman.'

'Lieutenant Dawlish!' she exclaimed. 'Oh, thank heaven it's you!'

Lieutenant Max Dawlish of the Royal Engineers, for it was indeed he, regarded her with surprise and no small amount of suspicion. Perfectly natural, really, as he had just been confronted by a woman he'd never seen before who clearly recognised him.

'Who are you?' he demanded. 'And what are you doing down here?'

'Looking for you,' she lied. The men, all with their rifles trained on her, were all Royal Engineers, and so must have been down there on some form of working party. It was an extraordinary stroke of good luck. If she could convince Dawlish and his men to come to Piccadilly Circus with her... 'I'm an associate of Doctor Travers. She sent me to find you.'

'You know Miss Travers?' Some of the suspicion cleared from Dawlish's face, but not yet enough for him to order his men to lower their weapons.

Anne nodded, slowly dropping her hands to her sides. 'We were at Cambridge together; she asked me to come in and help. I'm... Doctor Shaw.'

In the background a soldier was heard to murmur, 'Stone me, *another* of 'em?' Whether that was just scientists or specifically female scientists, Anne couldn't tell.

'Clarke!' Dawlish admonished. He glanced at her, narrowing his eyes. 'Miss Travers never mentioned you...'

'That's because she wasn't sure she could get hold of

me,' Anne said quickly. 'I only just arrived last night. She's come up with a way to stop the Yeti, and I volunteered to come down here and carry it out.'

'By yourself?' Dawlish sounded incredulous.

Anne wrinkled her nose in irritation. There wasn't time for this… 'No, not by myself. I came in with a squad from Warren Street, but we were attacked. I managed to escape, but the others… I knew if I could still find you, there was hope.'

The soldiers shared dubious glances, but she could tell that Dawlish was starting to believe her.

'How do we know you really are who you say you are?' he asked. Annoyingly, it was a reasonable question.

Anne sighed, thinking of a way to persuade him. She had no official papers, so the only thing available to her was familiarity. Quickly she recalled what she knew about Dawlish from the few times she worked with him during the Event. Something that could only be learned through personal interaction.

'Anne told me you swear in Polish,' she said bluntly. 'And keep humming *Living Doll* when you think no one's listening.'

There were several snorts of suppressed laughter from the squad behind him, and even in the dark Anne could tell Dawlish had gone bright red.

'All right, so you do know Anne Travers,' he said reluctantly, and waved for the men to lower their guns. 'So, Miss Shaw, what's this plan of hers?'

Anne cast a glance at Arnold, who was still regarding her with suspicion, although he had obeyed the order to stand down. There was no way to tell if Arnold had been taken over by the Intelligence yet, or whether it was actively listening in if he had. But if she wanted to secure Dawlish's help, there was no way she could avoid Arnold overhearing. On the other hand, the Intelligence had only really seemed to take an interest in their activities at

Goodge Street after its intended victim had arrived – so it was possible that its attention would be elsewhere, running Arnold on 'remote' for now. It was a risk she would have to take; but not just yet.

'I need to tell you first, lieutenant,' she said firmly. 'Then you can brief your men.'

That prompted fresh suspicious glances all around, including from Dawlish, but he nodded. At least he was familiar with the concept of 'need to know'.

'Help me over to that wall, Collins,' he said to the man supporting him, and Anne followed. The lieutenant braced himself against the brickwork, wincing, but nodded and the sapper retired to stand with the others.

Anne studied Dawlish with some concern. He was covered in what she recognised now as masonry dust, a shallow cut just beneath his hairline leaking slowly down the side of his face. Though he seemed fairly mobile, he was clearly in pain, and in need of medical attention.

'What happened?' she asked.

Dawlish gave an embarrassed grunt. 'Tunnel demolition; tripped and fell. Damned stupid of me, but I'll live. Tell me this plan, then.'

Anne was not overly convinced by the 'brave soldier' response, but she pressed on, lowering her voice so as not to be overheard. 'Before you left, Anne was trying to isolate the frequency on which the Intelligence was broadcasting, hoping to see if she could jam it. She managed to do so, but in addition she's been able to find out where it's coming from. It's at Piccadilly Circus.'

Dawlish's eyes widened to almost comical proportions.

'Then what's Old Spence waiting for?' he asked, excitement creeping into his voice. 'Why doesn't he attack now?'

'It's not as simple as that,' she said, then realised what Dawlish had just said. Her heart sank, realising that, of course, he didn't know. How could he have known out here in the tunnels?

Dawlish gave a derisive snort. 'It never is!'

'No,' Anne said distractedly. She took a deep breath. 'And I'm sorry to have to tell you, but Colonel Pemberton is dead.'

There was a beat of silence, in which Dawlish's gaze dropped to the track bed, his expression unreadable. Anne let him have the moment.

'A shame,' he said eventually, his voice carefully controlled. 'Good man; a very fine soldier.'

'Yes,' Anne agreed. *A very fine soldier.* The exact words Alistair had used.

'Don't tell the men,' Dawlish said firmly. 'Not yet.'

Anne shook her head. 'I won't, I promise.' She returned to the plan. 'Captain Knight reckoned a full-on assault would be too easily repelled, and end up costing too many lives. However, a small squad —'

'— going in on the quiet?' Dawlish finished. He raised his head, a new sense of purpose in his eyes. 'Get in there and destroy the place from the inside?'

'Not even as much as that; only one piece of equipment. It'll be a large glass and steel construction, shaped like a pyramid. The Intelligence had something like it in Tibet, serving as its focal point. If we break the pyramid, we destroy the Intelligence's link to the corporeal plane, we destroy the Yeti.'

Dawlish nodded his understanding. 'Might as well give it a shot,' he said.

Inside, Anne felt a sense of triumph. It seemed she would have her squad, but Dawlish really didn't look in great shape.

'Are you all right to go on?' she asked. She was sure his skin was turning paler beneath the grime.

Dawlish smiled, though, a glint of steel in his gaze. 'Absolutely. Piccadilly's on the way back, anyway. And this one's for the colonel.'

Anne could not help but smile in return. She had liked Dawlish. He had been nothing but polite to her from the start, calling her 'ma'am' instead of 'miss'. He had been nice as well; a little out of his depth when he told her how he'd been brought in to the whole set-up. She had never learned what had happened to Dawlish. In the clear-up afterwards he had been listed among those whose bodies had never been found. Perhaps his was another life that could be saved by her pre-emptive action.

'But first, can you vouch for each and every one of your men?'

Dawlish frowned, looking across at the other soldiers. 'Of course I can. Why?'

'Anne also discovered that the Intelligence doesn't only control Yeti,' she explained. 'In certain circumstances it has the ability to directly influence human minds and use them as spies.'

'What, double agents?' Dawlish looked alarmed.

'Of a sort; it's possible that they don't even know they're being controlled. Think, have any of you lost sight of the other, even for a moment?'

Dawlish hesitated. 'I don't think so.'

'What about A... Your staff sergeant?'

'Arnold?' Dawlish frowned, not only surprised but offended by the suggestion. 'Absolutely not!'

'We've got to make sure,' she said calmly, reasonably. She glanced over to the small knot of men, who were starting to shift around impatiently. 'We need to ask them.'

Dawlish's frown deepened, but he did not raise any further objection. She helped him over to rejoin the group.

'Right, listen up,' he said, once they were back in company. 'Has any man been out of sight of the others, even briefly?'

The men looked blankly at each other, but there was

no response. Then one sapper piped up hesitantly.

'Well, I went over there for a—'

'That's enough of that, Jones!' Arnold barked.

'I think we're all accounted for, miss,' Dawlish said quickly. 'We've been together ever since we've been down here, even after we came across those Yeti at South Kensington.'

Anne relaxed a little, but still cast a wary glance at Arnold. Maybe he hadn't been taken over yet. After all, they had never known where or when he had first died. If all went well then, like her father, he might well never fall under the spell of the Intelligence.

'Good, then you're probably all fine,' she said.

The squaddies looked at each other, baffled. They turned to Dawlish for an explanation, but in this they were disappointed.

'Change of plan,' he said abruptly. 'We're calling in at Piccadilly Circus along the way.'

'What for, sir?' asked one of the men.

Dawlish shot him an irritated look. 'We're doing a recce for Miss Travers, and Miss Shaw here,' he said. 'I'll tell you what we're looking for when we get nearer.'

Alistair tried not to stare at the man, but it was damned difficult. Welby had marked the sapper out as the driver of the truck; a thin, gangly sort with large ears, a prominent chin, and an incredibly strong Welsh valleys accent.

'Everything all right there, is it, sir?' Evans asked.

Another casualty, although not from this battle. It had been decades since he'd last seen Gwynfor Evans, and it had been an even longer time since he had seen this version of him; a rum-looking fellow with something bordering on an attitude. A born REMF if ever Alistair saw one, and revelling in his role as a driver. Alistair had often wondered how the man had ever managed to apply himself enough to be accepted into the Royal Engineers; he would have been just as happy in the RASC. Alistair probably should have asked him.

'What? Yes, of course,' Alistair said sharply. He straightened up, setting his mind back on track. 'Let's get underway, shall we?'

'Soon as you like, sir,' Evans said, a little resentfully. 'We're just about finished loading up.'

Resisting the urge to roll his eyes, Alistair walked around to the other side of the track and settled into the passenger seat.

The small convoy was made up of the ammunition truck itself and two Land Rovers, each manned by a small detachment from 33 Engineer Regiment, under the direction of Squadron Sergeant Major Stevens. While the truck would deliver supplies to Holborn, it would also deliver Alistair to his new command at Goodge Street. Or at least that was the plan - but it'd never get there.

Opening up the file of reports he had brought with him, there was a *thump* against the partition behind Alistair's head and a string of muffled curses as one of the soldiers banged his knee against the ammunition crates. Alistair allowed himself a small smile, but it was tinged with sadness. In an hour's time all these men would be dead – only himself and Evans would make it out alive. The urge to do something, say something was tremendous, but he fought it down; focused on the reports and held his tongue.

And prayed somewhere, somehow, he would be forgiven.

The word of command given, the men all jumped aboard their respective vehicles, the engines gunning into life. At the time Alistair remembered that he had let himself begin to speculate beyond this current crisis, beginning to wonder what life might have in store for him going forward. Even back then he knew he could not go back to 2 Scots; even if he had wanted to, he was not for a moment naïve enough to believe the Brass would simply let him loose back into the regular Army. His eyes had been opened, and he could never... *would* never close them again.

As the convoy set off from the Elm Park command post, Alistair leaned back into his seat, and wondered how much longer he would remain in 1969. Surely he would not have to live through the entire London Event again...?

The going was slower than Anne would have liked. She walked along behind Arnold and Clarke, Collins having resumed charge of Dawlish since, although he was now walking by himself, he was still prone to stumbling every now and then. Jones and the remaining soldier took up the rear.

It took them a good twenty minutes to get as far as Green Park Station, which was thankfully deserted, and then another quarter of an hour before they neared Piccadilly. All the time Anne's eyes kept being drawn to Arnold. The tension between his shoulder blades suggested he knew he was aware of her scrutiny, but he said nothing, didn't look around; just kept his attention fixed firmly on the tunnel ahead. There was still time to make this work; still time to save her father. Once she got to Piccadilly, everything would be all right...

As the platform came into view, Dawlish signalled for them to stop.

'Right, lads,' he whispered, as the men drew closer to hear his instructions. 'This is what we need to do. We'll take–'

But he never finished, his words suddenly cut off by a huge, fiendish roar from behind them. Anne turned, and muffled a scream as three Yeti emerged from the tunnel they had just been through. Where had *they* come from? Another roar, and she looked up to see more Yeti emerging onto the platform from the station entrance. The Intelligence knew. Arnold had betrayed them again!

With shouts of alarm, Naylor, Clarke and Jones scrambled to bring their rifles to bear, but the Yeti moved first. Mist shot from the web guns, and within seconds the three men were cocooned, dead before they hit the ground. A sob of grief ripped its way out of Anne's throat, and she backed away from the smothered corpses – stumbling straight into the arms of Arnold.

'We've got to go, miss!' he shouted, his expression fierce. His grip tightened around her shoulders and he dragged her eastbound, away from the platform and the Yeti. 'Quick!'

'No!' Anne fought him, broke loose from his grip and rounded on him furiously. 'You did this!' she shrieked. 'It was you all along!'

Behind her, the air was split by the sound of a gunshot. She turned just in time to see Collins fall, his face frozen in shock, fresh blood blossoming across his chest.

Dawlish stood over him, smoking gun held in his hand. He raised his head and turned to look at them, his face slack, emotionless, his eyes burning with malevolence. He trained the gun on Anne and Arnold.

'Drop your weapon, Staff Sergeant,' he rasped.

Anne felt the world fall apart around her. She had seen that expression, heard that voice before; from her father, so many years ago and tomorrow. *No…*

'Sir?' Arnold said, confused and fearful. His eyes darted between Dawlish and the Yeti, which were forming a circle around them. 'Sir? For pity's sake, what's wrong with you?'

'It's not him,' Anne said bleakly. She felt weak, all the breath knocked from her lungs. *No, it's horrible, just too horrible!* 'Not anymore.'

Dawlish nodded his head stiffly, two more Yeti emerging from the tunnels to flank him like bodyguards.

'I am the Great Intelligence,' he whispered hoarsely, air grating past appropriated vocal chords. He turned to look at Anne. 'And you... *know* me.'

CHAPTER SEVENTEEN
Don't Forget to Remember

ARNOLD STEPPED IN FRONT OF HER PROTECTIVELY, levelling his rifle at what had once been Dawlish.

'Stay back, miss,' he murmured.

Dame Anne could only stare at him dumbly, shaking her head. From being so full of anger that she thought she might burst, she now felt drained beyond measure, empty of both thought and emotion.

Dawlish, not Arnold. How could she have got it so wrong?

The Yeti behind them gave a menacing growl, and Arnold edged away, keeping the rifle trained on his former officer. Anne could tell he was weighing up the situation, calculating their odds of escape and finding them massively against. She couldn't fault him for his bravery; but there was nothing she nor he could do.

Even though there was no facial expression to read on its host's face, the Intelligence seemed amused at Arnold's attempts to resist.

'I would not do anything foolish,' it hissed. 'You may shoot me, but know that if you do, my Yeti will tear you to pieces. Surrender your weapon.'

As if to emphasise the point, the Yeti moved a step closer and growled, brandishing their web guns. Arnold only clutched the rifle closer to his chest.

Anne urgently laid a hand on his sleeve. 'Do as it says,' she begged. 'Please.'

225

They were probably dead anyway, but she had no desire to see Arnold torn apart by Yeti. And while the Intelligence believed it had a use for them, there might still be some slim chance of escape.

Arnold frowned at her. Surrendering went against his every natural and taught instinct, but between being heavily outnumbered and the pleading expression in her eyes, he recognised the folly in resisting. Reluctantly, he bent down and grounded his rifle.

'A wise decision,' the Intelligence said approvingly, as a Yeti stepped forward to take charge of the weapon. Dawlish turned and addressed Anne. 'My thanks to you, child. I do not wish for any unnecessary unpleasantness.'

Then it paused, seeming to reconsider.

'But no, not "child",' it said, pondering. 'Your soul is at odds with the sum of your years. You are not what you appear to be.'

Anne felt a flash of anxiety and hastily lowered her eyes to the floor. It knew. How, she could not begin to guess, but she only prayed that it had not discovered her real identity.

'No matter,' the Intelligence whispered when she refused to reply. 'I will learn soon enough.' It gestured with the gun towards the platform. 'Will you walk into my parlour?'

Arnold cast a questioning glance at Anne, but she could only shake her head; they clearly had no option but to do as instructed. As they moved towards the edge of the track the air was filled with electronic bleeping. The Yeti received new orders. The beasts turned, forming up around them, leading the way and bringing up the rear. The Intelligence followed, Dawlish's gun aimed at their backs. Prisoners and escort.

They were quite deep in the earth here, and Anne remembered with some trepidation the long, winding journey they would have to make up the emergency staircases to the ticket hall. That previous time there had been four of them captive, marched up the stairs in oppressive silence. However, as she and Arnold were herded through the archway marked 'Way Out', she became aware of a low, metallic grinding and the rumbling of machinery, and to her astonishment she saw that the escalators were working. The Intelligence must have reconnected the power to them purely for her and Arnold's benefit.

How considerate, she thought absently.

The Yeti growled at them to continue onwards.

It was certainly one of the strangest predicaments in which Anne had found herself in to date; travelling up an escalator in the middle of a squad of Yeti, listening to the ponderous creaking of the mechanism beneath their feet. The whole experience lasted less than a minute, but the pause gave her brain plenty of time to begin the process of self-recrimination.

Or would have, if Arnold had not taken the opportunity to quiz her.

'What's happened, miss?' He needn't have bothered trying to keep his voice down; with the Tube devoid of the usual chaotic din, even the slightest sound echoed off the tiled walls. 'What is that thing?'

Anne looked back over her shoulder, but she could not see past the Yeti behind her. She knew the Intelligence was still there, though; hiding in its stolen body, not wavering it in its aim.

'It's the intelligence that controls the Yeti,' she said. 'The Mist, the fungus; it's behind all of this.'

Arnold frowned, clearly having a problem taking it all in. 'How do you know all this?'

'Anne briefed me,' she said bitterly. Technically it was true; not that it really mattered anymore. 'Her father, Professor Travers, met it in Tibet, but was unable to destroy it.'

'What's it done to him?'

'Possession,' Anne said quietly. 'It can control people. I warned Dawlish, thought it might have taken you over, but…'

She faltered, unable to continue. *But I presumed too much, was too desperate to press on, trusted again and was betrayed. And now, I've failed again.*

The staff sergeant's face became unreadable, and for a moment he stared at the back of the Yeti in front of them.

'Will it let him go, d'ye reckon?' he asked quietly, after a moment. Anne could hear the careful edge of hope in his voice, and felt absolutely wretched when she could only shake her head again. She respected him too much to offer up empty platitudes or sugar-coated words.

'I'm sorry,' she said.

'S'alright, miss,' Arnold murmured softly. 'You weren't to know. None of us were.'

He was trying to be kind, but Anne winced, wishing he wouldn't. That only made it worse.

They reached the top of the escalators, and as the step beneath her came home Anne was almost flung into the back of Yeti in front of her. Arnold steadied her, then kept a protective arm around her shoulders as they were led into the ticket hall proper.

Everything was just as Anne remembered it. The circular ticket hall was lit by its emergency lighting, the dim glow catching the thin trails of Mist curling across the floor. Banks of computers were arranged around the walls, crudely lashed together, cables snaking in all directions. In front of Holden's famous Liner Clock stood the pyramid; its glass and steel structure gleaming menacingly in the half-light. *So familiar.* She half-expected to see her father waiting anxiously for her in the gloom, haunted by fear and regret.

She shuddered at the memories, cast a quick glance to the pyramid. Maybe it wasn't too late? Maybe she could...?

But the Intelligence didn't seem to be taking any chances. The Yeti took them past the Pyramid, around the side by the ticket office. Arnold tried to keep between Anne and the Yeti, but at a gesture from the Intelligence two Yeti stepped forward to separate them.

'Don't struggle, Staff Sergeant!' Anne warned. 'You'll only make it worse.'

Arnold stilled, having already begun to fight back, and reluctantly complied, allowing himself to be moved a few paces further away to her right.

Satisfied that Arnold was momentarily subdued, the Intelligence returned its attention to Anne, the gun turning with him. Anne shuddered again, disturbed to see it studying her through Dawlish's eyes.

'How long has it been?' she asked. 'How long since you took him over?'

She remembered Dawlish introducing himself in the workshop at HQ, his barely-concealed look of despair when he'd found Knight had ousted him from his bunk, his brave stand against the first Yeti when she insisted on getting a photograph of them. To think that, beneath all that, the Intelligence may have been watching and waiting...

'No so long,' the Intelligence hissed. 'An hour, perhaps, maybe more. I whispered to him in the tunnels, and his mind was... receptive. I called him to me, and he came.'

It turned to Arnold.

'This body died by my design at South Kensington,' it gloated. 'I saw in his mind your pathetic plan to slow my advance. I found where the roof of the tunnel was weak, guided his siting of the explosives and then held him in place, caused him to lose his footing. You did not see the life leave him before I brought it back.'

Arnold's face was a picture of rage. 'Murdering swine!' he spat. 'He was a good man, and you dare to stand there, in his skin!'

The Intelligence radiated an aura of smugness. It was... *pleased* at Arnold's anger.

'I am the Great Intelligence,' it breathed. 'I am Pure Consciousness, beyond such petty concepts as good or evil. Through me all shall be brought to enlightenment. But enough pleasantries; to business.'

In a flash the pistol's aim moved across to Arnold, and it fired.

Anne gave a cry of anguish as the staff sergeant fell to the floor. She darted forward, the Intelligence and the Yeti standing by impassively as she knelt down.

Arnold looked up at her, eyes wide with shock, hands clutching at his stomach. Blood pooled onto the floor from between his fingers, bright red against the white tiles.

'Miss...' he gasped between pained breaths. 'I'm sorry... Meant to... take care...'

'Don't.' Anne fought the tears that threatened to fall. 'Don't, you'll be all right. Stay with me!'

No, not again. Please, not again.

But it was too late. Already his eyes were glazing over, his skin becoming waxen. Another moment and his breath stopped altogether. He was gone.

Alistair stumbled, but managed to brace himself against the tunnel wall before he fell over. For a moment there he had suddenly felt faint, his thoughts temporarily scattered, and he blinked a few times to combat the sensation of dizziness. Fortunately it seemed to be dissipating quickly enough.

He had heard laughing. A laughter all too familiar to him. It was time. He closed his eyes briefly. He knew what was coming next – just around the corner was his destiny.

Alistair stumbled again, the gnome's laughter pulling him into the black...

Colonel Lethbridge-Stewart blinked, rubbed his temples. Odd, that. He thought he had heard somebody laughing.

He wasn't sure how long he'd been walking through these tunnels. It was hard to orientate himself in the dark, but he felt sure he was heading in the right direction. Over the past few days he had made a thorough study of the Tube map, and he was pretty certain he was now on the Piccadilly Line, somewhere between Covent Garden and Leicester Square. At that point he could change onto the Northern Line and reach Goodge Street that way.

As Lethbridge-Stewart resumed his journey, he wondered what had come over him just now. It had been a very peculiar sensation; not really like fainting, but more as if he'd momentarily lost focus, part of his mind going off elsewhere. Had he eaten breakfast that morning? Among the organised chaos of handing over control of Greater London to his successor, it was quite possible that he had missed out. Between that, the ambush, and then losing the rest of the men at Aldwych, he honestly couldn't remember.

These past two weeks had been hard going on them all; and Lethbridge-Stewart could not recall ever feeling so driven before in his life. It was as if there had been some guiding influence, both within and outside of himself, that had been pushing him relentlessly onwards – like when he had instinctively jumped at Pemberton's offer to recall him from Tobruk so that he could assist with the crisis over here. Perhaps that was why he had suddenly felt so exhausted? Yes, must be it. Events were taking their toll, but he couldn't afford to falter now;

especially with Pemberton gone.

Lethbridge-Stewart felt a momentary stab of grief, but then he brushed it firmly aside. There would be time to mourn his friend later; right now he needed to concentrate on the task in hand. As with any crisis, things were liable to get worse before they got better. All eyes in Central London would be looking to him, and while Travers and his daughter worked towards their scientific solution, he would do his damnedest to carry the day.

And he would not let Old Spence down.

From up ahead he heard a sort of scuffling, and what sounded like a cough.

Instantly alert, Lethbridge-Stewart drew his gun and retreated into a workman's alcove. Moments later a shabby figure dressed in baggy checked trousers and an ill-fitting dark coat shambled past. Lethbridge-Stewart frowned. A civilian? What the blazes was a civilian doing down here?

Quick as a dart, Lethbridge-Stewart stepped out of his hiding place and pressed the muzzle of his gun into the small of the little man's back.

'Stand perfectly still and raise your hands.'

Dame Anne felt herself shaking, and she balled her fists in the denim cloth of Arnold's smock. She was alone again, utterly alone in the face of the enemy. There was nothing left, no one else to turn to.

She wished Bill were here.

'Why?' she sobbed quietly to the air. 'Why?'

'I have a use for him,' the Intelligence whispered, answering the question it had not been asked. 'But also, it would not have done for him to overhear our conversation. You are... not right. I can sense it; a mind adrift in time and space, like me, but not of me.'

'I'm nothing like you!' she spat, still clinging to Arnold's body.

'No,' the Intelligence agreed. 'You are less. But still, you know me. You knew of my Yeti, my ability to bend others to my will, and you knew my connection to the pyramid. Only Travers knows these things, and one other – and he has only just arrived. Do you travel with him?'

'No!' Anne snapped. Because, of course, she couldn't possibly have learned any of this for herself…

'Travers, then,' the Intelligence said, considering. 'I failed to obtain him on his way into the city, but I did not think him so much of a threat. Could I have underestimated him? Does he know more of my secrets than I was led to believe? If so, then he cannot be allowed to share this knowledge further. He shall be dealt with.'

Anne felt a sudden chill close around her heart at its words, an awful realisation dawning. It had been her; her fault all along. She had prompted the Intelligence to go after her father. And then there was Arnold… He had been shot because of her presence here now. Again, she hadn't changed anything. She had fought to change history, when all of the time she was part of it. Always had been!

'No,' she begged. She felt sick, the world spinning around her. 'No, please, he's just an old man; a harmless old man. He's no threat to you.'

'And I would agree,' the Intelligence said. 'But your presence here proves otherwise.'

'Please, you can't. It will destroy his mind!'

'You are wrong,' it said gently. 'He shall become one with the Pure Consciousness, as will you, as will all in time. When the opportunity presents itself, I shall dispatch my Yeti. But first, I would know more of you. There is some connection between us, linking us to this time and place; I feel it stretching back through the years. You have foreknowledge that will be of vital use to me in these coming days. I would know what you know.'

Crouched there on the cold, tiled floor, kneeling over

Arnold's body, Anne saw that future. She couldn't let it know what she knew.

For a moment she thought she heard laughter, but she had to have been imagining it. What was there possibly to laugh about here?

All of her efforts had failed. Events were unfolding in the inevitable pattern, within which she had been a part all along. Despite her best intentions she had condemned her father to a horrible, lingering death.

It didn't matter. None of it. Whatever she tried... she was part of the sequence of events. Even poor Rachel, and why Malachi never spoke of her after the London Event...

No. She shook her head. No, she would not allow the Intelligence this victory. If it acquired the knowledge in her head, then there would be no futures. Not for any of them.

She had to end this.

She sprang up suddenly, ran past the Yeti and sprinted for the ticket barriers.

'Stop her!' the Intelligence shrieked, and the Yeti roared.

The laughter came again; louder this time, distinct, mocking her. Before her two Yeti loomed large and Anne changed direction, made a dash for the pyramid. She needed to... She had to try!

It flashed through her mind, then; childhood summer spent with her father, the formation of the Fifth, meeting Bill, their wedding, the birth of their son, all the times they saved the world... Her past, present and future all merged together, narrowed to one point in time.

She had to make things right again.

The laughter was ringing in her ears and through her head. The volume of sound was deafening. The roaring of the Yeti, the Intelligence's cries and the laughter all mingled into one overwhelming, soul-splitting cacophony. She stumbled, managed to lay hands on the pyramid, but a Yeti seized and flung her back across the ticket hall. She crumpled against a pillar, her head spinning. The Yeti closed in and she screamed, holding her hands up in front of her face in a last desperate defensive posture and waited for the claws of the Yeti.

Anne had been so sure, but as the claws struck her, the realisation solidified, whatever the gnome was up to, it wasn't what she'd thought… Perhaps, after all, it *was* about Alistair. She wasn't on some mission to fix the past, she was just along for the ride, and nothing she did made any difference.

Defeat numbed her.

And then she was falling, falling…

Into the black.

Her last thoughts were of Bill. Her darling Bill.

Wherever he was, she prayed he would make it out alive…

EPILOGUE

THE SMALL GROUP WATCHED AS THE THREE FIGURES
disappeared, making their way towards the platform
and, eventually, Covent Garden Station. Chorley glanced
back, and addressed Professor Travers. 'Where is he
going?'

Colonel Lethbridge-Stewart listened, his eyes casting
around them, at the chaos of the ticket hall. The Great
Intelligence had been defeated, although the cost was
high. Poor Staff Sergeant Arnold – his burned body lay
on the floor. Killed when the Intelligence's link to Earth
was severed by the intervention of that McCrimmon lad.
Several Yeti lay on the floor, too. Immobile.

'You mean this, uh, this time machine thing, it really
exists?' Chorley was saying.

'Well, I, er…' Travers looked to his daughter, standing
beside him, watching him with concern. The old man was
clearly tired. 'Oh, explain it to him, Anne, will you?'

Miss Travers tried to say no, but her father ignored
her. Instead he walked around the small group, and said
as he passed Lethbridge-Stewart, 'Colonel, I think we'd
better check up top, don't you?'

Lethbridge-Stewart almost smiled. 'Right, Professor,'
he said. Anything to get away from Chorley – although
he suspected that would prove harder than said. 'Evans!'
he snapped, and turned to follow Travers.

There was much work to do. As Driver Evans shuffled

236

after him, Lethbridge-Stewart heard Miss Travers attempt to follow, but Chorley was having none of it. He had questions, and she was the only one left who could answer them.

As the three men slowly worked their way up the immobile escalator, Lethbridge-Stewart took a quiet moment to reflect.

It was all over. The Great Intelligence defeated, London (and possibly the world) saved. They all did their part, the Doctor moreso than others, it turned out. Strange chap. No doubt they'd meet again. One day.

Hopefully, by then, he'd have everything sorted in his head. The last few weeks… Strange things had happened. A lot of good people dead. And he'd seen, first hand, the proof that life on Earth was a very small thing indeed. Lethbridge-Stewart wasn't too sure where he would go next, but he knew it wouldn't by Libya. The enemy may have been defeated, this time, but who was to say it wouldn't try again?

Resigned to it all, he determined that at the earliest opportunity he would have a long discussion with General Hamilton. They needed something a lot more ambitious than the Special Forces Support Group going forward.

And then there was London. So much left to do. An empty city, one full of dead soldiers and immobile Yeti…

It was over. And yet, at the same time, it was only just beginning…

The Laughing Gnome continues in…
The Danger Men.

THE FORGOTTEN SON
by Andy Frankham-Allen

DEAD LONDON. IT WAS A SIGHT COLONEL ALISTAIR Lethbridge-Stewart would never get used to.

He had been travelling from his little flat in Pimlico to the London Regiment offices in Battersea from where he was co-ordinating the re-population of London. It was a mammoth task, and one of the least enjoyable roles of being a colonel; he preferred to be out in the field, but after the last couple of weeks he had seen enough good soldiers die in London that for once he looked forward to returning to the office.

Nowhere was the evacuation more obvious than Carnaby Street. The centre of fashion for London, the street was usually full of young people; boys in their bell-bottoms and double-breasted jackets, and girls in mini-skirts and white go-go boots. Lethbridge-Stewart was far too conservative to fall into the latest trends, but he did admire the vibrancy of young people. And now, as he stood next to his car on that deserted street, he felt the lack of that vibrancy keenly.

It was simply wrong. All around him the city was still, despite the slight breeze. Barely a sound, not even the distant rumble of a dustcart. London was a city made to be loud, to be full of noise, of people. The lack of it was eerie.

Young people were emerging as the dominant presence in the city, overshadowing the more serious and less 'fab' gentry that were once the face of London. Lethbridge-Stewart felt a little depressed by the sight around him. The shops, usually open and full of life, were still closed. But now even the red and blue sign of *Carnaby Girl* seemed lifeless above the darkened windows, the colourful outfits in the windows of *Irvine Sellars* next door seeming almost drab and unwanted. Above the street Union flags blew gently in the breeze, as if they couldn't work up the enthusiasm anymore, and on the corner of the street where usually an ice cream cart stood was nothing.

Things were going to change, though. Friday 14th March would forever be remembered as the day that public life returned to London. Already the first trains were en route from the outer cities and towns, from the country, from wherever people could go after the unexpected and very abrupt evacuation weeks ago. The London transport system was, after days and days of false starts, once again underway – getting the buses back on the streets, and the Underground moving, was not as simple as flicking a switch. Businesses, the lifeblood of London, were slowly getting ready for the upcoming deluge – workers and business owners had been among the first to return to London, ahead of the millions of others that were only now starting to be herded back home. Of course, most still did not know why they had been evacuated, although a D-notice had since been issued it seemed the reason behind the evacuation was to remain a secret, muddied by politics and rumour. Just like the Great Smog of '52 all over again, only worse this time. So many more lives lost. Only a select few knew the real reason: top civil servants, a few government officials and high-ranking military officers. And Lethbridge-Stewart. He knew because he had been on the front line, one of the last men standing in Central London.

He still found it hard to entirely accept what he'd

witnessed. But he was a practical man, of course, and a pragmatic one at that. He had been there right to the end in Piccadilly Circus Station, had seen with his own eyes his men butchered by the indefatigable onslaught of Yeti, the foot-soldiers of an alien intelligence. There was no getting around it. Just as, now the Intelligence had been defeated, there was no getting round the unenviable task of restoring London to its usual glory.

First there were all the dead bodies to account for, hospital mortuaries all through the city filling up with hundreds of dead soldiers, and then they had to surreptitiously remove all evidence of the alien presence – the Yeti, the control spheres, the pyramid device that had exploded and killed the last receptacle of the Great Intelligence. So much work, more than anybody would ever know about, all to ensure that normality returned. Where all the Yeti and control spheres went was anybody's guess – once they left London they seemed to disappear, no doubt taken to some top-secret vault, the location of which a normal army officer like Lethbridge-Stewart would never learn. This suited him just fine. He was quite happy to forget all that had happened, but he knew that he never would. Pragmatic to the last. He had seen too much, and as the commander in charge of restoring London he was being kept in a position of easy surveillance. His superiors were watching closely, determining what they needed to do next.

It seemed nobody had anticipated this attack. Not even Professor Travers, who had encountered the Great Intelligence and its Yeti way back in 1935. But nobody was talking about that – both Travers and he had been debriefed on that score, and Anne Travers, the professor's daughter, had been sent off wherever the Yeti had been taken. A brilliant scientist, it seemed the powers that be still needed to pick her brain. As far as his superiors were concerned the two events formed one long-term attack, which had now been dealt with. Lethbridge-Stewart wasn't convinced. He had it on good authority that the Intelligence was still *out there*, whatever that meant. But such a warning was too ambiguous for the Brass, and it was decided that they would cross that bridge should they ever come to it. For his part, Lethbridge-Stewart wasn't convinced that dealing with such potential attacks on an ad-hoc basis was a practical or wise strategy, if he could even call it such.

It was out of his hands, of course. He was merely a colonel in the Scots Guards, and he had his orders. Get London back up and running. Though if it was up to him he'd have made damn sure London would never end up like this again.

To that end, it was time to be on his way. He climbed back into his car and turned on the radio. The sound that greeted him made him smile. Not to be defeated, Radio Caroline was back on the air, and with it the music that helped make London the city it was, even if there was hardly anybody around to listen. Small Faces were a far cry from the music he enjoyed – he'd have preferred to listen to Scaffold's *Lily the Pink* – but as his car continued on its way to Battersea he found himself developing a fondness for *Tin Soldier*. It gave him hope. It was his job to make London vibrant once again, and he was going to do just that.

'Now that's a sight I never thought I'd see,' said Lance Corporal Sally Wright as soon as Lethbridge-Stewart entered his office. She was standing behind his desk, looking out of the window at the street below.

'What is?' he asked, not bothering to question her unauthorised presence in his office. He really should have a word with his assistant and remind her that no one but he was allowed access to this office without his express permission. There were top secret documents contained in the filing cabinets, not to mention the reports still open on his desk from a late-night session. Not that Corporal Wright would ever look at such reports without permission, but that was hardly the point.

'Buses on the streets of London.' She glanced back at him as he put his briefcase on his desk. 'We may yet get to have our party,' she said, offering him the kind of smile she knew he could not resist.

But resist he did. Lethbridge-Stewart turned away and walked back to the open door, poking his head into the ante-office where Lance Corporal Bell sat at her own desk. 'Lay on some tea for me,' he said. 'Make that two cups.'

Bell smiled pleasantly. 'Yes, sir,' she said.

Lethbridge-Stewart narrowed his eyes and let out an *hmm*. Discipline was a bit too lax. He supposed he could put that down to two things: an exhaustive week and the early hour of this particular Friday. Not to mention how much work was bound to come their way over the next couple of days. They anticipated at least half a million flooding into the city over the weekend, and with them at least twice that amount of problems and complaints.

'Are the telephone staff in yet?' he asked, just as Bell picked up her own phone.

'Yes, sir. They started to arrive an hour ago. The switchboards are being set up all over London as we speak.'

'Good. We don't want two million phone calls coming to this office, especially not if one of them is the BBC.'

'Still complaining about not being able to film on the Underground, sir?'

'One of many complaints, Corporal. Evacuating London wasn't good for television programming, apparently.' That all said, Lethbridge-Stewart returned to his office and closed the door.

'What brings you here, Corporal?' he asked once he

had shooed Sally from behind his desk.

'Orders from General Hamilton.' She reached into her jacket and pulled out the orders. Lethbridge-Stewart took them, but he needn't have bothered opening them, since Corporal Wright proceeded to tell him what they said. 'He's reviewed your request, and has granted you full authority to initiate martial law until you see fit to rescind it.'

Lethbridge-Stewart raised an eyebrow and sat down. 'Anything Hamilton doesn't tell you?'

Wright smiled, her eyes twinkling. 'Everything, I imagine. And he didn't tell me – I sneaked a look.'

Upon checking the orders Lethbridge-Stewart noticed that they had already been unsealed. He glanced at the open reports on his desk. 'Anything else you have "sneaked a look" at?'

'Don't be such a prig, Alistair. You know you'd tell me anyway.'

That was debatable. 'Corporal Wright, I expect better from Major General Hamilton's adjutant, and when you're in this building I would remind you that you are on duty, and as such I am your superior officer. And,' he added, lowering his voice, 'the walls of this building are awfully thin.'

She looked around, and nodded. 'Sorry,' she said, her voice also low. She cleared her throat and was about to speak again when there came a knock at the door. Bell entered, bringing their tea. Once she had returned to the ante-office, Wright reached out for her mug. 'So, martial law? Is that not a bit extreme? Sir,' she added, with a cheeky smile.

Lethbridge-Stewart rolled his eyes. What was he to do with her? Marry her probably. 'I would normally have thought so, but we've had workers striking already. Too much work, not enough pay, and right now we don't have time to negotiate with trade unions. Over eight million people need to be returned to this city in the shortest time possible – the longer it takes, the more it will cost everybody, including the tax payers who are now striking. Once the city is up and running again, then they can do as they like. It will no longer be my problem. I am not a politician, and neither do I intend to play the part of one now.'

'Thus martial law.'

Lethbridge-Stewart nodded. 'Easiest way. Work to your strengths, that's what my father always told me.'

'There could be riots at this rate.'

'Not if I have any say. This is not Paris, Corporal, and right now we have control of the streets, and we will continue to until it's no longer our problem.'

The conversation was over and for a few moments they sat in companionable silence. Then the intercom buzzed.

'Sir, Major Douglas is on line one.'

'Thank you.' Lethbridge-Stewart picked up the phone, but before he could press the line-one button, Corporal Wright spoke.

'Dougie? Why is he calling you?'

'Because I need a man out there I can trust, someone with enough clout to see that martial law is maintained with a firm and fair hand.'

Wright looked confused for a moment, then she grinned. 'You knew Hamilton was going to approve your request.'

'Well, of course.'

She narrowed her eyes. 'And you knew he'd send me.'

Lethbridge-Stewart pressed the button on his phone, enjoying the look of surprise on Wright's face. Of course he knew; indeed, he had asked if Hamilton would send the orders via Corporal Wright. If she was going to be his fiancée, then he had to find any way he could to spend time with her. General Hamilton knew this, and happily agreed.

'Major Douglas,' Lethbridge-Stewart said, once the call connected. 'Yes, yes, Sally is here. Yes, you would think I planned this. Orders for you, and a question. Would you care to be my best man?'

It had been over thirty years and once again he found himself returning to the area in which the 'accident' occurred. He wasn't sure why; he liked to fool himself that Jack, his beagle, simply enjoyed the expansive area of Draynes Wood, but sometimes Ray Phillips wondered if there was some other reason he made the half hour walk from Bledoe every weekend. Wondered if there was something calling him back, never letting him get far enough away to forget.

He knew the risk of allowing Jack the freedom afforded him by Draynes Wood, but in all the time he'd brought the dog there, not once had they been near the area where Golitha Falls met the River Fowey.

There was a chill in the air. He wanted to say it was the weather, but he knew it was something more. He stopped at the edge of the woods, looking down at the gorge itself, the cascading water dropping some ninety feet to join the rest of the Fowey. The waters raged, and he remembered. The spring of 1938 and the day that changed his life. He shivered.

He looked around for Jack, and not finding him, for a moment worried that the small dog had jumped into the river. The current was especially strong at Golitha Falls, and Jack was old. He'd get swept away before Ray could even move. Fortunately, though, he spotted Jack a little way into the oak woodland, foraging through the bluebells and anemones that carpeted the ground either side of the gorge.

As he watched the dog snuffling away, a flash of light caught his eye. Ray placed his glasses on the edge of his nose and peered closer. He stepped back, overtaken by a sudden dread. In the far distance, just visible through the oak trees, was the old Remington Manor house. It had been deserted for thirty years, but now there was a light, a glimmer through one of the upper windows.

Ray shuddered. He was too old for this kind of nonsense, he knew, but deep down something in his gut turned.

He couldn't remain here any longer. He called Jack to him and walked back into the woods, in the direction of home. He'd get in his car, put on an 8-track, and take his dog as far from Golitha Falls as possible. There was loads of open land in Cornwall where Jack could roam free. He didn't need to walk through this woodland. He didn't need to be anywhere near the Manor. No, he would walk away from it all. He had dealt with his ghosts a long time ago.

But something made him stop. The same something that made him return here every weekend. He looked back up at the Manor.

The three boys who stalked Remington Manor were taking a risk.

Not that they would call themselves boys; they were young men, fast approaching eighteen years and, for Lewis at least, freedom from the suffocation that was Bledoe. Owain, twin of Lewis but often the polar opposite, blamed the third person in their little group, the intruder that was Charles Watts. He had returned to Bledoe (not that Owain remembered him ever being there before, but it seemed he used to often visit there when he was a kid) a few weeks previously, after being evacuated from London. He, along with the rest of his family, was staying with his nana. You couldn't have found a man less suited to country life than Charles – a city man if ever there was one. Like Lewis, Charles considered himself

one of those 'lemons', as Owain had heard them called –
a group of men who found their solidarity in like-
minded, working class men, with their tight jeans and
Ben Sherman shirts and braces, their hair cut
unfashionably short. Not that Owain much cared for
fashion, but allowing your hair to grow was in some ways
quite freeing. Something women had known since the
dawn of time.

Lewis had taken to this new image quickly, to the
point of permanently borrowing a pair of their father's
braces and getting the local barber, Mr Bryant, to cut his
previously long hair so it matched Charles'. He'd even
removed his precious moustache – much to Owain's
delight, since bum-fluff never looked good on anyone.

Their parents had not been happy, of course, although
their father had also found it oddly amusing, no different
than when the twins had a cheeky pint in *The Rose &
Crown*. Their mother was less amused and had attempted
to ground Lewis, but with Charles in town that simply
was not going to happen. They were seventeen and no
woman was going to tell Lewis what to do.

That was the biggest change in Lewis. They had been
brought up to mind their mother; her word was final. But
in the past week Lewis had started questioning
everything – almost every word she said. In his mind
their mother was out of touch with the real world beyond
Bledoe, and he had begun to talk more and more about
London, about joining in the movement against the
government there. 'We'll make it like Paris,' he said,
although what he meant by that was beyond Owain.
Bledoe was their home, and as far as Owain was
concerned what went on beyond was of little interest to
him, unless it was football, of course. French,
Londoners… what did any of them matter?

It had been Lewis' idea to explore the house, driven
as he was by boredom, and Owain resented that he had

to come along. He wasn't sure he trusted Charles to be alone with his brother, besides it was almost expected for Lewis and Owain to do everything together simply because they were twins. Like that secured some mystic connection. Certainly Charles seemed to think so. 'I would love to have been a twin,' he had told them the first day they met. Since then he hadn't stopped going on about it. 'If I hit Lewis, would you feel it?' As if Owain and Lewis was the same person!

Owain looked around. Both his brother and Charles had gone on ahead; they were already some way down the long landing, while he was only just mounting the final step of the large, although dusty, staircase. He paused, bored, and pulled out his pocket transistor radio. He was missing the league cup final for this.

He looked up briefly, to make sure neither Lewis nor Charles were paying him any attention, and twisted the small dial that turned the radio on. He kept the volume low and tuned into the match. It was bound to be an uneven game, what with most of the Arsenal players still recovering from a bout of flu, and, not surprisingly, as the radio tuned in Owain learned that the Gunners were being trampled all over by Swindon Town.

Owain must have got caught up in the game, because the next moment Charles was before him, snatching the tranny off him. 'What are you playing at?'

Owain sighed, bored again. He looked over at Lewis, who stood watching, his arms folded, carrying about him a look of disappointment. 'Can we go now? There's no one here besides us.'

'That's the whole point, innit?' Charles said. 'The Whisperer isn't here, you can just hear him. Creepy, huh?' He grinned and pocketed the transistor radio. 'I'll keep that, see if we can pick up some reggae on it later.'

Owain was about to complain. He didn't listen to music on his radio, that's not why he had it. It was for listening to football matches when his mum wouldn't tune the TV in to the BBC. Complaining would do no good; Charles wasn't the type to listen. Not unless Lewis had something to say.

'Do you both share the same bird when you have one?' Charles asked, breaking the silence.

Owain gritted his teeth.

Lewis laughed at this. 'Not at the same time.'

'Anyway, we're not exactly identical,' Owain mumbled behind them. Which was true, but they were obviously twins. Even a blind man could see that.

'That must be so much fun, man, imagine if —' Charles stopped abruptly. 'Did you hear that?' he asked, looking back the way they had come.

The three young men peered around. The long corridor was, of course, empty, the wallpaper bleached by the sun that came in from tall windows bereft of any netting. Cobwebs lined the coving along the top of the walls, dust covering the table and candlestick holders a few feet away.

Lewis glanced back, smiling. 'The Whisperer?' he asked.

'Of course not, moron,' Owain responded, giving his brother a dirty look.

Of course it wasn't the Whisperer, no such thing existed. Just stories told by parents to keep the kids away from a house that was slowly falling apart. Not that it worked obviously. They had both heard plenty of stories about it over the years, about the household driven mad by the whispering of the walls, and how one day a visitor came by to find the house empty, devoid of all life, everything in place as if the household had simply gone for a walk and forgot to come back.

That was back in '39, and since then nobody had claimed the Manor. It remained as it had been left, albeit with the gates and doors padlocked shut. Padlocks that had been broken many times by brave and bored teens – much like his brother and Charles.

'Then what?' Charles was now having fun. 'Should we go and look?'

Owain knew he couldn't say no; if he did he'd never hear the end of it. 'Come on then,' he said and stepped forward, the forced smile leaving his face as soon as his back was to Charles and Lewis.

They walked behind him, Lewis once again taking to humming another of his favourite tunes.

Charles started mumbling the words of the song, encouraging Lewis to hum louder. *'Shirt them a-tear up, trousers are gone.'*

'Don't want to end up like Bonnie and Clyde,' Lewis joined in. *'Poooooor me, the Israelite!'*

Owain was all set to complain when he heard it again. Was it a voice? He shook his head. No, that was stupid.

Lewis stopped, his body tense. 'Creepy. I definitely heard that.'

'Yeah, man, me too.' Charles looked up and down the landing. 'Creepy,' he added with a large grin.

Owain preferred it when Lewis didn't agree with him. Then it was just him being stupid, but if Lewis and Charles agreed then… there was something in the walls.

'Maybe we should just leave?' Owain suggested.

That was probably, looking back, not the wisest thing to say, as was immediately obvious by the cold look that swept across Charles' face.

'What are you, a Nancy-boy? There's nothing else to do, what with us not being allowed back to London. And we don't have ten-bob between us, so no chance of doing anything else.'

Lewis laughed softly. 'Come on, O', you're the cynic, remember? You don't believe in ghosts or any of that rubbish.'

'And you do now? Not exactly fitting for a bovver

boy.'

'I knew it! You read about London, too.' Lewis nudged Charles. 'See, told you it wasn't just me. Anyway,' he continued with a smug grin that matched Charles. 'We're not bovver boys. We're not looking for aggro, just letting people know we're not going to be one of the destitute struggling to make a living when the government is–'

Owain held his hand up. 'Yeah yeah, we're all working class heroes.' He shook his head and looked around the corridor again. 'Reckon we're all going a bit mad anyway. No voices here, except ours.'

It wasn't true, of course; he knew he had heard a voice, but he wasn't intending to let either of them bully him into staying any longer. If he was lucky he could make it home in time for the late news and watch the action replays of the match.

It has been years. How many it does not know. Trapped in the walls, hardly able to do anything but whisper, a bodiless voice, intangible. But now it can feel it, the soul it's been waiting for. Young, but strong. Strong enough to give it strength. This time, though, it will be different. It will plan, prepare, and do things properly. It will not be beaten again...

LETHBRIDGE-STEWART: THE LAUGHING GNOME – SCARY MONSTERS

by Simon A Forward

Sir Alistair Lethbridge-Stewart is nearing the end of his life and has just buried another old friend. Feeling out of sorts, he is somewhat surprised to find himself in 1981. Some mysterious force has pulled him backwards in time, into his own past, an adventure he has only vague memories of...

1981: London, a bomb detonates in a London pub and Brigadier Alistair Lethbridge-Stewart is among the injured. Moscow, a hijacked plane sits on the airport runway and Major Grigoriy Bugayev leads the assault against the six gunmen holding the passengers hostage.

These are the triggers that set the two military men on an international manhunt. Their investigations converge and uncover a group of terrorists whose roots reach back to sinister Cold War experiments, and something that was unearthed in ancient ruins in the New Mexico desert by one Sophia Montilla... and Anne Travers.

Terror is a contagion. It means to spread. And humanity is set on doing everything in its power to help it...

ISBN: 978-1-912535-07-1